THE BALANCE

Visit us at www.boldstrokesbooks.com

THE BALANCE

by

Neal Wooten

A Division of Bold Strokes Books

2014

THE BALANCE
© 2014 BY NEAL WOOTEN. ALL RIGHTS RESERVED.

ISBN 13: 978-1-62639-055-3

THIS TRADE PAPERBACK ORIGINAL IS PUBLISHED BY
BOLD STROKES BOOKS, INC.
P.O. BOX 249
VALLEY FALLS, NY 12185

FIRST EDITION: APRIL 2014

CREDITS
EDITOR: JERRY WHEELER
PRODUCTION DESIGN: STACIA SEAMAN
BOTTOM COVER PHOTO BY CHERYL RAE PHOTOGRAPHY
COVER DESIGN BY SHERI (GRAPHICARTIST2020@HOTMAIL.COM)

To my sister, Neenah, the most caring, loving, accepting person I've ever known. Although she left us in 2005, her spirit lives on through all who knew her.

CHAPTER ONE

I'm nineteen years old today. I will make my first visit to Level Twelve. I am in my room alone sitting on the chair by the edge of my bed. I gently press my finger to the wall and the screen appears. I check my scores on the city Central Link. They are higher than most kids my age. It isn't much, but this is one of the very few things that make us different at all. I sigh as I pull up a math game to help pass the time.

Later I go to the kitchen, press the tab to retrieve a food tablet and put a glass under the water dispenser. My mother is on the Central Link in the main room. She doesn't look away. My father is at work. I stare at the entrance to my grandparents' half of the living quarters. I want to knock on the door to see if my grandfather is ready, but I know that isn't appropriate. I swallow my tablet and go back to my room.

An hour later, there's a tap on my door. As I slide the door open, I see my grandfather, Adon, already walking toward the front door. I quickly follow. We leave the living quarters and walk through the dimly lit corridor. The plush material on the floor soothes my bare feet. We speak neither to each other nor to the people we meet. I have never spoken to my grandfather. We reach the first transport entrance and wait. As it comes to a stop, two people get off as we get on. We do not make eye contact or acknowledge them. They are wearing the same white robes as we are, the same robes that everyone in the city wears. We are the only two people in the transport, which zips around the enclosed tube.

I like to travel the tubes. With no windows in the city, this provides the only view of the sky, which is normally warm and bright, but not today. I notice the sky outside is not clear at all. I think Adon notices it as well. Suddenly there is a brilliant flash followed by a startling boom, causing my ears to echo with reverberating pulses. The transport stops and shakes violently, the inside filled with air as black as the clouds outside the tube, making breathing painful. I have never seen clouds this high before, never as high as the city. My breath erupts in a sudden sharp exhale as my lungs try to expel the shadowy substance.

"What happened, Adon?" I ask between coughs.

The air clears as the pumps disperse the toxic smoke. Adon stares out through the clear side of the transport. "I think it was lightning," he says.

Lightning? I have only seen lightning from above as I traveled around the tube, beautiful green and blue bursts from within the clouds thousands of feet below the city. The transport shakes again and I almost fall. I sit on the cushioned seat to brace myself, my fingers digging deep into the outer material. Adon still stares out the side of the tube away from the city, so I look to see what he sees. I see only myself. The darkness outside creates a mirror effect on the tube, a distorted reflection looking back at me, scanning my own eyes as if also searching for answers. I notice my shoulder-length, straight, pale hair, the same as every other male in the city, even my grandfather's. I see wrinkles on my face that should not be there, then I realize they are not on my reflection but hovering in the span of distance between us. There are lines that seem to be floating in air, little threads tracing across the normally unobstructed view of the sky. The tube is cracked, and the lines seem to be alive, growing, spreading.

Adon turns to look at me and his eyes convey confusion. "Brace yourself, Piri. I think we are going to fall."

This surprises me. I did not know this was possible, and the very thought makes my chest constrict. Fall? To where? To earth? I look upward as a transport flies through the tube above us. I assume all other eleven tubes are still functional. We are on the bottom level of the city, so there is nothing between us but empty air, forty thousand feet above the surface. I can see the next entrance a mere twenty feet ahead. Where are the maintenance people? I know they live on Level Eleven, but they should be here soon.

The tube's clear casing breaks even more, the lines darting across the cylindrical enclosure like lightning itself, stretching out in all directions. Then the space beside our transport explodes into a million shards of crystal, reflecting the dim light like twinkling stars as they spin off into oblivion. The transport seems to hover for a full second and then...weightlessness.

We plunge. I try to hold on to the seat, but it offers no comfort, for it is falling as fast as I am. Adon grabs me. I first think it is to give me support, then I realize it is to give him balance. My heart is beating faster, and I can feel its pulsations in my throat. It has never done that, and I am not sure of the ramifications. I see the darkness outside the transport as we fall through the storm, the black interrupted by fluorescent flares every few seconds as lightning continues to flash. Then we are clear of the clouds. I can see the giant column that supports our great city. Its smooth, gray exterior walls offer no markings and make it appear as if we are not falling at all, only floating.

Suddenly we are jolted as the transport points downward. Adon and I are thrown to the bottom, which is actually a solid wall up front. Only the sides and top, which form the enclosure, are transparent. I am on top of Adon. His expression is odd, and I can see his eyes are closed tight and watering. But our descent has decreased substantially as now we really do seem to be floating. The wind pushes us left then right as the transport sways like a pendulum.

I manage to stand and take my weight off Adon, who still lies motionless, his eyes now peering up at me without focus, staring into nothingness. I look out the side of the transport and see we have drifted a long way from the column. It looks so small now in the far distance, like a lone tree whose scanty leaves are covered in fog. I can see the landscape. We are getting closer to the surface, a desolate wasteland devoid of people, of water, of life. I wonder if they will send a rescue party in time.

We seem to float for a long time and then land with a thud as I am once again thrust into Adon. He does not make a sound; his eyes do not blink. The impact jars the lower sliding door open, breaking the seal and allowing the air outside to rush in. The wind is loud. The transport falls over and rests on its bottom as if it was still in the tube. I am on my side now and can smell the atmosphere. It is dense and cold and wraps its fingers around me in a frigid embrace. I do not move. My breathing is as fast as my heartbeat. I am not familiar with the sensation.

Several minutes pass and I lie there without moving. Then I hear a strange noise outside. I do not know what it could be. Is there life here? Some wild animals perhaps that we never learned about? Then I see it. It is hideous. It sticks its wooly head in the open door and sniffs, its tongue darting in and out of its open jaws revealing huge fangs. I have never even dreamed that such an abomination could exist. It rushes straight toward me, its dirty white fur covering its entire body, a long scraggly tail waving in the air behind it. This is how I will die, eaten by a strange beast on the surface miles below my home. I brace myself as the head of the beast presses right up against my face. It licks.

I finally gather the courage to open my eyes as the beast continues to stroke my face with its sticky tongue, its breath hot and foul. Perhaps it is deciding if I am satisfactory to eat. Then I hear another sound, and it startles me more because it is not the sound of an animal. It is the sound of…a human?

"What is it, Ash? What is it, boy?"

A figure appears in the doorway. It is a large figure, a human male draped in a cloak and hood. In one hand, he carries a long rod with a sharp metal point. Down across his back is a flat piece of curved wood held in place by a string that runs the length of his torso. Long sticks with strips of thin material attached to them rise from his back beside his head. He walks over to Adon first and bends down beside him. He then rushes to me as the beast steps back. "Come on. Got to get you out of here," he says.

He lifts me easily and carries me out of the fallen transport, managing to hold me and the long pointed rod. The beast follows. I can see now the beast is only two feet high. It seemed much larger from my previous viewpoint. In the light I can make out the face of my…I am not sure what he is. Is he here to rescue me or kill me? His face looks young, but his body is muscular and strong. I see his eyes, two luminous blue dots scanning the horizon. He appears to be as frightened as I. Yes, that is what I am feeling—fear. I look around but all I see is the rocky terrain and the source of our slowed descent, a large piece of red canvas attached to the transport with metal rope.

"Keep a lookout, boy," he says to the beast. He carries me about a hundred feet, then stands me up. I grimace in pain as I put weight on my feet. Like fear, pain is another new sensation. "Think your foot is hurt pretty bad, eh?" he says.

I look down and see my foot is covered with blood, mostly dried and almost black. Is it mine? The rocky ground digs into the tender flesh of my under-feet. I can also see my breath. It appears as a fog when I exhale, then it dissipates quickly.

"Got to find a place to hide for the night. It's almost dark and we'll never make it back. Scavs will be all over the place soon."

I have no idea what he is talking about. He lifts me up and carries me until he finds a crevice in the rocks. He stands me up again and motions for me to go inside. I fit through the gap easily, but he has to squeeze through. The beast follows. Inside is a small enclosure. He prompts me to go to the corner and joins me there. He holds tight to his rod but removes the flat stringed instrument and the pouch carrying the sticks and leans them against the rock wall. He looks at the beast and holds his finger up to his lips, the tip just under his nose. The beast seems to understand and lies beside us.

We sit hunched in the corner of our little cave and no one makes a sound. My robe is no match for the chill of the rock walls and dirt floor. Thirty minutes pass. Suddenly the beast lifts his head and sniffs. Then I hear a growling that makes me quiver. The beast lowers its head onto its front legs. Although it is almost dark outside, a shadow passes by the front of our hiding place, then another. I wonder what manner of creature it could be. A loud yell erupts away from us, the strong wind carrying the sounds across the area. They found the transport. We are still close enough to hear their guttural screams of excitement followed by the clangs and shattering noises as they go through the wreckage.

It is entirely dark when we finally cease to hear the creatures. I realize that my entire body is shaking. I have never experienced cold before. The boy offers his cloak and I accept. This grungy cloth provides some security between me and whatever is outside. It emits a strange odor, but it is amazingly warm. As I curl up against the wall, I feel my heart pounding. My foot is throbbing with pain but the pulses soon synchronize with my heartbeat.

As the cold and fear subside, I have time to evaluate the situation. Who is this person with the shaggy little beast? Where did he come from? Did he fall from the city like I did? Has this happened before? The transport was prepared for such an occurrence considering it had a device to prevent a direct descent, so maybe that is the answer. He speaks strangely, so he must have been here a while. I wonder if there are other survivors here. That thought suddenly worries me. If this boy fell from the city like I did, why was he not rescued? The more pressing thought is this: will I be rescued or left to die here as well?

I close my eyes.

CHAPTER TWO

I wake and see the faint light of day coming in through the front of our hiding place. The boy is standing at the entrance. His cloak is wrapped over me, and I see he is wearing a tunic very different from my smooth robe. It is shorter and made of an odd material. It appears to be very old and worn. Several pouches hang from a belt around his waist. His feet have some kind of flexible boards underneath, kept in place with straps across the tops of his feet and around his ankles.

"You awake, eh?"

I look up and see him smiling. His teeth are large and white with two pointed ones that look similar to the fangs of the beast, though not quite as long. As I examine his rough appearance, I do not think he ever lived in the city, which makes me wonder from where he and his furry friend came. The beast is just outside the cave.

"We got to go. Need to get out of Scav territory." He walks over to me with a small jug and removes the top. "Water," he says.

I am very thirsty. I turn it up and drink slowly. It tastes plain and stale but my body needs it.

He helps me up, then wraps his cloak around me and ties it tight. My foot is swollen and the pain is still sharp. Once outside, he straps on the pouch holding the sticks but facing to his front this time. It is the same with the flat wooden thing, the string now across his back. He bends his knees, leans forward, and motions for me to climb onto his back. I hesitate, but remembering the sounds from last night, I know I do not wish to stay here, so I climb up. He grasps his rod and we begin walking, the beast leading the way.

We walk for an hour as I hold on around his neck. As my foot throbs, I know this is not a dream. I scan the morbid panorama and realize I am not going to wake in my own bed. The gray clouds melt into the rocky horizon, the colors running together so I cannot tell where the earth ends and the sky begins. I never knew life existed on the surface and staring out across this forbidden wasteland, I now wonder *how* they do it. Yet I have already encountered this human, his beast, and the horrible creatures known as Scavs.

I am lost. Part of me wants to jump down and run away. Part of me wants to give up. We are walking beside a seven-foot-high rock wall when the beast suddenly stops and points his nose toward the wall.

The boy sits me down and puts his finger to his lips like he had done with the beast last night. I am unfamiliar with this gesture but think I understand. I remain silent. The boy clutches the rod with both hands, his eyes scanning the top of the wall. "How many, boy?" he whispers.

The beast scratches the ground once with his front foot.

A scream like the ones from last night rips the air, making my whole body flinch. A creature flies from atop the wall, its eyes glowing red. It is much larger than the boy, but the boy rams the metal end of the rod into its stomach and pins it to the ground. The creature does not die from the penetration. As blood gushes out of its midsection, it snarls and reaches down to its waist, its legs kicking wildly. In one quick motion, the boy pulls the point from the creature's stomach and thrusts it into its neck. The creature lies still.

My heart is racing once again, and my breath rushes in and out of my lungs. I stand to get a better look and am shocked at what I see. The creature is humanoid, wearing a garment that goes from its waist to its knees. Blood runs from its open jaws and I see its jagged teeth. The entire body is more muscular than the boy's and is covered in black paint. Its coarse hair is wild and pitch black. Around its waist is a belt from which dangle several lightly transparent round bubbles. They seem to be made out of skin of some sort. The creature's long thick fingers are barely resting on one of the bubbles.

The boy rubs the metal end of the rod on the creature's garment to remove the blood. He leans down but I cannot move. He smiles to reassure me. "It's okay now. You're safe."

Somehow I do not feel safe, but I climb on again. We continue for another hour.

"Almost to the forest," he says. "Be a little safer then."

Moments later I see the forest, with its beautiful green growth underneath and a brilliant green canopy above. We enter through the trees and keep going. He puts me down and I walk, but very slowly. He offers to carry me again but I refuse. I do not know where he is taking me, so I feel no hurry to get there. I have to rest frequently. I can see our progress alarms him as he and the beast continue to survey the forest. The weather is warming as the day progresses, the sun making the green canopy glow as it illuminates the forest floor. After we are deep into the forest, the boy stops and helps me over to a small boulder so I can sit. He takes a sip of water and hands me the small flask. I quickly drink. I have never known thirst before.

"You hungry, eh?" he asks.

I nod. He takes a brown chunk of something out of a small pouch and hands it to me. I stare at it. It has a rough texture and looks more like a tool than food.

"Meat," he says.

I try to bite into it but it is repulsive. He laughs. He goes back into the pouch and pulls out another chunk of something; this one is red and looks much softer. I bite into it. It is sweet and bold, making my tongue curl and mouth water. I must be making a strange face because he laughs again. I never knew my mouth could produce sensations like these. I eat the entire piece. He hands me another, which I take willingly.

"Least you like fruit," he says. "Still a long way from home but don't look like we'll make it at this pace. No worry. Be safer sleeping in the forest tonight."

I have not even thought about where we might be going or

how long it will take us to get there. I wonder if I should have left the transport. But then I remember the creatures. After we rest a few minutes, we begin again. The boy seems to walk without tiring, though this is not the case with me. But he is patient and does not push. We go on for hours like this with me needing to stop frequently and rest or wait until the pain subsides. The light in the forest wanes. The boy finds a spot between two trees and we lie down for the night.

"Can't risk a fire," he says, "but you can have the cloak again."

I find it odd that I am sharing space with a strange person on the surface when I was never this close to anyone in the city, but the alternative is unthinkable. Soon we are in the same position as before and I eventually drift off to sleep. I wake many times in the night as I hear the sounds of the Scavs echoing through the trees. Often I close my eyes only to slip into a shallow sleep and see the image of the creature flying off the embankment again, its teeth clinched and eyes blood-red, jolting me awake. The trees echo the barbaric sounds of the Scavs. They are never close but definitely in the forest, messengers of death from the rocky perdition. The beast continues to sniff the air but never makes a sound.

Early morning arrives and we are off again. After hearing the creatures all night and realizing the dangers of our slow pace, I agree to let the boy carry me once more. By midday I can see the clearing through the trees. We exit the forest into an open field of soft, tall grass swaying in the wind, a considerable contrast to the terrain on the other side of the forest. I can see for miles. There are no trees, and I can even see the column to our city in the distance. I notice large, square, flat stones spread out all over the landscape resting on stone walls four feet high. A wooden shaft protrudes upward at least six feet from each flat stone with four flat wooden rectangles running from the top to the bottom of the shaft, each spinning in the wind. Just like back at the rocks, the wind is still blowing strong and the sky is still overcast.

As we near the first stone structure, an older man appears and waves. The boy returns the greeting. Soon we are getting the attention of more people and all stare as if wondering who we are—or who I am. The stone structures have steps going down to a door, and I see some people coming out of the doors and assume these boorish structures to be living quarters. That confirms that the boy is not here by accident; people live on the surface. Why is this something I never knew? We pass children playing games in the grass, laughing as they run at each other. I see more animals like the beast, all the same size and color. The beast rushes up to every other beast we see and greets them with a shared sniff, then rushes back again to take his place ahead of us.

A little while later, the beast darts toward another stone structure. The boy follows and descends the four steps to the doorway. He pushes open the door and we enter. My eyes adjust to the dimmer light. The room is very small with three doors, one each in the other walls, and the air is clammy and stale. He sits me on a wooden bench by the front door. An identical bench is across the room. I look to the ceiling and notice the light is coming from the same flat round stones we use in the city. The boy takes off his array of tools and weapons and leans them against the wall. He takes his cloak from around me and hangs it on the wall next to the door.

"I'm home," he says with a louder tone.

A grown man walks into the room followed by a small girl. Each is dressed similarly to the boy, wearing a tunic made of odd and worn material, except the man has a long red strip of cloth hanging from his belt. The beast rushes to the man and begins to jump up on his leg. The man looks at the boy with wide-open eyes. He rushes to him and throws his large arms around him and begins to squeeze. The little girl also attacks the boy, albeit from a lower standpoint. Why are they trying to hurt him? And why would he come into this place if he knew he would be in danger?

"No," I hear myself shout. "Please do not kill him."

CHAPTER THREE

The man releases the boy and all three of them laugh at me. I am confused.

"Who's your friend?" the man asks.

"Don't know," the boy says. "First time he's said anything."

The little girl comes over, sits by me, and smiles. The man looks back at the boy. "I'm sure you two are hungry. Get changed and cleaned up, and I'll see to your friend. Then we'll make something to eat."

The man walks over to me and reaches down for my swollen foot, which is still covered with dried blood. I jerk my foot back.

"It's okay. Just want to see how bad it is."

His words are reassuring, so I let him lift my foot and examine it. He slides a small padded stool under my foot. "Chiquita, go and get me some water and a rag," he says. The little girl jumps up and runs into another room.

"What's your name?"

"Piri."

"Nice to meet you, Piri. My name's Vet. I'm Niko's papa. And this little monster," he says as the girl comes back with a small vase of water and a worn cloth, "is Chiquita." He holds his hand up by her head to signify her height, or lack thereof.

"My name is Ana," she says as she gives her father an evil stare.

"I'm sorry, her name's Ana. Just prefer to call her Chiquita." He looks back to me. "Not sure what you were doing out there in Scav territory with no footwear or cloak, but it ain't safe out there."

"I believe you," I say as he washes the dried blood from my foot.

He smiles. "Where you live, Piri? Sure your parents are very worried."

I think of my parents, but worrying is not something they do. "I live in the city." I point upward. His mouth drops open as he stares at me, and I wonder if I said something wrong.

Niko comes back wearing another tunic just as worn as the other one. But the timing was good as his father turns his attention to him.

"Couldn't believe when your hunting party came back and said you'd decided to travel alone into Scav territory. What in the world were you thinking?"

"Sorry, Papa," Niko says. "When I saw that thing falling from the sky...you should've seen it. It was hanging from a huge red thing that looked like an upside-down bowl. Had to see what it was. The wind pushed it farther away than I wanted, but I thought it might be a gift from the Fathers."

Vet looks back at me and smiles. "Might be. You live in the city in the sky, eh?"

I nod. Ana and Niko are stunned.

"And you bleed?" Niko asks.

Ana holds her hands out beside her and waves them up and down. "I thought you could fly."

I do not say anything.

"How did you end up on the surface?" Vet asks.

I explain how Adon and I were in the transport. I tell them about the lightning.

"What happened to Adon?"

"Already dead when I got to them," Niko explains.

"Who was he?" Vet asks.

"Adon was my grandfather."

Everyone looks at me with sad eyes. "I'm so sorry," Vet says.

Ana, who has taken her seat beside me again, squeezes my hand. "I'm sorry, too."

I am confused. Why are they sorry? They had nothing to do with the accident.

Vet turns his attention back to my foot, which is now clean. "Don't think it's broken and the cuts are minor. Swelling should go down in a few days. Let's make something to eat."

He places his hand on my shoulder and leads me to the room where Ana had retrieved the water. It is a larger room and the flat stones in the ceiling are closer together, which makes them illuminate brighter. I hope this means they have other comforts from home here.

"Take him to the washroom," Vet says to Ana.

The girl leads me to a small room. I am glad to see it is a bathroom. She shows me how to press the levers to activate the water for the seated and sink areas. It is primitive but operational. After a few minutes, I feel somewhat refreshed. I am given a tunic, complete with belt and two pouches, to replace my torn and stained robe. Its texture feels horrible against my skin. When we walk back into the kitchen, they sit me at a wooden table which has four wooden chairs, one on each side. Ana pulls a chair up beside mine and sits there. She continues to stare at me. Vet and Niko remove things from shelves.

"Your teeth are so pretty," Ana says.

"They are?"

Vet leans over the table and looks at me, so I open my lips to display my teeth. "Noticed that, too. They're small and perfectly even with no pointed teeth at all," he says.

"He doesn't like meat," Niko says.

Vet looks at me and nods. "Explains the teeth. Don't eat meat at all up there, do you, eh?"

I shake my head.

Vet smiles. "Makes sense. All we send you are vegetables and fruits."

I look at him but have no idea what he means. He notices my confusion.

"We're the ones who provide your city with fresh crops," he says. "Didn't you know this?"

I shake my head. "I did not even know there was life on the surface."

He looks very confused. He walks over, pulls up a chair and sits down on the side of the table to my right. "Everyone once lived on the surface, even the Fathers. That's where your people came from. According to The Book, you were the original Chosen Ones. The city in the sky was constructed for you to live away from the perils of the surface."

Nothing he is saying is familiar to me. "What book?"

"*The Book.* The Fathers from the city in the sky created The Book for us Children to learn and it gives us the rules to live by." Vet gets up and goes into another room and returns with The Book.

"Do you read books?" Ana asks.

"No."

"How do you study?" Niko asks.

"From the wall."

Ana laughs. "You write on walls?"

"No. We use the city Central Link. It has all the information we need. Anywhere in the city, you touch any wall and a screen appears. That is where we get our information to study or to find program schedules and things like that." I look at the dreary stone walls around us. "I guess you do not do that here."

"Hardly," Vet says. He opens The Book to the first page and points to a map. "This is the land where we live. It's called Canus."

I look at the map but all I see is a simple sketch.

"You don't study this?" he asks.

"No. We study math, engineering, physics, social responsibility, language, and things like that."

He points again to the map. "To the north is the ocean. First chapter of The Book explains that there was a sad time in our history, many thousands of years ago, with violence and immorality. The Fathers were chosen to live in the sky, so the city was constructed. But the evil didn't go away, so the Fathers punished us by making the oceans rise. Canus was a lot larger at one time. The green area in the northern part of Canus is where you are now. It's called The Garden. The land outside the forest to the east, west, and south is just desert for thousands of miles, and Scav territory. Above The Garden to the north are the cliffs and beyond that is where the Scavs live. They have tribes to the east and west along the coast, at least that we know of. Small inner circle close to the northern border is the base of your city. The five lines make up our four provinces. We know the column is forty-eight hundred feet across but we don't know how large the city is."

I do. "The city is five thousand feet across and three hundred and sixty feet high." I look closely and see the lines coming from the circle that represents the column of our city. The one on the left begins at the west side of the column and goes to the western point of the inner area through the forest. The one on the right goes to the eastern point. The other three lines equally divide the areas in between.

"We live in the eastern province," Vet says. "Each province is governed by three Elect."

Ana strokes my hair. "Your hair is so pretty. Never seen hair this color. Are you the only one with hair like this?"

I smile. "No, everyone has hair this color." I notice that my shoulder-length, straight, pale hair and gray eyes are unique in this room. Niko also has long, straight hair, but it is very dark, and his eyes are dark blue. His father, who is the same height as Niko, about ten inches taller than I, has the same color eyes and hair, but it is shorter and very curly. Vet is much broader than Niko, and his arms are larger but not as defined. He has very thick eyebrows. And the little girl, Ana, has a curious face, as smooth as the walls in our city, with big curious brown eyes. Her hair is light brown, long, and flowing down her back and shoulders with wondrous waves, albeit tangled and messy at the moment. Their skin, however, matches my own—a medium olive tone. The big difference is the height and size. I am five feet even, the same as every adult inhabitant of the city, male or female. The only difference is the hair of the females, which is about a foot longer than the males.

Ana taps me on the shoulder and I turn to look at her. "Papa is an Elect," she says.

"You are part of the government?"

Vet nods. "Sí. That's what the red sash here represents." He lifts the red strip of cloth hanging from his belt. "We ain't just governors; we're also ministers and doctors. You'll get to meet them all tomorrow. Have to let them know about you so we can decide how best to get you home."

Thank goodness. I want to go home. "My father is also part of the government in the city. That is why we live on the bottom level. The levels represent the social statuses. Government workers are the lowest standard. Maintenance is Level Eleven."

Vet laughs. "Government is the lowest and maintenance is the highest?"

I nod. "Yes, maintenance is the highest achievable profession. Maintenance requires a great amount of engineering study. They keep the city in structural order. Level Twelve is the entertainers, but you have to be delivered to that family to become an entertainer. That is where Adon was taking me—my first visit."

Niko places a dish on the table. It is filled with different types of food like the red stuff he let me eat earlier. "You want me to send the signal for the meeting, eh?" he asks.

His father nods. "Sí. But first, let's eat."

Niko takes his seat and they all join hands. Niko has to reach across the table to grab Ana's hand since she is still sitting beside me. Ana takes my left hand and Vet takes my right. I do not know why. But then they close their eyes and Vet begins to speak softly.

"We thank the Fathers for this meal and for all the good things they bring to us. And we thank them for our new friend and ask for their guidance in getting him home safely. Gracias, Fathers."

"Gracias, Fathers," Niko and Ana repeat.

After that, they open their eyes and begin picking pieces of food from the dish on the center of the table. I pick one and begin to nibble on it. It is different from the red stuff I had earlier but still as tart and sweet. My taste buds are once again in a heightened state. I enjoy the sensation. "Are these some of the crops you send to us?" I ask.

"No," Niko says. "These are fruits and berries from the forest. We are forbidden to eat the Fathers' crops."

I hear a knock on the door and a voice yelling out. "Niko? Are you home?"

Ana rolls her eyes. "Great. It's Ari." She looks up at me and whispers, "That's Niko's mate."

CHAPTER FOUR

Niko walks to the door and opens it. A girl rushes in and throws her arms around him. "Are you loco? Tag told me what you did."

They come into the kitchen and Niko sits again as the girl sits in his lap, her arms again around his neck, her long, straight black hair flowing across her shoulders and draping down in front of her. Her eyes are green. This perplexes me, not just the physical aspects of everyone, but in the city I do not remember ever touching anyone. Here it seems they cannot stop.

"This is Piri," Niko says, motioning to me.

The girl stares at me with a scornful look. I wonder if I have taken her seat.

"He's from the city in the sky," Ana says.

"I thought they were invisible," the girl replies. "What's he doing here?"

Yes, I must have taken her seat.

Niko ignores the question. "I have to go send the signal for the Elect." He gets up and goes into another room and returns with a large, neatly folded cloth. He walks toward the front door and the girl follows.

"Can me and Piri come?" Ana asks.

Niko stops and turns around. "Sure."

The girl's expression gets worse.

I shake my head. "I do not think I can walk very far."

"It's okay," Vet says. "We'll all go and take the carrier. It's not far."

We go outside. The girl, Ari, is still glued to Niko. He does not offer to carry me so I walk as best I can. We go only about five hundred feet and come to the carrier. It is a flat platform about ten feet long and four feet wide with side panels that come up about three feet on the front and sides. It sits about two feet off the ground and rests on a flat metal track.

"Use this to haul crops in, also," Niko explains. "This runs down the middle of our province and through the middle of the crop fields. We add the back panel when we fill it with crops."

We all climb onto the carrier as Vet goes to the controls in the front. He makes sure we are secure, presses the control stick forward, and the carrier begins to glide along the track, slowly picking up speed until it is moving very fast. We pass many homes and people, most waving as we go by. I can see the distant column getting larger as we travel toward it, and as we get nearer the column, the more homes I see.

Niko explains as if he was reading my thoughts. "More people like to live closer to the column. It's less distance to the fields and less distance to travel on the seventh day."

Ari stares at me again. I wonder if I have taken her spot on the carrier. I try to look away, out over the land. The homes do get very crowded. Then the land becomes almost barren as the carrier comes to a stop, just dirt as far as the eye can see with dried stalks protruding from the ground.

"This is where we harvest the crops for the Fathers," Vet explains. "The crops are dead now, but when the weather begins to get warmer, the fields will turn green and fill with crops. This is also where we bury the dead."

That answers my next question as I see several groups of people spread out over the fields standing around rectangular holes dug into the dirt, perfectly positioned between the rows of withered stalks.

Niko hops off the carrier and walks over to a tall pole. He attaches the large cloth to a rope and pulls the other rope, making the cloth rise high in the air as it waves and snaps in the wind.

"Now others will run up their flags across the land and get word to all the Elect," Vet explains.

Niko boards again and we begin the journey back the way we came.

"Do you eat the crops we send?" Ana asks.

"We do not eat crops."

Vet once again looks confused. "What do you eat?"

"We do not have a word for it," I say. "We have small square tablets that we take many times a day with water."

"What about the babies?" Niko asks as he climbs back into the carrier.

"It is the same, just dissolved in water."

Suddenly Vet stares up at the sky and sniffs. "Uh-oh."

Niko looks up and sniffs the air as well. "Yeah, it's coming. We better get off."

Vet stops the carrier and everyone jumps off the end. Vet helps me off. I do not know what is going on.

"Come on," Vet say. "Gotta get away from the carrier."

"Why? What is happening?"

Ana points upward. "Storm coming."

As we get about a hundred feet from the carrier, everyone lies flat on the ground. I do as they do but I am still unsure as to why. The answer does not take long in coming. Large water drops begin to fall from the sky, pelting the back of my tunic and drenching my hair. I can feel the dirt under the tall grass turning to mud. I am not sure why they feel the need to lie down during this event but I soon understand as a lightning bolt lights up the sky and cracks with the same sound I heard before in the transport. I cover the back of my head with my hands, my face pressed against the wet ground, as several more streaks of light erupt with thunderous declarations. I am shivering and wishing it would end. It finally clears a mere minute after it began. We all get to our feet and go back and board the carrier. I am soaked through and still shivering.

"We have to get off the carrier," Vet says, "because lightning is attracted to metal and to the tallest objects. When we're away from the forest, we have to make sure to get as low as possible."

I wonder how people can live like this.

We get back to their home where Ari hugs Niko for the tenth

time and leaves. We all put on dry clothes and come back and sit at the table.

Then Ana asks a question that does not make sense. "Have you met my brother?"

I look across the table at Niko and nod.

"No, not Niko," she says. "Have you met Bren?"

"Who is that?"

"He's my oldest son," Vet says. "He was chosen. Lives with you in the city now. Sure there are so many people, you ain't met them all."

"Why do you think he lives in the city?" I ask.

Niko answers. "A year ago, he was one of the Chosen. He only entered because his mate was chosen. He was so lucky; he got chosen the next week after his first time entering. All the Chosen Ones go to live in the city in the sky. You must see them in some areas of the city."

I have never seen anyone who looks like these people. Everything they say is so confusing. I do not answer.

"I'm eight. How old are you?" Ana asks.

"I am nineteen. I just turned nineteen. That is why Adon was taking me to Level Twelve. We are not allowed to go before."

Vet and Niko look at me funny. "I thought you were younger," Niko says. "I'm nineteen."

"How many people are there now in the city?" Vet asks.

I know this one as well. "There are one hundred and forty-four thousand."

"That's how many there are now?" Niko asks.

"That is how many there always are."

"Think you must be mistaken," Vet says. "We send four hundred people every seventh day. Your population must change frequently. For instance, they're missing two people right now. How do they account for you and your grandfather?"

That is a good question. Adon was already retired, so it would not really have an effect. But what if I die or never get back? How would they compensate for that? I concentrate on my fruit. I do not know what to say.

Vet does not let it go. "How does your population stay the same? Can you tell us about your family in the city?"

I think of how to explain. "First of all, no one touches anyone. We study from the time we are two, and we are taught that emotions are undesirable and create disruptions. Therefore, we concentrate on understanding our responsibilities as citizens of the city and studying to be the most productive citizens we can be. Before we turn twenty, we choose our profession. My scores are among the highest of my age, so I am going to choose Maintenance. When we turn twenty, our spouses are assigned by the Central Link, and we are married to others from the same chosen profession. The husbands move to their wives' living quarters and their son is delivered."

"On the day you're married?" Vet asks.

Niko is also shocked. "You wife is already pregnant before you marry?"

"I do not know about pregnant. The son is delivered via carrier. The husband and wife then go to work, and the son lives with the wife's parents in their half of the living quarters. Ten years later, the daughter is delivered. When the daughter arrives, the son moves into the parents' quarters and the daughter lives with the grandparents. When the daughter turns ten, she moves in with the parents. The son, who is then twenty, marries and moves into the grandparent's quarters. The mom's parents are then eighty years old and move out and report for the end. That is when they expire. So the population never changes."

Vet and Niko are staring at me as they try to process the information. I feel as though I have said something to upset them. Thankfully Ana does not comprehend everything.

"Maybe we look like you when we go to the city," she says.

Niko, Vet, and I all look at each other as we consider the possibility.

"So, you have a little sister, eh?" she asks.

I nod. "All families consists of two grandparents, two parents, and two children, the boy always being ten years older than the girl. I am surprised that you had another brother. I did not know families could have more than two children."

Niko laughs. "Our family's small. My friend, Ferg, has six brothers and three sisters."

"Twelve people total?"

Niko nods. "Your sister a pain like my sister?" Niko asks with a smile.

Vet laughs and Ana scoffs.

"I do not know. She is ten years younger and lives with my grandparents. I have never met her."

Everyone seems stunned by that news.

Ana smiles. "You miss your mama, eh?"

"I miss my home," I say. Then I realize something. "Where is your mother?" The room grows silent and faces turn down. I feel again as if I misspoke. "I did not know not to ask," I say.

Vet pats me on the hand. "It's okay. She was taken several years ago by the Scavs."

I can tell it is painful for them. "What are they?"

"Vile people," Niko says. "They only eat meat—any meat they can get their grubby hands on. That's why the forest is so dangerous."

"But is that not your territory?"

"They don't care," Niko says just below a shout, causing his father to look at him sternly. Niko drops his head as if in shame for raising his voice.

"We got to go into their territory, too," Vet says. "That's the only place to hunt. All the lizards stick to the rocky areas and desert terrain because it's warmer. That's where we find meat and eggs. And we got to go to the forest to pick berries and gather fish. It's a constant struggle keeping enough to eat for everyone. Some families don't have strong sons, and we got a lot of sick people."

"Guess people in the city never get sick," Niko says.

"No."

Vet puts an end to the interrogation. "Think we've asked Piri enough questions for now. Let's let the poor boy eat."

Vet seems to be wise and caring.

As night falls, Vet shows me to Bren's old room and tells me I can sleep there. All the lights stay on. The stones in the bedroom are farther apart, so the light is not as bright as the other rooms. I crawl into bed and fall fast asleep, weary from the day's events. Sometime in the night, I am woken by that dirty beast creeping under the covers with me. I do not move. It snuggles up right against my back and slides its leg over my waist. I reach down to move his leg and feel the tiny fingers. It is not the beast. I turn over. In the dim light, I see Ana smiling at me.

"Can I sleep with you, Piri?"

I do not know what to say. Does she not have her own bed? In my silence, she snuggles up against me. "I'm really glad you came here," she says.

I am not sure how to respond. I am not glad. My foot still throbs, and I am miles from the safety of my home. I try to go to sleep

CHAPTER FIVE

I wake to an odd smell. Ana is not in bed with me anymore, and I wonder how long I slept. I get up and go back to the table where I find the entire family. They are all busy doing something, so I sit back at my spot at the table. They all look around and smile, then continue working. They set more fruit and a plate of white round balls on the table. They take their seats as Ana sits again in the chair she had pulled over beside me.

"These are eggs," Vet explains, handing me one. "We harvest them every year as the weather begins to get warm, right before we harvest the crops. We keep them cold so we can have them almost all year. We boil them in water and eat them."

I bite into it and my teeth penetrate the cushiony texture. It is squishy but tastes good. Inside the white, there is a yellow part that tastes even better, so I eat it and some fruit. I drink a full glass of water.

They give me some things to wear on my feet. They are called sandals. I learn that the beast is called a dog. His name is Ash. He follows me around almost as much as Ana. They give me a cloak to wear over the tunic. We set out for the meeting with the Elect. Ana does not come along. She stays with another family.

"Where is the meeting?" I ask.

"At the column. That's where we always meet," Vet says.

We make the walk to the carrier again. Niko carries me on his back as Vet carries Niko's weapons. The long one, I learn, is called a spear and the other is a bow. The sticks with thin strips on the ends are called arrows.

The carrier speeds along as before. We stop to pick up the other two Elect from this province, each with his own armed guard. This time, however, we do not stop at the edge of the fields. When we reach the column, I notice a giant door with a section missing at the bottom just large enough for the track, which continues on inside. We get off the carrier and travel west along the southern side of the column. We pass the second carrier and continue on. Once we are at the southernmost point of the column, we come upon the eighteen others waiting for us. Vet introduces me to all of them.

The armed escorts, including Niko, go off to the right and left to stand guard for Scavs. Although they say a Scav has never intruded upon a meeting, they do not take chances. When just I and the twelve Elect are left, Vet explains to them the reason for the meeting. He tells them of my accident and explains that I am from the city in the sky. They are all amazed.

"You're one of the Fathers?" one asks.

It still feels odd being referred to as a Father. I had never heard that term used in that manner until Vet used it, but I nod.

They gather around me and look me over. Each one is carrying a copy of The Book and each one displays the same red sash from his belt. Several reach out to touch me as if wondering if I am really flesh and bone. I try to back away as they crowd me.

"Okay, you've seen him," Vet says. "What we need to decide is how to get him home."

"How are we supposed to do that?" one asks.

"We can't send him in with the crops. If it's totally automated, he would be killed. The Fathers would not like that," another says.

"I thought we might send him in with the Chosen Ones," Vet offers.

The other eleven stare at Vet as if he said something terribly wrong. "That's against the rules," one says.

"But the Fathers couldn't possibly be upset if we broke the rules for the greater good, could they, eh?" another chimes in.

Pretty soon all are talking at once.

"Wait!" Vet shouts. "Let's go one at a time. What say you, Maren?"

A woman takes a step into the middle of the circle. She is older than the rest. Her hair is lighter than mine. In fact, it is completely white. "I believe there are two problems with that. First, as pointed out already, we don't know how the Fathers would respond. I would love to get little Piri home, but not at the expense of anyone here. The second thing is—would any of you be willing to sacrifice a spot on the carrier for him? Many of our children wait years for a chance to be chosen. Would you deny one the right to take that opportunity if they finally get it? And if we send more than one hundred from each province, we come back around to breaking the law."

All nod in unison.

This continues for an hour as they discuss the only two possibilities they have been able to concoct. Finally an Elect steps forward who appears to be much younger than the others. "I think I have a possible solution."

"Very well, Shon," Vet says. "What's your idea?"

The young Elect looks around as if he is nervous. "Can't we just send a note with the next group of Chosen, eh?"

Everyone, including Vet, nods. They vote on it and it is decided. They also decide that for my safety, they will not tell anyone that I am from the city. We disband and everyone goes back to their homes. I wrap the cloak around me as tightly as possible as the carrier zips along the track, the strong wind almost pushing me over at times, so I sit again with my back against the side.

When we get back to Vet's home, it is midday. Niko and Vet go out with a hunting party. "Only have a little while longer to hunt," Niko explains. "The lizards will sleep underground when the weather gets cold."

Cold? I thought the weather was already cold, and it scares me to think it will get colder than it is now. I am glad that Ana stays home with me. She is nice to me. I sit in bed to rest my foot and she brings me water and fruit. Then she surprises me again. She brings me The Book and asks if I will read it to her. I must admit that I have been curious about The Book. She crawls into bed with me and lays her head on my side. I hold The Book in my lap. It is thick, made of some kind of odd material. It appears to be very old but in amazingly good shape. I open it and read.

"In the beginning, Canus was a giant land mass in the world, stretching from the warm oceans in the south to the icy plains of the north. But the people had become too many and too violent, so the Fathers were chosen to live away from the violence, and the great city was constructed in the sky. When it was completed, they left the surface to the Children and lived high above the clouds.

"But the evil continued to spread amongst the Children, so the Fathers rained down fire to punish them. The skies turned black and many of the Children died as a result. Peace returned to the surface, but it did not last.

"As the evil returned, the Fathers had to punish the Children again. This time they made the oceans rise and flooded the great land of Canus, leaving only the desert lands that remain now and The Garden. The Fathers created The Book to guide the Children from that day forth, so they would not allow the evil to return. As long as the rules are obeyed, the Fathers will be happy with the Children."

Ana is holding me tightly and shivering at the words. I close the book. It confuses me. I never knew it existed. I have never heard any of these stories, and they are horrible stories filled with irrationality.

She looks up and smiles. "You know any games, Piri?"

The only games I know are mathematical games on the city Link. I shake my head.

She teaches me a game where she picks an object in the room, and I have to guess what it is. She tells me I am colder if the object I guess is far away and warmer if I begin to get closer. It is not a challenging game since their rooms have very few objects in them. We play until we drift off to sleep.

We are roused from sleep by Ash jumping on the bed and licking us both in the face, apparently a favorite pastime of his. It tells us that Niko and Vet are back from the hunt. We get up and walk outside to find them.

Niko greets us as he walks past to enter the home and put away his weapons. Vet is standing over two giant creatures. They are hideous, each about five feet long and covered with dark green scales. They have spikes running down their spines, and their tails are the longest part of their bodies.

"What are those?" I ask.

Vet smiles. "These are lizards. This is where the eggs came from this morning. They're a great source of meat. Along with fish, they are our only source. We use the skins to make sandals and arrows. Take one and share it with others," he says as Niko comes back out.

Niko obeys, taking one of the scaly creatures as he walks away.

Vet takes a knife and cuts the skin away from the remaining lizard. Ana and I go back inside so we do not have to watch.

Later that evening, Niko cooks some of the meat for dinner. I stick to the fruits.

As we eat, Ana continues to ask questions. "Are you coming to worship with us tomorrow?"

"I do not know. Am I?"

Ana and Niko look to Vet. "Think it best he comes along," Vet says. "The rules say everyone must attend."

"We cannot break those rules," I say. That might be my first attempt at sarcasm.

Vet simply smiles.

That night as we go to bed, Ana automatically follows me. We go to sleep in the same positions as she curls up in my arms. I once again fall into a deep sleep.

We set out for worship early the next morning, and I wonder if anyone ever sleeps late on the surface. Niko offers to carry me again but I decide to walk. My foot is not hurting as much anymore. Vet used a forked limb to construct an aid to help take pressure off my foot. He added cloths to the fork area, and that slides under my arm, allowing me to shift more weight to the stick as I walk. Ana walks close beside me. I do not see any other people during our walk. "I thought everyone had to go to worship," I say.

Niko nods. "Sí, unless you're very sick or dying, or about to have a baby. The people who live way out here must start many hours before daylight. It's a very long walk and only the Elect and their families are allowed to ride the carrier."

I find myself relieved that Ari is not a family member of an Elect. There is something about her that makes me uncomfortable. Like before, we ride the carrier and, like before, we pick up the other two Elect, only this time they are joined by their families, making the carrier a little more crowded. Everyone still stares and smiles at me. As we near the area of the crops, we pass people walking. Some carry babies, some pull carts with wooden wheels, but all wave and smile. There are so many little children, women with babies, and women with swollen bellies who seem to have eaten too much. I see some people sitting on their homes.

As we glide through the crop areas, we pass a tall boy who waves enthusiastically and begins to run before we ever get to him. "Today's my day. I can feel it," he yells before losing his balance and falling face first to the ground.

"Slow down, Payo," Niko yells as we pass. "You're going to hurt yourself."

The others on the carrier laugh. "Way to go, Tonto," one yells. Other boys walking by him laugh, throw balls of dirt at him, and call him Tonto as well.

Vet laughs, too. "Hope it's his week. That boy's been dreaming of being one of the Chosen since the day he turned fifteen."

"You have to be fifteen years old?" I ask.

Niko nods. "We're allowed to add our names to the mix when we're fifteen and have to remove them when we turn nineteen. The Chosen can only come from the Children between those ages. Payo just turned eighteen, so he's getting worried he won't be chosen."

I remember Niko saying he was nineteen. "So, you have had to remove your name?"

"Never entered," Niko says. "Would love to go to the city and see Bren, but I'm needed too much here. I really hope Payo makes it, though, because his mama and papa are dead now, and he lives with his older brother. He's more of a burden since he can't hunt."

"Why can he not hunt?"

"It's not that he can't," Vet says. "He just can't hit anything with a bow and arrow."

"That's not completely true. He did hit his brother once," Niko says as he, his father, and several others on the carrier laugh.

I still do not understand the Chosen One concept. "If you are not chosen between fifteen and eighteen, you never make it to the city."

"Only after we die," Vet says. "And only if we lived a good and productive life."

The concept just got more confusing. I am certain there must be a misunderstanding. I have never seen people from the surface, the Children they call themselves, in the city. And I certainly have never seen dead people from the surface in the city. Even if they did somehow change appearance to resemble the people in the city, the population would still change. But I do not want to say anything to undermine something they believe in so much. I look down at Ana and she shrugs her shoulders. I am glad I am not the only one confused.

CHAPTER SIX

We reach the column and I can see all the way to the rocky border. There is no forest this far north. Although the rocks are miles away, it still frightens me to stare out toward them. Then I see it but I am not sure if it is real or my eyes playing tricks. I see it again…and again—patches of black movement among the rocks. Then I realize what it is. "Oh no," I say, pointing to the rocks. "Scavs."

No one seems alarmed, not even Ana, and most do not even look in the direction I am pointing.

"It's okay," Niko says. "Today is the seventh day. Scavs don't attack on the seventh."

"Why?"

"The Book," Vet says. "They also follow the rules of The Book, which forbids bloodshed on the seventh. They travel to their northern camp for worship, just like we travel to the column for worship."

Somehow I did not think the Scavs were civilized enough for something as organized as worship or intelligent enough to follow any rules. But it does make me feel better. The crowds of people become thicker as we near the column. Drums are everywhere and many people huddle around fires to stay warm, some holding their copy of The Book. We reach the giant door again and everyone except the three Elect gets off the carrier. As Niko helps me off, I scan the view. There are people as far as my eyes can see, an ocean of heads, hair, and eyes. Seeing this many people is strange to me, for now there are more in my view than live in the city, and with so many diverse appearances. As I step off, I can only see the people in the front as the adults are taller than I am.

One of the Elect raises The Book high and calls for prayer. "Dear Fathers. We come together today on the seventh day to give thanks for all the wondrous things you do for the Children. We strive to obey your laws and to lead productive lives, so that we might one day take our place among you. Gracias. Amen."

As he speaks, his words are repeated in whispers, beginning with the first row of people in the crowd and drifting backward, all the way I assume to the very back rows.

After the prayer, the second Elect on the carrier steps forward holding The Book. "Today, I'm going to read from page twenty-three of the fifth chapter." He opens The Book to where he had it marked and begins to read. "Do not seek personal gains so you might brag to your neighbor. For such things are not pleasing to the Fathers. But go about your life in a humble way, doing what is right and just, not trying to be any better than others, and you will be rewarded. Those who obey the rules and live their lives in a simple manner will never really die, but will be lifted up to the city for all eternity."

I watch as the words are whispered back and everyone nods in agreement. He continues reading other sections of the book and then turns it over to Vet. Vet also walks to the end of the carrier with The Book held high and reads from passages he had marked for today. "Do not fight among yourselves or seek revenge if done wrong. Know that if someone does something wrong to you, punishment will come to him when he dies, unless he makes it right to you. But if you try to take revenge, that which is reserved for the Fathers, your punishment will be worse."

I do not know what to think about The Book. Did it really come from our city in the sky? Why are these things I have never known about? After each of the Elect has read his portion of The Book, it is time for the drawing for the Chosen Ones. They step off the carrier and a large bag is brought up and given to Vet. He sticks his hand in, pulls out a small cloth, and reads the first name. "Mani Cloe."

The name is repeated throughout the crowd, not whispered like before, but almost yelled. A loud scream is heard and everyone looks to see who it is. A young boy makes his way through the crowd as everyone parts to give him an aisle. He comes up with a huge smile on his face and is instructed to get onto the carrier. This continues for hours as Vet continues to pull names from the bag. Finally, one hundred kids are packed onto the carrier. Parents come forward, reaching up to take their children's hands one last time, tears of joy running down all faces.

Vet walks up to one of the kids on the carrier and hands him a rolled-up cloth. "Give this to the first person you meet inside." He turns and gives me a nod. I know it is the note explaining that I am here with questions about how best to get me home.

I stare upward at the giant column to where it disappears into the clouds. It does not seem fair that these outsiders are going to my home and I am not allowed to go. I wonder if I should have been more demanding. As the commotion and crying dies down, we wait. Vet gets onto the carrier and maneuvers it forward to just outside the great door, then climbs off. I look to Niko.

"We're waiting on the time for the door to open and receive them," he says in a whisper.

And that is what happens. The giant door makes a loud screech that makes me jump. It rises as the kids on the carrier try to stare into the darkness. As it opens fully, the carrier moves forward, taking them into the void, and closes behind them. The crowd turns and walks away as a few parents still cry and stare at the massive closed door.

"That is it?" I ask. "Worship is over? We go back now?"

Niko nods. "It's over, but we have to wait a while. The Elect will meet again, as they do every seventh day after worship, so we have to wait here until Papa returns."

The family members of the Elect talk amongst themselves or find other ways to occupy their time. It is already late in the day and I think of those who had to walk from the outer areas, those who left many hours before daylight and will get back home many hours after dark.

Niko motions for me to follow him. Ana grabs my hand and comes along. We walk around the column toward the north side.

He points to faded paintings on the column. The paintings are of flowers, I believe, and they go on as far as I can see.

"Mama did these," Ana says.

"Really?"

Niko nods. "Sí. She did this every day of worship while Papa and the other Elect met. These were her favorite flowers. They grow everywhere during the warm days. Mama called them 'Kablooms' because they look like tiny explosions."

I stare at the artwork. Some are very faded, suggesting they were done many years ago. But some are still very clear and they do indeed look like explosions. They are about the size of a human head, red, with many jagged leaves stretching outward. The insides are yellow with streaks darting off in different directions, blending into the red. The images seem to go on forever around the base of the column. "How far do they go?"

Niko smiles. "All the way around to the west entrance door, I think. She couldn't just stand around and do nothing, so this is how she passed the time. During the warm months, Mama always picked bunches of these to keep inside the house."

"Niko does it now," Ana said.

From the look on their faces, I can tell they miss their mother very much. It is a startling revelation to me. I did not know people shared such reciprocity with each other. I wonder about the repercussions of these emotions; how it must affect their lives, their judgment. I think it must be a huge liability.

The noise of the giant door opening makes me jump again. It is the empty carrier returning. We rush back around to see if there is an answer to the message. I almost expect one of my people to be in the carrier to guide me back home. But it is empty.

"It might take them a few days," Niko says.

I nod. Then I see that the entire crowd has not dispersed. About fifty remain, standing motionless, staring at me. They began to walk closer, some reaching out their hands.

"You're one of the Fathers?" one asks.

Niko steps in front of me. "Where did you hear that?"

I hear Ari's name whispered by several members of the crowd. They flow around me like water, forming a circle and still closing in, still reaching out with desperate fingers. The circle tightens, and I feel trapped.

"Step back!" Niko yells.

They ignore him and press forward. I feel hands touching my head, my back, and my face. "Stop!" I yell.

Vet returns and pulls everyone back one at a time. They finally move away and I feel as though I can breathe again. Vet sends them on their way. "Sorry about that," he says. "They think you might have powers and touching you will help them, I guess. I was trying to avoid this."

As the daylight fades, we mount the carrier and head home, dropping off the other Elect and their families as we travel. I sit back against the side and Ana sits beside me. I close my eyes. Then I feel the carrier slowing, but it does not feel like we should be to the end. I hear Vet and Niko whispering. I look up and see an older woman standing on the track, a young girl in her arms. The girl appears to be several years older than Ana, and larger. It is an amazing sight. The woman is frail, her bones visible in her shoulders and chest, yet she cradles the girl with all her might. I wonder how long she has held her like this.

The carrier comes to a stop a few feet from the woman. "You can't block the carrier like this," Vet says. "Go on home."

Tears run down the woman's narrow face. "Please. My daughter's very sick. You couldn't help her. No one can. But maybe a Father can." She stares at me. "Please touch my child."

Niko and Vet turn to look at me as well. I do not know what to do. "I cannot help her," I say.

The woman walks to the back of the carrier. "I've carried her four miles to meet you here. Please touch her."

I do not understand how that could possibly help, but I get up and walk to the rear of the carrier. I get on my knees and look at the girl. Her eyes are barely open, and her breathing is labored. There are red sores all over her body. I do not want to touch her, but everyone seems to be expecting me to do so. I reach out with my hand and put it on her forehead. She is burning hot. I hold it there for several minutes and bring it away.

The old woman smiles. "Gracias," she says and walks away. I watch her as she carries the girl with much effort.

Niko assists me in getting up and going back to my spot as Vet maneuvers the carrier onward. As we near the end of the track, I realize I am starving. We have not eaten once all day. I will be glad to get to their house and eat. The carrier stops and we walk to the house, Ana holding on to my hand as always, which does not help me balance the walking aid on the other side. I am uncertain why she does it, but who am I to question their customs? It is completely dark out, the only light coming from the doorways of homes.

We reach Vet's house and walk inside, but instead of sitting down to eat, he kisses both Ana and Niko on the forehead. "Buenas noches," he says.

"Are we not going to eat?" I ask.

Vet smiles. "We can't eat on the seventh day."

My expression must reflect my thoughts.

"You get used to it," Ana says.

She and I go to bed and Niko and Vet do the same. Ana snuggles up against me as usual. I try to go fast asleep, but my stomach is making sleep difficult. I have never felt this way before, and I dream about my own home and wish I had a handful of our food tablets right now. My stomach makes a funny noise and Ana giggles. Of all the things in The Book that seem crazy to me, not eating all day on the seventh day is clearly my new most misunderstood rule.

CHAPTER SEVEN

Our toes are only a few inches apart, and Ana bumps my feet and laughs. She is a bizarre little girl. She is easily amused. We sit outside the house on the short walls that form the walkway to the steps. The walls rise up about six inches off the ground, I assume to keep the rain water out. It is cold outside early this morning, but we were bored staying inside.

Ash lies beside Ana as she scratches his head. He seems to like that.

"You sad, eh?" Ana asks.

"Sad? Why do you say that?"

Ana looks down at her feet. "Because it's been so long. We've been to worship three times now and sent three messages and no one has told us what to do."

I have been surprised that not one message has been returned. Are they receiving them? Do they not need the population to remain the same? Or are they satisfied with all the new Chosen Ones and decided they do not need me? At least the people here do not approach me to touch me anymore as they have learned that I have no magic powers. This they deduced from the old woman who stopped the carrier as her story spread throughout the land. I learned the girl died before she made it back home.

Ash lifts his head. I turn to see the clumsy boy walking up to us. I cannot remember his name.

"Hola, Payo," Ana says.

"Hola, Ana. Hola, Piri."

I wonder how he knows my name but I nod and greet him. He just stands there for several seconds staring at me. He is almost a foot taller than Niko, lean and muscular, but every movement conveys a sense of awkwardness and lack of coordination. His hair is brown like Ana's but thicker and comes down over his eyes. He constantly brushes the strands from his vision. His teeth protrude with gaps between them. I notice one of his legs is covered with a black substance that runs about halfway up his lower leg. His sandal is completely black.

Ana sees it too and puts her hands over her mouth as if trying to muffle her laugh. "Payo, did you step in a pit again?"

His face is red as he looks down at his leg. He keeps his face down as he nods.

"It's okay," Ana says. "I've done it, too."

He looks up and smiles. Then his smile disappears. "I have a message for your papa."

Ana slides off the edge of the little wall and opens the door to the house. "Papa, Payo is here and needs you."

Vet and Niko walk out of the house. "What is it?" Vet asks.

Payo squeezes his hands together as if he is nervous. "A hunting party was attacked on the west side."

Vet looks alarmed. "How many were in the party?"

"Eight."

"How many Scavs?" Vet asks.

Payo looks at me and Ana then back at Vet. "Three."

Vet seems to realize his own demeanor might be making things worse, so he smiles. "Okay, thanks, Payo. You go on home and wash your leg. Be careful of those pits now."

Payo smiles. "Sí, I will. Bye, Ana. Bye, Piri." He turns and walks away.

We instinctively look to Vet, who looks at Niko. "This is strange," he says. "I've never heard of Scavs attacking a party that large. And this is the third weird story we've heard recently. Six days ago, Scavs were spotted in the forest in the southern part of The Garden, a place where they've never been seen."

"What do you think is going on?" Niko asks.

Vet shakes his head. "Don't know."

I see the girl, Ari, approaching. She runs to Niko and throws her arms around him. "Are we ready to go?"

"You going after fish today?" Vet asks.

Niko nods.

"How many are going with you?"

Niko looks embarrassed to answer. "Eight."

"Double it," Vet says. "Don't want to take any chances."

"Sí," Niko says.

"What's going on?" Ari asks.

Niko takes her arms and removes them from around his neck, which she does not seem to like. "Scav attack."

Ari looks worried then looks at me and smiles. "I think Piri should come along."

Everyone looks at me. I have no idea what she means, but I am ready to do anything other than sit around the house. "Sure," I say.

"Can I come?" Ana asks.

"Sorry, Chiquita," Vet says. "You know you're not old enough yet."

Niko retrieves his spear and bow and arrows from the house along with a large sack. I wonder if he uses the weapons to catch fish. I feel sorry for little Ana, who crosses her arms and pouts as I walk off with Niko and Ari. We walk due south and I can see the forest to our far left along the horizon. We come to a group of seven other boys, all with the same weapons and all with the same kind of sacks.

"Hola, boys," Niko says as we walk up.

They all smile and return the greeting.

One steps forward with a really big smile. "This is the one you told me about, eh?"

Ari laughs. "Yes. This is Piri. He came from the city in the sky. Piri, this is my brother, Tag."

Her brother extends his hand. He is only a few inches taller than I am. His hair is shorter than the other boys and sticks straight up like black spikes. His chest, shoulders, and arms are much larger than Niko's with protruding veins running the length of them. He has a large scar spanning the distance from underneath his left eye to his chin. As he continues to hold his hand out, I realize he is waiting for me. I extend my hand and he shakes it roughly.

"Nice to meet you, Piri," he says.

"Listen, boys," Niko says. "Scavs have been acting funny, attacking groups of eight, so I want all of you to go find one other person to go with us today."

They all look alarmed but hurry off to find someone, all except Tag.

"What about you, Tag?" Niko asks.

Tag walks over and puts his burly arm around my neck. "Already have."

I want to move his arm but decide not to, even though I know I would not be any help against those creatures.

When the others return, each with another person, we set out for the forest. My heart beats faster as we near the line of trees. I still remember the night I spent there, and the memory is not a pleasant one. Before we enter the forest, the group spreads out into a large square. I do not know why.

Niko must see my expression and explains. "Scavs use bombs to knock people out. Then they carry them away. That's why we spread out."

I think back to the creature Niko killed. "Is that what they keep around their waist in those clear bubbles?"

Niko nods. "Sí. It's something they make from seawater. When they remove it from their belt, there is something in the tip that reacts to the air and it takes about three seconds to ignite. That sets off the clear substance in the bubble, which creates a very large explosion. If one goes off near you, it will knock you senseless."

I begin to rethink my decision to go fishing. I might be bored at the house, but I wouldn't be in danger. I can see the worn trails through the forest and realize it is a path taken frequently. Ash leads the way with his nose in the air. Another dog belonging to one of the other boys brings up the rear, his nose also in the air as they sniff constantly. As we walk, Tag comes up alongside me and takes my hand, something Ana does frequently. I look at the others. I see two boys also holding hands and Niko and Ari are as well. I realize it must be another custom, one pertaining to the forest.

Niko looks back at us, particularly at Tag. He almost seems angry. I wonder what Tag has done.

Finally we come to a small clearing in the forest, and I behold a beautiful sight. It is a large body of water, a stunning lake about five hundred feet across. The only areas that disrupt the symmetry are two peninsulas that dart inward on both sides, forming almost a perfect figure eight, leaving only about two hundred feet from each bank. I have never seen an image like it, at least one not on the Central Link. It is breathtaking.

Niko walks right up to the edge of the water as the others take defensive positions. The water moves along the bank as it laps the dirt, forming ripples and foam at the point of contact. Niko moves a rock and pulls out a hollow vine. He motions for me to come over. I notice no one is holding hands anymore except me and Tag, so I pull my hand away.

"Blow into this," Niko says.

I look at the dirty vine and shake my head. Ari laughs. She takes it from Niko and pulls it up to her lips and blows into it. After each breath, she holds her thumb over the opening. She does this for a while then points out into the water. I follow her finger and look out over the shiny surface. I see it, but I am not sure what I see. There seems to be a large white balloon just below the surface about fifty feet from the bank. Ari continues to blow and it partially rises out of the water. She then takes a piece of wood and plugs the end of the vine as Niko pulls the balloon toward us. As the balloon gets to within ten feet of the bank, Niko wades out, reaches beneath it and pulls a large box out of the water. It is about three feet in all directions and constructed of small sticks forming a cage of sorts. There are small rocks inside, and that is not all. As he brings it completely out of the water and walks back onto land, I can see the bottom is alive with funny-looking animals, fish I assume, flopping around as if wondering where their water supply went.

Niko stands it up on what appears to be the back side and removes the front panel. He holds it up for me to see. "See how this side is made? It has these sticks going inward, which makes the fish believe it's a huge opening. They swim inside but this side forms a small hole and they don't think they can get out, so they stay in the box." He takes the fish and empties them into his sack.

When all of the fish are removed, he replaces the front panel, wades back out into the water, and gives it a push. The balloon is still filled with air, so it slowly drifts back out to where it was before. Ari removes the plug from the vine and the air rushes out of the balloon, causing the box to sink back to the bottom. He puts the vine back in place and covers it with the rock.

After he finishes, Niko grabs his spear and bow and he and Ari take a position on the outside perimeter as Tag goes to find his own balloon box to repeat the procedure. I guess he realizes I am not going to help, so he calls out to his sister. She goes to help him retrieve his fish. Niko and I take a seat on some rocks and Ash sits in front of us as he continues to sample the air with his nostrils.

I look around the trees with an uneasy disposition.

"Don't worry," Niko says. "Been coming to fish here a long time. Used to come with Bren. I sure miss him. Bren was awesome. He used to beat me up all the time."

"And that is a good thing?"

He laughs. "Yeah, it is. I mean, he's a lot stronger than I am, so he could have really hurt me. But he never did. It was just for fun, or maybe to teach me to be tough."

I think about that. "Are you tough?"

Niko holds his chin high in the air. "You know it." He laughs.

Knowing how they miss their mother, I wonder if it is the same. "Are you sad that he was chosen?"

"Sí," Niko says, "but happy, too. He was so sad after Jeni was chosen."

"His mate?"

"Yeah. He put his name in the very next day. He stayed around the house for days after, crying."

"Crying?" I ask. "This was the boy who used to beat you up?"

He nods, then looks at me funny. I do not know why, but it makes me feel a little strange, almost equivalent to the feeling of fear, but still a far cry from that feeling. Whatever it is, it makes me a little uncomfortable and I stare upward at the sky.

Ash jumps up and growls, snapping me out of the trance.

"Scavs!" Niko yells and places an arrow in his bow. "How many, boy?" he asks, but Ash just whines. I think there are a lot of them.

The fishing stops as everyone grabs their bows and loads an arrow. Niko walks backward toward the group, his eyes still scanning the line of trees as Ash continues to stay poised, pointing his snout toward the forest. Soon everyone is in a large, partial circle with the water behind us. No one speaks or moves, only watches. I see the other dog also pointing toward the forest in the opposite direction. I wonder if this means we are surrounded. I turn to look back in the direction of Ash's stare and see a dark figure run from one tree to another.

"Saw one," Niko informs the group.

An hour passes as no one moves and at least a dozen more sightings are witnessed. The days are not very long and judging from the overcast sky, the sun is drifting toward the western horizon.

"Okay, boys, let's head out," Niko says. He places his bow on his back and grabs his spear.

Some of them grab the bags of fish. Half of them continue to hold their bows and the other half take the spears, most of that half holding two spears. We remain in a loose circle and walk back toward the forest from where we came.

My mind is once again consumed by fear as we enter the darker area under the forest canopy. One of the Scavs yells, but no one reacts; they just continue through the forest. The Scavs are so close I can hear them walking on the brown leaves that now partially cover the forest floor, their guttural sounds suggesting they are just beyond the scope of our vision through the trees. We march on until we come to the clearing. As we enter the grassy field free of the trees, they all form a line and walk backward, their bows and spears still aimed at the forest. Only when we are almost out of sight of the trees do half of them turn and walk forward. As we near the first homes, everyone turns forward and a collective sigh of relief is felt.

"We're okay now," Niko says to reassure me.

It does not. I keep turning to look behind us. Tag comes up and takes my hand again.

When we reach the point where we all met this morning, the fish are divided up and everyone goes about their way as if nothing happened. Tag finally releases my hand and Niko and I walk back to his house.

"Are you sure we are safe now?"

Niko nods and smiles. "Sí. The Scavs never come this far. We're okay."

But I can see in his eyes that this was not a normal encounter. This is confirmed when we get back to his house and he explains it to his father.

"Were you able to complete the fishing?" Vet asks.

"No," Niko says. "We still had many more boxes to go."

Ana comes over and takes my hand.

Vet looks at the bag of fish. "Go and give some to the ones who need it most."

Niko nods. "We still have time before the water freezes to go back for more."

"No," Vet says. "The cold will be here soon and I don't want anyone going out there now after what happened."

CHAPTER EIGHT

There are more fire drums going this seventh day. The weather is bitterly cold, and I can barely feel my hands and feet. I hold my hands closer to the fire but that makes them hurt. I can find no comfortable distance from the flames to hold them. I take Ana's hand in mine as I try to share the heat of my almost burnt hands with her. Even though we are bundled up with cloths wrapped around our legs and feet, a cloak, and a hat called a tuque with a silly little ball on top, I cannot keep from shivering violently.

"It is not the things in this life that concern us," Vet says as he reads from The Book, his words being whispered back through the crowd. "Everything we endure in this life makes us stronger and adds to the pledge of everlasting life when we die. The Fathers, who shower us with their love, have promised us no more suffering, no more sadness, and no more pain."

I think the Fathers promise a lot. If they wanted to shower the Children with their love, why then are they not allowed to worship at home on days like this?

When worship is over, we do not walk around and look at the flower art on the column; we huddle close to the fire. When the carrier returns from delivering the Chosen and Vet returns from the meeting of the Elect, we take the carrier home, but much slower since the air is too cold to travel fast. This is the seventh worship I have attended, seven letters we have sent about me being here. No one in the city seems to care. I am beginning not to care. As we reach the end of the track, strange white puffs fall from the sky, floating, sometimes dashing horizontally in the wind.

"It's snow," Vet says.

By the time we reach the house, the entire ground is covered. It is strangely beautiful. Although it is dark outside, the snow makes the landscape fairly visible. As we enter the house, the air inside is noticeably colder than it has been. I wonder how they stay warm.

Vet walks over to a little shelf in the center of the wall with the light producing discs. I had noticed these in each room but did not understand it. He turns one around to face the other and pulls his hand away quickly as the light shines very brightly. It is so strong I can instantly feel the warmth it is producing, and Ana and I walk over and raise our hands to warm them.

"I had no idea these put out heat if you got them this close together," I say.

"Really?" Vet asks. "How do they heat the city in the sky?"

"I do not really know, but I know it is not this way. The temperature always stays the same in the city. But I am glad they put out heat, and I am glad you have enough of them."

Vet walks to another shelf. "Oh, we have plenty. I guess these were abundant in nature. Some of the empty houses have tons of them stored."

"Can I do it?" I ask as he reaches for the next shelf.

He smiles. "Sí. Come on."

I do what he did. I turn the one disc around to face the other, but I did not know how fast it would become hot and it catches me off guard, causing me to drop the disc on the floor.

Everyone laughs and Vet picks it up and does it himself. But it does not work. There is no light and no heat. He looks closely at the disc. "Oh, it's chipped. I guess it can't work if it's chipped."

I feel guilt. "I am so sorry."

He laughs. "It's okay. We got more in the storage room." He looks at Niko, who goes and retrieves another. Vet puts it in place, and the heat-producing light comes to life.

"The storage room is where we keep food throughout the winter," Vet explains. "It's also where the well that provides our water is located, far underground. The windmill on top of the house brings the water up and keeps the storage area cold and provides water for the washroom and kitchen."

After all of the shelves are producing heat, the warm air engulfs me like a cloak. I still have not become accustomed to fasting on the seventh day, but not being cold helps a little. As always, we all go straight to bed.

"Good night, Ana," I say.

"Buenas noches, Piri."

I close my eyes but, like most nights, Ana wants to talk for a while. I do not mind. But her topic catches me by surprise this time.

"When I grow up," she says, "I want to be just like you."

"Why?" I ask sincerely.

She looks up at me and smiles. "Because you're so smart."

A smile crosses my lips. "I am?"

She nods and drifts off to sleep.

I wake the next morning and am surprised to find Ana still curled up against me fast asleep. I have gotten used to being the last one up. I am starving but do not want to wake her. I lie there unsure what to do. Finally, she opens her eyes and smiles. "Are you ready to get up?" I ask.

She shakes her head and closes her eyes again.

"Your father and brother might be expecting us to eat with them," I say. At least that is what I am hoping.

"No," she says without opening her eyes. "We stay in bed much longer during the cold days."

Figures. The one morning where I do not mind getting up earlier just to eat is the day they decide not to get up. But my stomach is grumbling. Ana looks at me, smiles, and puts her finger across her lips for me to be silent. She slips out of bed, leaves the room, returns, and crawls into bed again. She has a devious smile as she opens her hands and reveals three pieces of dried fruit. We split them. I go back to sleep. I think the day is half over when Ana wakes me. We go into the kitchen, and I see that Vet and Niko have just gotten up as well.

We sit at the table and hold hands as Vet thanks the Fathers. I notice the amount of food placed on the table is about half what is normal. Vet sees me staring.

"Got to be careful during the cold days," he says.

"How many cold days will there be?"

"Never can tell," he answers. "Sometimes it's thirty, sometimes one hundred." He directs his gaze toward Ana. "Which is also why we don't sneak food."

Ana grits her teeth and looks up to me. I say nothing. I take a piece of fruit and bite into it. Then I feel something under my nose. I wipe it with my finger and it is sticky. I think it came from the fruit.

Vet laughs. "You got a runny nose. Here, wipe it with this." He hands me a cloth. "Stay bundled up. Don't want you catching a cold."

I am confused as I wipe the substance from my upper lip. "How can I catch the cold?"

Niko and Ana laugh. "Not *the* cold," Niko says. "*A* cold. It means you could be sick."

I do not like the sound of that. I go to the washroom to clean my face, but no water comes from the tap. I go back and tell the others.

"Snow's getting deep," Vet says. "It's blocking the windmill."

Niko looks upward. "I better go clean the roof."

"No," Vet says. "Let's eat first. You got plenty of time."

Niko gets up. "Want to make sure Piri has water."

Vet smiles.

Like when we get ready to go to worship, Niko takes long rolled-up cloths and wraps them around his feet and exposed legs. He puts on two cloaks over his tunic, places his tuque on his head, and fetches a tool of some kind from his room. It is a flat piece of wood, about two feet long, a foot high, and only an inch or so thick. It has a wooden handle protruding out of it. He goes to the front door and we all follow. As he opens the door, the snow falls into the house. We have to clear it before we can close the door again.

"What is going on?"

Vet points upward. "The snow's getting so deep that it's keeping the windmill on the roof from spinning. That's why we don't have water."

I hear scraping sounds above us as Niko uses the tool to push the piled up snow off the roof. When he comes back in, he is shivering. He takes off the snow-covered wraps and cloaks and Vet drapes a blanket over him.

Niko looks at me and smiles. "I'll be okay."

I did not realize I was staring and quickly look away.

He looks at his father. "Let me warm up a bit, and I'll go do the others."

"What others?"

Vet nods to Niko then looks at me. "There are elderly couples who live nearby that have no sons to do this for them. We can't let them be without water. Everyone who is able helps the others who are not."

True to his word, Niko wraps his feet and legs again and leaves the house. While Niko is gone, there is a knock on the door. Vet opens it to find Ari and Tag.

"What are you doing out and about?" Vet asks.

Ari smiles. "Just came to visit Niko, and Tag wanted to see Piri."

Vet looks at me as if confused, then back to Ari. "Niko is gone to clean roofs. Come on in the kitchen."

We all go and sit at the table. Thankfully Ana sits by me again as Tag takes Niko's seat across the table and continues to smile at me. Vet looks at Tag the same way Niko did, and I cannot help but wonder why everyone seems to be angry with him.

"So," Tag says, "you don't have a mate in the city?"

I shake my head.

He smiles even bigger. "Good."

Ari laughs.

Niko returns and seems a little distraught at seeing the two of them here, or maybe just Tag. He changes his wet clothing and comes back to the table. Ari quickly plants herself in his lap again.

"They make a cute couple, don't they?" Ari asks, looking first to me, then her brother.

Niko ignores the question. "The snow is getting deeper. You two should be heading back."

Ari frowns but they take their cue. I cannot help but notice that the tension seems to lighten as soon as they leave.

Throughout the rest of the week, Niko periodically goes to clear snow or to deliver food as Ana and I never leave the house. Only when Niko leaves do we even get a glimpse of the outside. Vet takes this opportunity to teach Niko and Ana from The Book. As I am fascinated with The Book, I sit in and learn as well.

One day as we are gathered around the table, Vet slides The Book over to Ana to let her read. She puts her tiny finger on the page and glides it along as a guide. She reads slowly. "All things are provided by the Fathers so that the Children may live comfortably. But only hunt and kill in small numbers, so that your food may continue to thrive. Only pick fruits and berries in small numbers, so that they may grow in abundance the following year. Always keep the balance so that the land will always reward you."

"And what does that mean?" Vet asks.

Ana closes one eye and looks upward. "Uh…it means we can't pick all the berries and stuff in the forest because we have to leave some to make new ones the next year."

Vet smiles. "Very good, Chiquita. Niko, read page twelve of the first chapter."

Niko takes the book and reads, but much faster. "Although the Fathers had provided the Children with all they needed, some were not content. Vee, who lived thousands of years ago, disobeyed the rules of the Fathers and picked one of the forbidden crops from the Fathers' fields. When it was discovered what she had done, the Fathers punished the entire land, raining down fire and destroying many lives." Niko looks at me. "That's why we don't dare eat the crops from the fields."

I understand. At least I understand the words. I still do not express my concerns about the probability of the people in the city being able to accomplish the things in The Book.

The week progresses in the same manner with the snow not going away. Sometimes Niko goes out to help the elderly or deliver food, and sometimes Vet is summoned to help others. But for the most part, we stay in and study The Book. On the eve of the sixth day, the snow is deeper than ever. As we are preparing for bed, I think about the seventh day. "We do not have to go to worship in this weather, do we?"

Vet simply nods.

This is crazy. I know how difficult this is going to be for the older citizens. I go to bed that night but cannot stop thinking about it.

Vet wakes me and Ana early the next morning, and we spend a while wrapping ourselves with the rolls of cloth. I notice Niko is not present.

"He's clearing a path," Vet says.

"What do you mean?" I ask.

He explains. "It's very hard to walk through snow this deep, so we use the carrier to plow through the snow and make a clear trail. Most people will walk over to the rail and follow the track all the way to the column."

As he finishes that sentence, Niko comes in and takes a seat. He is wrapped up tight, but the trip down to the column was clearly not a comfortable one.

We leave a little earlier than normal since we will not be going full speed. We are all wrapped up with as many cloths and cloaks as we have available, plus that weird hat called a tuque. But it helps keep my ears from breaking off, so I wear it willingly underneath my hood. Seeing the older people walking in this weather makes me angry. I wonder if the Fathers even know what they are putting these people through. I stare out over the horizon as we near the column. The white snow makes the Scavs easier to spot, black dots of evil against an alabaster backdrop, as they continue to make their journey in this awful weather as well. I do not agree with this nonsense at all.

Like always, Vet goes off to meet with the Elect as we huddle around a fire to keep from freezing, waiting both for the return of the carrier from delivering this week's Chosen and for Vet to return. As I try to keep myself and Ana warm, my thoughts are no longer on the connection or love felt between the Children. My mind is focused on anger and wondering why my people have not come for me. Why have they not sent one simple letter instructing me to get on the carrier with the Chosen and come home where it is never cold and I was never hungry?

Then it dawns on me. Why do the Fathers make the Children go to worship every seventh day when it is not something we ever did in the city? Why do they make the Children fast on the seventh, claiming it to be a rule, when we did not ever refrain from eating on the seventh day, or any day for that matter? Why do the Children have all these rules that the Fathers ignore? And most importantly, why do they use fear to keep them doing it? The more I think about it, the angrier I become. I do not believe the threats in the book. As advanced as we are in the city in the sky, I truly do not believe we possess the technology to deliver the punishments mentioned frequently in The Book. And even if we could, I am not sure I want to return to a place and a people who could do such things. But I know I do not want to stay here in this cold, and it is this paradox that makes me the angriest.

CHAPTER NINE

Other than going to worship, which is an exercise in despair, we stay indoors. I am not sure which is worse: pushing through the snow as the cold air penetrates to my bones, all while listening to the redundancies of the threats propagated by The Book, or staying home. If I did not have Ana to keep me company, I do not believe I could take being shut in like this. As we sit and eat the limited dinner one night, someone knocks on the door. Ash does not even get off the floor, so we know it is safe. Plus, Scavs have never come into the home areas, and I doubt seriously they would knock.

Vet goes to the door and we hear him speaking but cannot make out the words. He comes back and walks through the kitchen and into his bedroom. Niko walks to his door.

"What's going on?" Niko asks.

Vet walks out of his room as he continues to wrap up. "Someone is sick, an older citizen, so I need to go by and check on him."

This is something that happens fairly regularly. Many times before the cold days, people would come and get Vet for this purpose. But tonight is bitter cold and dark as well. Vet puts on his tuque and walks to the front door. Niko follows.

"It's completely dark out," Niko says. "You want me to come with you?"

Vet shakes his head. "No, I know the way." He opens the door and disappears into the white covered darkness.

Niko comes back into the kitchen and sits. I can tell he is worried.

"He does not have any light to guide him?" I ask.

"No, and it's very dark out."

I look up at the ceiling at the two stone discs. I know they have extra ones and wonder why he could not just carry two of those and keep them the right distance apart. I guess that would make walking through the snow difficult. And I learned the hard way that they can burn you if you get them too close to each other. Then I have an idea. I get my walking stick from my bedroom. Ana and Niko are looking at me as if wondering what I am doing. I remove the cloths from the forked area and look at Niko. "Can you carve out a precise hole in this wood?"

Niko looks confused. "Sí, I think so. Why?"

I hand him the stick and go to the storage room. I take two of the discs and return. "Can you carve out a hole that these would fit into very tightly?"

He smiles. "Sí. I see what you're saying." He takes one of the discs and traces a line on each branch of the fork for guidance, then takes his knife and begins to carefully cut away the wood inside the lines. He looks up and smiles at me and Ana.

"What's it going to be?" Ana asks.

"You will see," Niko says. He stops several times to insert the disc and, when it does not quite fit, he removes it and continues working. Finally he gets one side carved out just right and places the disc in the hole. It is a tight fit, so he taps it gently. We already know they can chip and not be useful anymore. The disc slides tightly into place. I drape the cloth over it and he begins on the other side. Once he gets that disc in place, he holds up the stick from the shaft with the fork in the air. I remove the cloth from the one disc and an instant ball of light appears.

He and Ana laugh. "This is great," Niko says. "I'm going to carry this to Papa right now." He goes to his room and comes back all wrapped up and wearing his tuque. He takes the makeshift torch and goes out the door.

"You're so smart," Ana says.

I simply shrug. I walk back to the storage room and take two more of the discs. I place one in each pouch I have on either side of my belt. I am not sure why, but it seems like something that could be useful. I go into the first room and sit on the bench by our bedroom door. Ana sits by me.

"Let's play a game," she says. We play *Guess the Object* again. I go first.

"Is it Niko's bow?" Ana asks.

I shake my head. "You are cold."

"Is it the bench over there?"

"Still cold," I say.

"Is it this bench we're sitting on?" she asks.

"Warmer."

Ana starts to get excited. She sees Ash lying on the floor in front of us. "Ash?"

"Still warm," I say.

She continues to guess everything she can think of: our tunics, our sandals, the floor, and the wall until she gets frustrated. "I don't know. Can you give me a hint?"

"Okay, sure," I say. "The object I am thinking of is really small."

She looks confused as she scans the room, then her eyes light up. "Oh, I get it. It's you."

I shake my head. "No, silly. It is you."

She giggles. We continue to play.

Halfway through our game, Vet and Niko return. Vet is carrying the torch. He props it against the wall and Niko grabs the cloth again and places it over one fork, covering the disc and causing the light to disappear.

"You came up with this, eh?" Vet asks.

I nod.

"That's very good. Very useful," he says. "Don't know why no one else has thought of that."

I do not know either. I do not think it was that inventive, but I am glad it worked.

Niko and Vet sit on the bench across the room from us, the one I sat on my very first day here, as they remove their wraps.

"Can we tell stories?" Ana asks.

Vet smiles. "Sí. Who wants to go first?"

This is a fairly common occurrence, and I have been fascinated by it ever since my first time listening as they reminisce with stories from the past. In the city, every day is the same, so this is not something that would be interesting to do. But here, life is different—very different.

"You go first, Papa," Niko says. "Tell us about when you met Mama."

"You have heard that one many times," he says.

Before I realize I am saying it, the words jump from my lips. "I have not."

Vet looks at me and smiles. "Okay, I'll tell that one." The room grows silent as everyone sits perfectly still while Vet's eyes seem to take on a faraway focus. "Was only fifteen years old when I went with my mama and papa to the Market. We sat to watch a show, but there wasn't enough room on the bench, so I sat by an older couple behind us. Then this girl about my age walked up and just stared at me. I had taken her seat and was sitting by her parents. I didn't want to get up, so I just scooted to the end of the bench and she squeezed between me and her mama. I started watching the show, and suddenly she scoots over real fast and sends me flying right off the bench. I jumped up and was going to push her off but everyone was laughing so hard, I started laughing myself. And when I looked into her eyes, I was hooked. She was smiling at me like no one had ever done before. I was glad to learn that she lived in our province. We started spending a lot of time together, and the rest just happened."

Ana begins to clap.

"What was her name?" I ask.

"Dali," Vet says with a smile. "Okay, who's next? Niko, your turn."

Niko looks up at the ceiling. "Okay, I got one. It's a little scary."

Vet laughs. "No. You're not going to tell that silly story again, are you?"

Ana shakes her head.

My curiosity is piqued. "What? What is the story?"

"This really happened," Niko explains before he begins. "Was out with a fishing party. Was standing watch as someone else retrieved his trap. Heard something kind of faint, but it was real. Looked through the forest but didn't see anything. Could tell Ash was nervous, but he wasn't acting like when Scavs are around. Didn't know what was happening. Then I looked up and saw it." He pauses and waits.

"What?" I ask. "Saw what?"

He smiles. "Don't know what it was. Was silver and shiny. Was in the sky just below the clouds, like it was floating in the clouds or something. I could see the reflection of the ground on the bottom of it. There were also lights on the bottom."

"What did it do?"

He shrugs. "Nothing. Just disappeared into the cloud and I never saw it again."

I am intrigued. "What was it?"

"His imagination," Vet says, causing Ana to laugh.

"They never believe me," Niko says. "But I know what I saw."

Vet pats him on the head. "Yet no one else in the entire fishing party saw this thing. Think I dropped the poor boy on his head too many times when he was a baby."

Vet and Ana laugh, as does Niko. "Ain't my fault what the others didn't see," he says.

"Okay, Piri, your turn," Vet says.

"What? Me? I do not have any stories to tell."

"Tell us about the city," Niko says.

"There is nothing to tell."

Vet smiles. "Tell us your earliest memory."

I tilt my head upward as if that will somehow make my thoughts clearer. "Uh, I remember being very small and sitting in front of the screen in the main room. My grandfather is sitting beside me, and he is telling me to watch the screen. There were these fake people, like artistic drawings to look like real people, and they were explaining the importance of being a citizen of the city."

"What were they saying?" Vet asks.

I shrug. "I do not remember exactly. But as I got older, there were similar programs with real people always teaching things like the importance of concentrating on your studies and becoming a productive member of society—that sort of thing."

"There's got to be more," Vet says. "Do you guys go places together, do things together?"

I shake my head. "No, we do nothing like that. My mother stays in front of the main screen in the main room. My father works most days and when he is home, he stays in his room at the Central Link there. I stay in my room and study. We do not eat together or go anywhere together. My parents sometimes go to Level Twelve, as do my grandparents, but I have never been anywhere besides our living quarters and occasionally around the city in the tubes."

"That seems very lonely," Vet says.

I shrug. I have never thought about it.

Niko smiles. "What about the day you fell from the sky?"

"Sí," Ana says.

I think about that day. I guess I do have a story. I begin to tell them how it all happened, but I realize even that does not sound as good as their stories. "Adon and I got into the tube and he pressed the button. There are twelve separate entrances to the tubes around the perimeter of the city. The tubes work by creating a vacuum, which zips the transport along the tube." All eyes are fixed on me. This is fascinating. I begin to mimic their elevated voices when describing certain points of the story, and I am amazed to see them leaning forward, glued to every word. I discover that telling stories is as much fun as hearing them. I even find myself embellishing.

"The clouds were really dark outside and lightning was flashing all around us. Suddenly it struck the transport, making it come to a stop. Smoke filled the air and we began choking. We could see the tube cracking and cracking more. I knew what was about to happen. Then it broke and sent us hurtling to the ground. Once we hit the ground, I thought I would die for sure. An ugly beast rushed into the open transport to devour me."

All eyes are opened wide. Ana is squeezing my hand. I reach down beside my leg and pet Ash. "Yes, this ugly beast right here rushed in. Then," I say, pointing to Niko, "an even uglier beast came in."

Vet, Ana, and Niko all erupt with laughter. I have never made people laugh before, not intentionally, and never before coming here. I have never heard anyone laugh before arriving here. But what surprises me most is that I feel a sense of satisfaction by making them laugh. "But, alas, I was rescued and here I am."

Everyone claps. I know my face is red, but that was really fun. When I finish, Ana gets up and walks over to Vet and whispers in his ear.

Vet smiles. "Sí, you can sing a song."

Ana turns and walks to the center of the room. She holds her hands together in front of her and looks at me. She begins to sing, her tiny voice filling the air.

"When the wind blows and makes the sky blue
That's when I know that I'll always love you
When the night comes and darkness comes too
That's when I know that I'll always love you
When the rain falls and the weather is cool
That's when I know that I'll always love you
When the grass grows and covers with dew
That's when I know that I'll always love you
When we are playing under the trees
That's when I know that you'll always love me."

When she finishes, she walks over and gives me a hug. I hug her back, but I know it is more mechanical than reflex. I do not know what I have done to make her feel this way. It seems that there are no deeds required amongst the Children to make someone like you, and I find that really strange.

"That was beautiful, Chiquita," Vet says. "Did you make up those last two lines?"

Ana nods. "Sí, just for Piri."

"That's a song our mama made up for us," Niko says. "She used to sing it to us all the time. Well, except the last lines."

"You really came up with the last part yourself?" I ask.

She nods. "Did you like it?"

Actually, I cannot understand what the weather and grass have to do with how you feel for someone. The lyrics did not make sense to me, but looking into her face, I know they made sense to her. "Yes, I really liked it."

She hugs me again.

Chapter Ten

I have read The Book completely through and it disgusts me. It is written as if was not intended for adults as the Fathers repeat their own greatness, offer the same unbelievable rewards of life in the city, and threaten the same impossible punishments. I guess that is why the surface people are called "Children," since they believe every word of it. That confuses me even more. Vet and Niko are intelligent people. They might not have had the chance to study the things we are presented with in the city, but they are not dumb by any means.

At least this dreary period of time is coming to an end. After forty days, the snow is melting, which is good. I have never known depression before. But if being here on the surface has unleashed positive feelings I have never felt before, why then would I not expect increases in negative feelings? I am glad the cold days are almost over. I am not sure which is worse, the snow or the lightning, and I do not think I could take being locked up in this house much longer. And yet, leaving the house is worse. We have all lost weight as the food has been rationed since we are never certain how long the cold will last.

On top of all this and being dragged to worship every seventh day, the situation is worse than it appears. Several older people died from starvation or the cold, some of them while attempting to go to worship. Many sightings of Scav tracks in the snow along the edge of the forest have been reported, and I can tell by Vet's expression that something is not normal. A part of me has begun to enjoy the camaraderie of my new friends, but the constant threat of Scavs, cold, starvation, and the feeble devotion to the rules of The Book has taken its toll. Vet has stopped sending the letters with the Chosen Ones, and I have not asked him to continue. It seems I am neither missed nor needed back there.

One day as we are eating, I think Vet decides it is time to try to shed the cold-day blues. "Let's eat a lot and go outside and play," he says.

Niko and Ana look surprised, but we are all willing. "Can we spare the food?" I ask.

"Sí, we can," Vet says and laughs. "The air is warm enough that the ice over the water has probably thawed enough to fish, so we're good."

He and Niko set out a large plate of food as Ana and I look on with watering mouths. We eat to our hearts' and stomachs' content. Afterward, we bundle up and go out into the fresh air. It is cold but not unbearable like before. The snow is almost all gone, and the once grassy ground is now soft and muddy. Within minutes, our feet and legs are brown. Others come out of their homes and join in. Before long, we are all completely covered with mud. I find myself laughing. I never knew laughter was an involuntary reflex. I just assumed everyone here did it on purpose. Vet is a wise man indeed.

Niko is covered from head to foot with only his eyes and teeth not darkened. He pulls his hair out into sticky globs and chases me and Ana screaming that he is a Scav. We run and laugh.

When we have tired, we stand outside the house as Vet brings us a bucket of warm water, heated over a fire in the stone pit in the kitchen, to wash the dried mud from our bodies. Ana and I cannot stop giggling as we splash the water on one another. Afterward, we go inside and put on clean clothes.

Later that day, Ari and Tag show up again. Tag takes Vet's chair without asking, and Ari latches onto Niko as usual. I am very surprised to find myself disliking this girl, especially whenever she selfishly demands Niko's attention. This puzzles me. I have come to understand fear and laughter, but these feelings regarding Ari I can neither describe nor identify. Besides her exaggerated displays of affection, every time she speaks to me, she is usually less than friendly.

"So, Piri," Ari says, "you never had a mate?"

I shake my head.

She laughs as she looks me up and down. "Well, I can see why."

"Don't act that way," Niko says. "They don't do things up there the way we do. They don't have mates until they get married."

Ari seems upset at Niko for defending me. "When do you get married then?"

"We get married when we turn twenty," I say.

"But you're here now," Tag says. "So you get to choose a mate."

I look around as I ponder those words. Am I *here* now? I look to Vet.

Vet smiles. "Piri is welcome here as long as he wants to stay."

I smile.

"Would you like to go for a walk, Piri?" Tag asks.

Vet and Niko both look at Tag with stern eyes. I have seen this look from them before, and it confuses me. I am unsure of the purpose of walking just to be walking, but I say yes, although there is something I do not like about this person. I do not know what it is I do not like, but it is there nonetheless. Maybe it is the feeling I get from Vet and Niko when Tag is around.

Tag walks to the door and I follow. I turn to wave at Ana, who returns the gesture. Tag takes my hand again as we walk. "You look great today," he says.

"Why do you say that?"

He laughs but does not answer. We continue walking. I find that the silence is unnerving, and I want to talk as we walk but nothing comes to my mind. Usually I am at least curious about a person but such does not seem to be the case with Tag. He leads me to a home that appears to be vacant. We walk around to the rear of the house, and he sits with his back against the wall, motioning for me to join him. I sit beside him. We sit for several minutes in silence.

"Glad the cold is over, eh?" he asks.

I nod.

"I think it's sad you never had a mate," he says. "I don't have one now, but I have lots of people who want to be my mate."

I don't say anything. I just look out over the landscape. He continues to tell me how much he is in demand and how wonderful a mate he will be. He explains how strong he is and how great a hunter and fisher he is. It's almost as if he is applying for a profession, and I am the city Central Link. Then he does something completely unexpected. He leans over and puts his mouth on mine. I pull my head back, confused.

"What are you doing?" I ask.

He does it again, his sloppy tongue darting out like Ash's. It is disgusting, and I cannot breathe. I push him away.

"What's wrong?" he asks.

"That!" I say. "What you are doing. I do not like it."

He laughs and leans over and does it again. And again, I push him away.

"Please stop," I say.

He smiles. "Everyone says that."

I think about that for a second. "That is because everyone wants you to stop."

His smile is still on his face, and now he begins to shake his head back and forth very slowly as if to argue with my last statement. I know now he will not stop no matter what I say. I want to get away from him. I try to stand, but he grabs my arm forcefully—maybe even angrily—and yanks me back down. His strong hand is wrapped firmly around my arm, and he continues his assault upon my face and mouth. I know they have many customs here, but I do not care for this one and try again to get away. His grip tightens, then his free hand crawls all over me. It wanders over my face and chest, down my legs then back up, and even inside my tunic. It is not painful per se, but it bothers me more than any pain I have ever felt. I am disgusted by it. And by him.

He releases my arm to slide his hand behind my head, and I seize my opportunity to pull away. I stand and quickly walk back toward Vet's home. Tag follows me, so I begin to run. He chases for a while shouting obscene statements at me, but I keep running. I just want to be away from this person.

I know I have done wrong and will possibly make everyone mad at me, but so be it. I have tried to be receptive to all the strange customs here since I am a guest in this land, but at the moment I do not care. As I near Vet's house, I look back and see that Tag is nowhere in sight. I am sure it will not take long for him to tell everyone of my wrongdoing. I go inside and see Vet and Ana sitting at the table.

"You're back?" Vet asks. "Are you hungry?"

"No," I say. "I am tired. I am going to take a nap."

I go into my bedroom and lie across the bed. My mind races as I go over what just happened. It has taught me a valuable lesson. I know now that my feelings are not just something I have to learn to adjust to, but something I need to learn to listen to as well. I knew there was a reason I didn't like Tag, and I clearly sensed that Vet and Niko did not like him either. But still, how could I have known? And since I did agree to go on this walk with him, how was I to know what that meant, what was expected of me? I am too confused and too mentally exhausted. I drift off and sleep for hours.

When I get up, it is already dark. I go into the kitchen. I find that I am apprehensive. I hope I have not offended or embarrassed anyone. I sit at the table and Ana smiles at me. I smile back. Luckily no one mentions it. I am unsure if they know, or they are just being polite by not saying anything.

Niko is there but not Ari. I guess she is home. I am certain Tag will tell her of my behavior. Niko hands me some fruit. I reach out to take it.

"What happened to you?" Vet asks.

I look at him but do not know what he means.

Niko takes my hand and pulls it toward him. "What happened?"

I look and see what they see. A large brown and blue area reaches out with fingers of its own, circling around my upper arm. My arm is bruised. I do not know what to tell them. I look to Vet then to Niko. "I am sorry." That is all I can think to say.

Niko's eyes are aglow and his face is red. His jaw muscles are clinched and pulsating. I can tell he is furious with me.

"I am sorry," I repeat.

He releases my hand and puts both his fist on the table and leans in to stare at me. "Did Tag do this?"

Wait. He is not mad at me? I look to Vet but he is also awaiting my answer. I look back to Niko and nod.

Niko walks quickly to the front door and disappears. Vet and Ana look very sad.

"I am sorry. I did not mean to do anything wrong."

Vet shakes his head. "No, child, you did nothing wrong."

No more is spoken of it. We finish our meal and sit up for a little while. There are no stories or talk of anything. There seems only to be a gloom in the air. I go to bed that night not knowing exactly what is happening. Niko has not yet returned, but I am glad I have Ana to comfort me.

CHAPTER ELEVEN

The next morning, all seems to be back to normal as everyone continues to avoid the subject. The only evidence at all that something is amiss is the bruise on my arm and the larger bruise on the side of Niko's face, going from his left eye down past his nose. But they all seem content to forget about it, and I am glad.

The next day, Vet tells me about something new, at least new to me. "It's getting close to time for the crops to begin blooming," he says. "Tomorrow is the first day of Market."

"Yay!" Ana screams.

I smile at her enthusiasm. "What is that? I know it is where Vet met your mama."

"It's fun," Niko says.

"It *is* fun," Vet says. "People set up and sell clothes and all kinds of crafts. People put on shows and plays."

It makes me think of Level Twelve back home. "Are we going?" I ask.

Vet nods.

"Wait," I say. "How do you pay for stuff that people sell?"

"Any way you can," Niko says. "I already have a lot of credit with many of the Market folks because I deliver meat, eggs, and fruit to them."

"People trade everything," Vet explains. "Some make clothes, some weapons. Some even make fancy foods from the fruits. And the shows are a lot of fun. But if you kids don't want to go this year—"

Ana puts her hand over her father's mouth as Niko and I laugh.

We go to bed that night, and Ana is so excited about going to Market. She wakes me the next morning, and she is still excited. I must admit that I am excited, too. We go in and sit at the table.

"Don't eat too much," Vet says. "You'll want to try as many of the treats at Market as possible."

"Thanks for the advice," I say. I do not eat a lot.

We walk to the carrier. The weather is fairly cool but comfortable. We take the carrier to the edge of the field, the column still quite a distance away. The fields are brown and don't seem to be ready to produce crops yet. We walk due west from there, pass the other track and continue. Before we can even see it, we can smell it. The air is filled with the aroma of meat, but there is something else I cannot identify. It is very pleasant, like fruit but in a magnified sense. As we near, we can see and hear the crowds of people. The Market is a large square area several miles across. Tables and small huts adorn the perimeter. We walk between two tables and enter the Market. It is amazing. The ground inside the Market is dirt, packed firm from the crowd walking on it every year. Everyone is smiling and having fun. A man approaches us throwing several round objects in the air. I duck behind Niko.

Niko laughs. "He's a performer—a juggler."

Ana holds tight to my hand. I am glad. I would be afraid to lose her in this crowd. Even I would be afraid to be lost in this crowd. "Stick with Niko," Ana says.

Niko leads us to a table with an older man and woman sitting on a bench behind the table. They get up as we approach, and the woman walks around the table to give him a hug. She then holds open her arms and Ana runs into them.

"Who is your friend, Niko?" the older man asks.

"This is Piri."

The woman walks over and puts her arms around me. I have gotten used to seeing everyone hug each other but not counting Ana, this is my first. I cannot help but smile. "I am Lia and this ugly man is my husband, Liko," she says.

I smile at them both.

"What you got for us today?" Niko asks.

That excites the woman even more as she begins to wave her hands in the air above her head. "Oh, I got everything. Look and see. I got Berry Bread and Fruit Squares, your favorite."

"What would you like to try, Piri?" Niko asks.

All eyes turn to me, and I feel embarrassed and special at the same time. The way Niko is smiling at me makes me remember that day by the water. "Uh…what do you suggest?"

"Try the Berry Bread," Ana says.

I nod. "Okay, but I do not have anything to pay with."

Liko laughs. "You don't need anything at this table. If we gave you everything we had, we couldn't pay back Niko for all he does for us."

I try the Berry Bread. It's incredible. The fruits were something my taste buds had never encountered, but those do not even come close to this. The bread melts in my mouth and the fruit flavors ooze out of it and across my tongue. I close my eyes as I savor every bit of the first bite.

Everyone laughs. "I think he likes it, Niko," Lia says.

"Yes, I do. I've never had anything like it."

I give the rest to Ana, who smiles and quickly bites into the sweet bread. She mimics me as she closes her eyes. We all laugh.

I do not know where Vet went, but we follow Niko around all day. So many of the people here know him and owe him. We sample many kinds of wonderful treats. My eyes scan the Market and absorb the scene. I see many couples holding hands, some composed of opposite genders, and others composed of the same. I realize it is not just a custom pertaining to visits to the forest. This amazes me since all couples in the city are male/female, but no one here pays any attention. Of course, in the city, it is not an emotional endeavor.

Then I see a sight that makes me take a deep breath. Across the way through the crowd I see Tag. He is walking with his sister, Ari. I find myself staring. I can't stop looking at Tag's face. Both sides of his face are black, and he has a huge cut across the bridge of his nose still stained with blood. It must be a deep cut. They turn and notice me and begin to walk toward us. I feel my stomach churn. I guess I have lost Niko for the day. I'm not sure what Tag will do, however, and pull on Niko's tunic. They walk directly up to us. Ana holds tightly to my hand.

I am surprised to see that Ari and Niko do not even look at one another. I'm also glad about that. All eyes are on Tag, who has his head down. Finally he lifts his swollen face to speak.

"I am very sorry, Piri," he says. "I have asked the Fathers to forgive me, and now I ask you."

Ari stares at me, awaiting my response.

"Yes, Tag, I forgive you."

He nods and the two turn away, both still avoiding eye contact with Niko. I remember The Book saying that if you do wrong to a person, you must make it right, or you will never go to the city in the sky. I feel better, not just because of Tag, but because Ari and Niko do not appear to be mates anymore. I guess Ana and I won't lose our guide today after all.

We run into Vet again, and he is carrying many new tunics and cloaks. "What do you think, Piri? Are you enjoying yourself?" he asks.

"Yes, very much. The food is very good. You were right."

"They're about to perform a play," he says. "Do you kids want to watch that?"

We all agree, so he leads us to a clearing in front of a wooden hut. Several low benches are positioned in front of the clearing. A few people are already seated, so we sit on a bench as well. The four of us take up one of the benches. Soon others occupy the other benches, and some people who arrive after us stand behind the seated crowd.

The show begins when a man comes out of the hut. He is wearing a lizard mask over his face and wears a long tail to complete the image. A hunter with a bow comes out next. The bow is not real and neither is the flimsy arrow. He seems to be as awkward as the boy, Payo, tripping over everything. People laugh at his antics. Ana is laughing so hard, I have to make sure she doesn't fall backward off the bench. The hunter sees the lizard and aims his bow. The arrow almost floats across the air and hits the lizard on its tail. The lizard jumps two feet off the ground.

Now it is Ana who must make sure I don't fall from laughing so hard. Everyone is laughing. I look at Vet and see tears falling down his eyes from laughing. I look at Ana as she literally bounces on the bench with laughter. It is a magical moment. I can't imagine how anything could be more meaningful and wonder if the performers on Level Twelve in the city can make people laugh like this.

I turn to look at Niko and his expression takes me off guard. He is not laughing or even watching the show. He is watching me and smiling. I realize I'm not breathing and quickly inhale and exhale deeply. I can't turn away. I know I am missing the show but, for some reason, nothing feels more important than this moment right now. I don't know what to do.

Suddenly Ana is snatched into the air and I turn to find her. The lizard performer has her and is holding her up as a shield between him and the hunter who is aiming another arrow. "No!" I yell, grabbing her and pulling her out of his arms. The lizard actor throws his arms up, screams, and runs away with quick short steps.

The crowd goes wild with laughter. Ana is laughing so hard at my reaction that her head is tilted back, and I find it hard to hold her. Vet grabs her head and helps me, although he is laughing at me also. I realize I just made a fool out of myself and can't help but laugh as well.

When the show is over, the two performers stand together and bow to the crowd. Everyone claps their hands. Then, unexpectedly, the lizard performer, who has removed his mask, points to me with both hands. The crowd erupts with more applause as several stand and face me when they clap. I know my face is red.

After the play, it is late, so we head back to the carrier. We are going home with new clothes and several bags of goodies.

"I saw many people displaying new tunics and other cloth items," I say to Niko and Vet. "How do they make those?"

Vet explains. "There are several types of plants that grow in abundance throughout the forest, and they produce balls of fluffy material. The clothes makers take it and string it out and weave it together. Other than leather from the lizards, that's where most of our clothing comes from."

I suddenly realize that I don't even know where our robes come from, the ones we wear in the city.

As the carrier slides along the track, I realize I am tired and sit on the floor with my back against the side wall. Ana sits between my legs, and I put my arms around her. She is also tired and falls fast asleep. I remember feeling sorry for Niko throughout the cold days as he carried food and cleaned roofs for others, but now I am thankful he did. It has been a great day. Niko takes a seat across from us. I look up and our eyes meet again. I am glad. I have begun to enjoy him looking at me. This is the best day I've ever experienced.

We walk from the carrier back to the house. When we get close, we see several people waiting outside the door. Vet and Niko pick up the pace. Ana and I continue our stride and let them go ahead. As we arrive, Niko is letting Ash out of the house. He has been in there all day and rushes to find a place to relieve himself. Niko then walks back over to where the three men are still talking with Vet. It is dark out, but I can see the serious looks on everyone's face. They turn to leave and we all go inside. Niko's and his father's expression are not the same as before. I know something is wrong.

"Let's get cleaned up and ready for bed," Vet says.

"What has happened?"

Vet looks at Niko, who takes Ana's hand and leads her to the washroom. Vet then looks back at me. "Scavs," he says, making my chest tighten again. "They attacked another fishing party today."

CHAPTER TWELVE

Ana and I run around the house chasing one another. The sun shines bright and a gentle breeze blows. She laughs as I chase her. I turn to run away from her as she chases me. I stop hearing her laughter. I turn but she is nowhere to be seen.

"Where are you?" I call out.

There is no answer. The sky quickly turns cloudy. Something is wrong. I run all the way around the house but can't find her. Then I hear her calling out to me, sounding as if she is behind another one of the houses, but there are hundreds of them around me.

Then a large Scav steps from behind a house, its eyes shining bright, its jagged teeth visible, then another appears and another. Soon they form a large circle around me, stomping up and down, side to side, as the entire circle begins to rotate quickly, their faces laughing. They keep circling and closing in.

"No!" I shout as I suddenly wake and sit up, my breathing short and fast, my tunic soaked with sweat even though I'm freezing. I look over and see Ana still asleep. I'm glad my bad dream didn't wake her. This has become more and more frequent. I never had bad dreams before coming here.

The next morning, after the first visit to the Market, tensions are once again high due to yet another Scav attack. I'm a little relieved that it isn't just me, but it does make me feel a little bad considering I asked Niko for a favor. We are going back to Market tomorrow, and I didn't want to go empty-handed and rely on Niko's labors for trades. I didn't own anything to trade, nor had I acquired any credit by doing good deeds, but I did have an idea that had already proven valid.

Ana and I are tossing a small padded ball around, laughing and enjoying the beautiful day, although nothing like the day in my dream, when I see Niko and Payo approaching, carrying the items I had requested—three small forked trees.

"Those look perfect," I say as Niko hands one to me. "Thank you both. You did go into the forest with a large group of people, didn't you?"

"Just us two," Payo says.

I stare at Niko. "Are you crazy?"

Niko shrugs. "Didn't actually go into the forest. Found these right on the edge. Plus, we had Ash with us, and he would have let us know if anything was around."

"It was still foolish," I say. "You have plenty of people you could ask to go with you." I see Payo's face is full of sadness as I chastise Niko. I do not want to make him feel bad. I know he will blame himself. "It is not that I care if anything happens to you, Niko, but I certainly do not want anything to happen to Payo."

Payo smiles and Niko laughs.

I still do not like that they went to the forest, even the edge, with just the two of them, but I am happy to have the forked trees. "Can you do these like before?" I ask.

Niko smiles. "Sure. Come on, Payo, you can help." They go into the house to retrieve six of the round flat stones and come back to work outside.

Ana and I stop playing to watch. After they complete the first one, I hold it up to inspect it. It works perfectly. I hand it to Ana, who marches around in circles carrying it high above her head. She stops and lifts it as far up as she can. I stare at it for a moment, then look at Niko. "I just had an idea."

"Oh no," Niko says. "We haven't even finished this one."

I laugh. "I don't mean for Market. Look at this."

He stops carving, and he and Payo focus on me.

"These make great torches," I say, "but they could be used for so much more. If the sticks were larger, we could stick these in the ground all around the province to keep things lighted at night. You could put them around the Market area or around the game areas you told me about. You could play after dark. You could have night games."

Niko stares at me with his mouth open. "That's a great idea."

"It is a great idea, Piri," Payo says.

"Thank you. Thank you both."

Before long, I have three more of the torches like the one I made for Vet, the one he still uses every time he goes out at night.

The next morning, I can hardly wait to get started. After we eat, we head out for the carrier. Payo catches up to us. "Can I go to Market with you?"

"Of course," I say, answering for everyone, and I watch as it brings a smile to his face.

As we enter the Market, Vet and Ana go to watch a show as Payo sticks with me and Niko. I am glad to have something to trade, but then think of my friend.

"Here, Payo," I say, taking one of the torches from Niko and handing it to him.

His eyes get big. "Really?"

I nod.

Niko laughs as Payo quickly rushes off to find something to barter.

Several hours later, Niko and I are still together. My torches are gone, and I now carry a full loaf of Berry Bread and two new tunics for me to wear. The day has already been great. I have sampled many varieties of flavored water and other treats. I also saw a bunch of small dogs like Ash, only just big enough to wiggle around on the ground. Niko brought more arrows than normal, and I learned that there are many games at Market and most require one arrow to compete, games like knocking over containers with a ball or trying to get a ball to fall into a container. I sense Niko has been trying to impress me and that makes it even more fun, although he has not been overly successful.

I spot Payo across the way, and he is still carrying the torch from booth to booth, still searching for the perfect item. I can't help but smile. Then I see a table with a familiar face. It is the oldest Elect.

"Hello, Piri," Maren says as she walks around the table to greet me with a hug. "This is my spouse, Jin."

Jin is also an older woman but still beautiful. She hugs me as well while Maren shakes hands with Niko.

"What do you have here?" I ask.

"You got to try this," Niko says. He hands me a small piece of hard bread.

I bite into it and nod. It isn't really that good.

Niko laughs. "Now try it with this." Jin hands him a small container and he pours a translucent golden substance onto the bread. The substance is thick and layers on top.

I put the entire piece in my mouth and my taste buds go crazy. "Oh my goodness. What is this?"

Maren laughs. "It actually comes from bugs."

"Really?" I ask, although I have no idea what a bug is.

Niko nods. "Yes, from flying bugs with stingers. You find them mostly in the southern area. Do you want some?"

I frown. "Yes, but I do not have anything else to trade."

Maren laughs. "Don't worry. It's gratis."

"Oh no," I say. "How about I split my Berry Bread with you?"

The spouse likes that idea, so I unwrap the bread and trade half of that for a small container of the golden delight. Suddenly someone bumps into me. I turn to see a large man carrying two signs. "The End Is Near" is written on one and "Death Is Coming" on the other.

He leans down and looks me in the face. "Do away with your wickedness," he yells.

It startles me so much I back into the table. Niko steps up and puts his arm between us. Maren also comes to my rescue.

"That's enough," Maren says. "Go on, Boro, move along. Go preach your message somewhere else."

The guy stares at Maren with an evil look, then turns and walks away.

"What was that about?"

"Sorry about that," Maren says. "That's Boro from the west province. He's always trying to scare people. He wanted to be an Elect but was never chosen, so he pretends to be. But he takes The Book a little too seriously. He has twelve kids, and they all are usually out trying to scare people. They even show up at funerals and tell the mourners that their family member died because they were wicked and the Fathers wanted them to die."

"That's terrible," I say as I watch the crazy man wander off.

We say good-bye to Maren and her spouse and continue on. Then I see the perfect item, and I wish I hadn't traded my torches so quickly. I walk up to the booth and admire the craftsmanship. "These dolls are beautiful," I say to the woman. "I really want one for Ana. What do you normally trade for?"

She smiles. "They're not for trade." She points beside the table. I see a large man standing inside a circle drawn into the dirt. The circle is about fifteen feet in diameter.

"I don't understand," I say.

"It's a game," she explains. "If you can push Dax out of the circle or knock him to the ground, you win a doll. If he pushes you out, you get nothing."

I stare at Dax. He's the largest person that I've ever seen. His arms are larger than my waist.

"It only cost one arrow to enter," the woman says.

My eyes light up. I quickly grab an arrow out of Niko's pouch and hand it to her.

"Are you loco?" Niko shouts. "That guy will kill you."

"*Me?*" I ask.

Niko's mouth drops open as he understands.

Dax laughs. "Come on, sonny boy. Let's go."

People gather around and begin to cheer, which brings more people around. Niko gives me a look of disbelief, hands me his arrows, and steps into the circle. Dax towers above him.

"We got us a contest," the woman shouts. "When I say 'Go,' you try to push Dax out of the ring or make him fall to the ground. Whoever leaves the ring first loses. Ready? Go!"

Dax lunges at Niko, who ducks under his massive arms. Niko circles around trying to keep his distance.

"Go after him," I yell.

Niko stares at me. Dax rushes again and again, Niko ducks him then rushes behind him and jumps on his back, his arms wrapped tight around Dax's neck. Dax laughs and just stands there as if to show everyone what a silly maneuver that was. Then he rushes backward toward the edge of the circle, which proves his point.

I find myself jumping up and down cheering for Niko, although it looks like it's almost over. But Niko releases his grip and falls to the ground and lies there to let Dax continue over him. As the big man passes, Niko jumps off the ground and lunges into his midsection, using Dax's own momentum against him to shove him toward the edge.

"Yes!" I yell. "You're going to do it!"

Dax suddenly sticks his leg back, stopping the momentum completely, his foot only inches from the line of the circle. He grabs Niko around the waist and tosses him like a toy. Niko actually makes a full rotation in the air and falls to the ground five feet outside the circle. The crowd cheers.

I rush over to him. "Are you okay?"

Niko looks up at me, and I can't help but laugh. A shadow consumes us, and I see the victor. The giant reaches down, lifts Niko off the ground, and brushes off the dirt.

"You did real good, sonny," he says. The crowd cheers again.

Niko smiles. "Thanks."

"You big loser," I say to Niko, making Dax laugh. Then I look up at him. "I do believe you're scarier than Scavs."

Dax laughs so hard, he bends over clutching his stomach.

"Can we go now?" Niko asks.

I smile and nod. I give him back his arrows. As we turn to walk away, Dax taps me on the shoulder. He is smiling, pointing to the woman, who is waving me back. I walk back to her.

"That was a wonderful effort your mate put on. Here." She holds out a smaller version of the dolls, but still as beautiful.

"Really?"

She nods, so I accept. I walk back to Niko with a huge grin. "Thanks, mate."

He laughs.

As the day passes, we find a bench to rest while waiting for the others to join us. Then I see Vet and Ana coming toward us carrying several wrapped items, edible goodies I assume. I learned that the Elect usually have automatic credit with most of the Market folks since they do so much for others. As they near, I hide the doll behind my back.

"We got some great stuff," Ana says as she runs to me and throws her arms around me.

"Me, too," I say and bring the doll from around my back and hand it to her.

Her mouth opens wide. "For me?"

I nod.

She takes the doll and hugs me again. Yes, it was well worth Niko getting beat up.

We walk toward the carrier, and I realize we are not all here. "Where's Payo?"

"Here he comes," Niko says.

I turn and see him coming. I can't help but laugh. "Payo," I say as he catches up to us, "why didn't you trade for something?"

Payo looks at the torch still in his hands. "Well, I couldn't find anything nicer than this."

CHAPTER THIRTEEN

My feet are completely off the ground as Niko tightens the grip around my neck. I struggle to free myself. Others are in the forest but not close enough to help me.

"Do it!" Niko orders.

I try to free his arm from around my throat but he's too powerful.

"Do it now," he commands.

I bring down my arm in a swift motion, and my fist connects with his mid-frontal area, causing him to release me and double over in pain.

"Like that?" I ask.

Niko doesn't look up. He stays bent over with one hand on his knee and the other hand holding out toward me. Finally he manages to look up. "I said to pretend," he says in a higher voice than normal.

I can't help but laugh. "I'm sorry. I was just too excited."

He stands up and takes a deep breath.

"And that works for any guy who might be attacking me?"

"Sí," he says. "And it probably doesn't have to be a guy. Anyone will react to that and hopefully give you time to get away." He limps over to retrieve the bow.

I am grateful he is teaching me self-defense. I am more grateful that we haven't seen Ari or her brother again. I notice one of the pits and sit by it. "What is this stuff?" I ask.

Niko walks toward me carrying the bow and four arrows. "Just stuff. There are small holes filled with it everywhere."

I stick my finger in the blackness and pull it out. The stuff sticks so hard to my fingers that it creates a foot-long extension from the pit before breaking off, leaving my finger covered in the goop. I try to wipe it on the grass, but it doesn't come off easily. I wonder how long it took poor Payo to remove it from his leg. "And you don't use this for anything?"

"Like what?" Niko asks. "It doesn't harden. It doesn't burn. We've never found a use for it."

I hold my finger to my nose. "It smells like it would burn."

Niko shakes his head. "No, we have tried. If you put some on a stick and hold in the fire long enough, it pops really loud, usually blowing off the end of the stick. But it's not something we have a purpose for. Now stop wasting time and let's get back to practice."

I stand up wearily. "I don't want to practice. I'm not good at this. I haven't hit the target one time." I look around the forest at all the others who are wandering around searching for the first signs of fruits and berries. The attacks from Scavs have increased, though no one knows why, but there is safety in numbers as the Children come out in force to restock the food supply. "Can't we just pick berries? I'd even go fishing again if you will just stop making me try to shoot that bow."

Niko's expression displays a little sadness and a little anger. "Come on, try again. This could save your life one day."

I know he's right, but I lack the skills to use the bow accurately. I am amazed, however, at how much stronger I've gotten since being here, so using the bow is simple enough. Hitting the target is the part that eludes me. But I am still stubborn. I flop back down on the soft grass and stare at the sky. It is still overcast but very bright.

"Have you ever seen the sun?" Niko asks.

I nod and lower my brow. "Why? Have you not?"

He sits beside me and shakes his head. "No, it never shines through. What does it look like?"

"I have only seen it as I have traveled around the city in the tubes. I can't tell you what it looks like since it's too bright to look at, but you can feel the warmth. The entire roof of the city converts the strong rays into power, so it provides quite a gift to the people in the city."

Niko looks at me and smiles. It's an odd smile.

"What?"

He takes a cloth out of his pouch and hands it to me. "Here. This is for you."

I unwind the cloth to find a small replica of a Kabloom flower carved out of light wood. There are two strings attached to the backside. It is only about an inch across and made of very thin wood, but the details are amazingly intricate, and the painted surface captures the flower well. This I judge going by the paintings his mama did on the column. I still have yet to see the first real one, although Niko says they will be blooming soon.

"It's to go around your neck," Niko says. He takes the strings and slides them around both sides of my neck. I can feel the heat of his breath on my ear. I hope it takes him a while to tie. "There you go," he says, pulling back.

I hold it out in front of me and stare at it. It's beautiful. "From which person at the Market did you get this?"

He looks hurt. "I made that."

I smile. "Oh, sorry. I love it." Then I remember something and decide to have fun with Niko. "I read about this in The Book. When someone chooses a mate to marry, he gives a gift that represents a vow to be together and faithful forever. Are we married now?"

Niko's eyes and mouth are wide open. His face is a shade of red that I didn't know a person could make. "What? No...I, uh... wait..."

I can't help but laugh, allowing Niko to realize I was joking. He falls back onto the ground with his hands over his face as he begins to laugh as well.

"Piri?" a voice calls out.

I search the forest for the familiar sound. "Over here, Chiquita."

Ana and Vet come through the trees, Vet holding a small container of berries. Ana has her hands behind her back.

"Any luck?" Niko asks.

Vet nods. "A little."

"I found something, too," Ana says. She brings her hands around the front to reveal a small Kabloom flower.

"Oh, you found one," I say, taking the tiny flower from her hands.

"It's the first one," Ana says with a smile. "I'm going to put it on the table like Mama always did."

"Great idea," I say. "I have one, too." I hold up the necklace for them to see.

"Where did that come from?" Vet asks.

I nod toward Niko.

"Are you getting married?" Ana asks.

Niko falls back on the ground again as we all laugh. "I'm going to throw you in a pit," he says as he jumps up and runs toward Ana, making her squeal and run behind Vet.

We walk back out of the forest as others conclude their first day of harvesting. Some carry berries, others fruit, and still others carry bags of fish.

"The crops are starting to grow," Vet says. "In a few weeks, we'll be picking crops for several months."

"Sounds like fun," I say.

Niko and Ana both shake their heads vigorously. "No, not fun at all," Niko says.

I have already learned from reading The Book that picking crops has the same rules as attending worship: everyone other than the dying and those giving birth are required to participate. This year would add an additional twist. The fields were always considered sacred, like the seventh day, and no Scav had ever attacked anyone in the fields, not while picking crops nor while burying the dead. But that has changed. Scav attacks have been on the rise, not just in intensity but in areas never before heard of, like the southern areas and even a couple of times in the fields at funerals. I know it weighs heavily on the minds of all the Elect, especially Vet, who seems particularly perplexed at the situation. Perhaps having lost his wife to Scavs makes it more personal to him.

I see a group of people pushing a load of trees out of the forest on a makeshift wagon designed for such a venture. It reminds me of my idea, which I had shared with Niko and Vet, and both had seemed impressed. Since trees are like every other resource, and you can only cut so many every year to ensure the continuation of the forest, I wasn't sure I would be allowed to try it, but the Elect had given their consent.

"When can we try my invention?" I ask as we walk.

"That silly thing?" Niko says.

Ana punches him.

Vet smiles. "Tomorrow. Everything should already be by the lake. I think everyone's excited about it."

I try to hold back the smile, but I am unsuccessful. I've never had an idea like this before, not of how to make things work better. It's bigger than the torch idea. It's not something I would have ever done in the city in the sky. And I'm certain I would have never felt these strong emotions that I am constantly feeling here: gladness, sadness, joy, sorrow, love, fear, and now dare I say...pride. I never even knew I had an ego.

After we eat and go to bed, I find I can't sleep and yet a new feeling takes control of my mind—anticipation. I try to focus on Ana's breathing, hoping that will convince my mind that it's time to sleep, but it doesn't work. I am too excited about tomorrow.

The next morning, Ana wakes me. I am so tired from not falling asleep until very late, but I jump out of bed and we go into the kitchen. Niko and Vet have breakfast ready and we eat.

"Sleep well?" Vet asks.

I nod, although it isn't true.

The weather is nice and warm as we leave the house and head back to the forest. I see others coming behind us, and they rush to catch up and join with us. I see others ahead of us already entering the forest. There are many spears, bows, and dogs. Ash seems happy to have many friends along as he makes sure to greet each one, and in not the most appropriate manner, making Ana laugh. Ana only comes to the forest on days like this when there are numerous people. On normal hunting or fishing days, she either stays home with Vet or with another family.

We retrace the same route to the lake. I am surprised to see more than a hundred people already standing along the banks. I didn't know it was going to draw such a crowd and now I'm nervous. A boy about Niko's age walks up to greet us.

"This is San," Niko says.

He smiles and waves. "Hola, Piri. We've already collected the fish and we have everything ready."

I smile. I see all the fish traps on the bank, the inflated balloons still attached on the tops with the hollow vines curled up beside them. Hopefully after today, the balloons and vines will no longer be needed. Trees and pieces of wood are scattered on the ground, and I am shocked to see the support structure already constructed.

"Look it over," Niko says. "Make sure these locos put it together correctly."

Everyone laughs.

I stroll around the structure. It consists of four posts eight feet high, two side by side, three feet apart, and the other two eight feet away, also side by side. They are connected by posts running across the length and width at the top and two feet above the ground, tethered to the frame. The bottoms of the upright posts have been sharpened to a point.

"It looks right," I say.

"Okay," Vet says. "Who are the brave volunteers?"

Two other strong young men step forward to join Niko and San, and all four take off their sandals. They step up and grab the construction, one boy on each corner.

"Just give 'er," someone yells from the crowd.

They grab it, lift it into the air, and walk toward the edge of the water. Everyone cheers, even the ones with loaded bows and readied spears on the perimeter. The four-man team wades into the water about waist deep and sets the structure down to rest.

Niko looks over to me. "Go stand on one side to make sure we get it where you want it."

Ana, Vet, and I walk to the left side of the lake. People move over to make a trail as we walk out onto the peninsula. I give a wave to let them know to continue.

They carry it out to where the water is up to their chins and set it down again.

"It's about to get fun," a man yells from the crowd, making everyone laugh again.

Niko nods to the others and they continue, their heads going underwater. The structure seems to float through the water as the weight keeps them submerged. They set it down and climb up the post for air.

"Are you boys okay?" I call out.

They all smile and wave and go down again, and the structure moves once more. They come up for air. "How much farther?" Niko asks.

"Only about ten feet," I shout.

They go back down and move it the remaining ten feet and return to the surface.

I squat down to look across to the other side, then I point in the direction they have been moving. "Okay, the back side needs to move that way about two feet."

Niko and San stay up while the other two go down to move it.

"Perfect," I say as they come up again.

The four boys climb up on top of the structure. Four other young men, who have been standing on the bank awaiting their task, pick up four nice-sized rocks and carry them out to the structure. They are able to bounce and swim to get the rocks out to the first four boys. Once they hand them off, they return to the bank, their tunics soaked completely through.

Niko and the others use the rocks to drive the four sharpened posts deep into the soft ground of the lakebed. When they are finished, they toss the rocks into the water. This cues other boys to start sliding four large trees, trimmed of all limbs, out to the boys on the platform. Once the trees have been positioned three feet apart, one side resting on the platform and the other side resting on the ground on the bank, they are tethered to the structure and spiked into the ground.

Vet puts his hand on my shoulder and smiles at me. I can't stop grinning.

Next are the finishing touches. Slabs of wood are laid out across the trees and attached, forming a bridge all the way across the lake. Everyone cheers as the last pieces are put into place and several men walk all the way across to display its strength and celebrate its completion.

Niko and San walk across onto dry land, although their tunics are still wet. Niko looks at me, and I can't help but smile as his long hair now looks even longer and darker, coming down over his eyes and sticking to his forehead. His tunic is heavy with water that streams from loose fabric along the bottom, running down his legs to his muddy sandals. "Let's try it out, boys," Niko says.

Other young men grab the fish traps and remove the balloons and vines, leaving only a small rope attached to each. Everyone else gets off the bridge to allow the boys to walk out with the fish traps. They spread out across the bridge and all drop the traps at once, holding onto the ropes. Then they all pull up the traps as everyone cheers again.

"That's incredible, Piri," a voice behind me says.

I turn to see Maren, the white-haired elderly Elect who has come all the way from her own province to witness the event.

"What used to take all day can now be done in minutes," she says with a smile. There is no mistaking the approval in her eyes. "That will make fishing faster and much safer, something we really need right now. Will you help the western province make a lake bridge?"

I nod and blush. Many of those in the crowd have gathered around and are smiling at me and nodding. Some squeeze by others just to pat me on the back. I never knew I could feel this way. As my eyes search out Niko, I find the one smile above all others, the one coming from the soaking wet boy who saved my life. I'm not sure if it's that he helped complete my design, or it's just seeing him wet that seems to delight me, but I know now that this is the life I want.

CHAPTER FOURTEEN

W oe to those who break the rules, for they may bring the wrath of the Fathers down upon their entire province."

I watch as Vet holds The Book over his head and waits for the crowd to whisper the message back. Half a year after falling from the city, I now consider this home and never want to return. I feel alive here, even a celebrity of sorts, at least in the general bridge construction area. I have overseen the construction of two other successful bridges. I now know most of the names of the people that congregate around Vet's family, and I love going to Market. However, I still don't like coming to worship and hearing the constant threats propagated in The Book.

I didn't like coming during the cold, and I don't like coming now that the crop plants are over seven feet high, making it impossible to see anything. The stalks are a brilliant green with yellow round balls growing on them, most the size of a grown man's fist. It is one more week before harvest, before the Children will spend all day, every day but the seventh, picking the Fathers' crops. I look through the stalks as far as I can see at the abundant yield, knowing how wrong it is that the Children often face starvation and not one of them benefits from all this food that they pick. But at least the Scavs still obey the rules of the seventh day, never attacking during worship.

As the crowds disappear and the new batch of thrilled Chosen enter the column to begin their life in the sky, Ana and I repaint some of her mama's faded art, something we have begun to do as the Elect meet after worship ends. Niko keeps us supplied with paint, which he makes by mixing the actual pollen from the Kabloom flowers with water. It isn't hard since we keep fresh flowers on the kitchen table now, something they still do to honor their mama. We make paintbrushes from the stringy tips of the mature crop stalks.

Looking at the column reminds me of a question I want to ask. "Who made all the homes we live in?"

"We don't know," Niko says. "We assume the Fathers made them for us, but The Book doesn't say that for sure, only that they provide us with everything we need. Do you know?"

"If I knew, I wouldn't have asked you."

Niko laughs. "We are not allowed to read or write anything not from The Book."

"You should be able to record your own history," I say.

"Yeah," Ana says. "Do you study your history in the city up there?"

As I ponder the question, I realize that I know nothing about our history either. "No, actually we do not. We study math and science and life in the city, but I've never read anything about our history on the city Link. I never thought about it before, but it's odd. I guess we're not supposed to know our past either. In fact, I learned more about the creation of our city from The Book than I ever did before coming here."

As we travel toward home on the carrier that evening, I can't help but wonder why we do not learn about our past in the city. Is that forbidden? Will we discover something we don't need to know? As I question these things, I look up and see Niko pointing to the south and hear others talking. I see a storm far away over the southern forest, and I can see the lightning bolts searching for their targets on the ground. The loud sound that comes with the lightning now takes a while to hear because it is so far away. Vet does not stop the carrier, so apparently there is no threat.

We get home and go to bed. Ana drifts off to sleep quickly and I'm glad. I am always ready to get up the next morning so we can eat. I also sink into a fast sleep. It doesn't last.

"Piri. Get up."

Niko is standing over the bed. I rub the sleep from my eyes. "What is it?"

"Come on. Get up. We have to go. Get Ana up."

He leaves the room, and I reach over and shake Ana, "Get up, Ana."

She looks over as if wondering what's going on. I don't have the answer. We get up and go to the main room. Vet and Niko are waiting by the door. Niko has his bow and spear and holds a long stick with a small flat piece of metal on the end.

"What's going on?" Ana asks.

"The forest is on fire," Vet explains.

We follow them outside. It is barely daylight. We walk toward the south, and I can see the smoke billowing upward on the horizon. Others are coming out of their homes with buckets and tools like the one Niko carries. It is miles away, and I wish there was a carrier but all those go toward the column.

"How did this happen?" I ask.

Niko answers. "Lightning. If it strikes a tree, it can start a fire. Have to put it out or it will spread and destroy the berries and fruits we pick. If they burn, it will take years for them to put out again."

We walk for hours until we come to the forest. Others are already at work. I see many with the red sash and recognize the Elect from the meetings. I think all of them are here. Some are just volunteers, but the Elect are required to be here, I think. We join in. The stronger women and men attempt to dig a ditch in front of the fire. The winds are blowing wildly to the east. I am given a bucket like many of the younger ones. Our job is to watch for fires starting up past the dig line. This happens often as the winds carry embers far across the line. When we see them, we douse them with water. Many times the diggers come by to drink from the buckets as well.

This goes on and never seems to end. We go to a lake nearby to refill our buckets, but we can't catch all the blowing embers. New fires grow, and the diggers have to dig new lines.

I keep Ana by my side and try to keep Niko and Vet in sight. We follow as they get deeper and deeper into the forest, their tunics now a gray color from the smoke and soot. Several older people have to leave the forest to get away from the heat and smoke, coughing uncontrollably as they search for fresh air outside the forest. The wind pushes the cloud of hot fumes toward us, and Ana and I try to cover our mouth with our clothes.

We seem to be losing the battle as new fires keep popping up elsewhere in the forest, and the diggers continue to readjust their lines.

Ana and I are standing far away from the diggers but still close enough to see them through the trees. We are very deep into the forest, and soon I see the clearing through the trunks, the light flooding the area beneath the canopy. I know the barren land is just beyond. Then I see a line of men just outside the forest holding spears and bows.

As Niko and Vet work to create the fire line, we stay directly across from them, exiting the forest when they make their way through to the clearing. The light coming through the overcast sky makes me and Ana squint, but we see them, and Ana grabs my hand tightly. About a hundred feet away, staring back at us, is a group of at least fifty Scavs, their long arms and evil heads swaying back and forth, their mouths open like a hungry man staring at food. I can't move or look away. I have never seen so many in one place and wonder if this is all of them. I know their camps are way north past the cliffs, near the ocean, and I realize how far they have come. I wish I could drop the giant trees on top of them.

Staring at the horrid group, I can't shake the feeling that they are all staring directly at me. I know it must be my imagination. Then one leans over to another as if whispering and points his jagged finger in my direction. Maybe I am not imagining things.

"It's okay."

I look up and see Vet.

"They won't try anything, so we're safe," he says.

I see Niko going back through the forest, making the line wider. I look back to Vet. "Should I take Ana home?"

Vet shakes his head quickly as he stares out at the group of creatures. "No. Wait until we can all go home together. You two are tired, eh? Go on back through the forest and wait for us on the other side. I think we just about have it beat."

"What if you don't get it out before dark?"

"We'll have to stay until we do," he says. "We don't have a choice. But really, I think we're almost finished."

I stare out at the gruesome sight one last time, then lead Ana back through the forest. When we reach the other side, I can tell by the light that it is already late afternoon. There are not many hours of daylight remaining. Then it dawns on me—that's what the Scavs are waiting for. If the fire continues into the night, the diggers and bucket keepers will be easy targets. I cringe at the thought.

Ana and I sit in the grass on the Garden side of the forest along with many others taking a break from the tedious work. I notice that all faces are spotted with areas of black. I take the edge of my tunic and try to clean Ana's. She smiles and then lays her head on my chest and falls fast asleep. Soon I join her.

"Let's go."

I feel someone bumping my leg and wake to see Niko standing over me. It is still daylight but barely. Ana and I get up.

"Is it over?" I ask.

Niko nods. His face is pitch-black, but I notice several puffy red dots.

"What happened to your face?"

Niko touches one of the swollen areas and grimaces. "Stepped on a nest of stinger bugs."

I frown. I feel bad for him. "Like the ones Maren uses to make the golden stuff?"

He nods. "I'll be okay."

Vet joins us, his face black as well but no stings.

We start the long walk home along with hundreds of others. I feel a little safer in a big group. Plus, the men with spears and bows bring up the rear. As we get halfway home, it is dark out. Suddenly a grisly scream penetrates the stillness. It makes me jump. Then there is another and another. It is the Scavs. I don't know if they are communicating with each other or crying out in anger since we were able to finish and get away before dark. The truth is, I don't want to know. I'm just glad we're going home.

My legs, neck, and back are so sore I find it hard to walk. Vet is carrying little Ana, who is sound asleep again.

"Wanna ride?" Niko asks.

I would love a ride but cannot bring myself to be a burden to someone who has worked so hard all day. "No, I'm fine." I can't help but smile at the gesture. I see Niko's eyes and teeth almost glowing in the faint light. I'm sure my smile is flashing back at him.

When we get back home, they let me and Ana clean up first, and I put her to bed. Vet goes next, and I sit at the table with Niko. We stare at each other in complete silence. He has never failed to amaze me with his strength and goodness. While it's true that I have discovered many people here on the surface that stand out with character and selflessness, I still think Niko shines above them all. Maybe I'm just a tad prejudiced.

Vet comes out of the washroom and Niko takes his turn.

"We should all sleep well tonight," Vet says.

I smile and nod as he turns to go to bed. I think about going to bed as well but decide to wait. A few minutes later, Niko comes back to the table wearing a new tunic and cleaned up from the fire. He sits at the table and I smile.

"What?"

"At least you don't look like a Scav anymore," I say.

He laughs quietly. Although we're both completely exhausted, we stay up for hours talking.

CHAPTER FIFTEEN

The days pass. I learn that fires are very rare. I'm glad. There is so much hardship here, yet still so much to enjoy. We play games, pick berries and fruits in the forest, and I have even learned to enjoy fishing, especially since it is much easier now.

Even worship doesn't bother me as much as it used to. I listen to the Elect read their verses and watch other batches of excited Chosen Ones go off to their destiny. The days between worship are carefree and wonderful. On the day after the fire, Niko and I take a walk alone, another pastime that has become common, much to Ana's disapproval. She can't understand why she can't come along, but to her credit, she suffers in silence, waiting for us to return so she can once again claim my attention. Unfortunately, she is not the only one who doesn't understand that we wish to be alone.

"Hola, Piri and Niko. Where you going?"

"Hola, Payo," I say. "How are you?"

"Good. I was hoping to get picked at last worship. Thought it was my day for sure."

Niko smiles. "Maybe next week, Payo. You have to have faith."

Several seconds of silence pass as Payo continues to walk directly behind us.

"Well, buenas noches, Payo," Niko says. "It's getting late, and I have something to show Piri."

"Oh, that's okay," Payo says. "I don't have anywhere to be. I can stay with you."

I smile at Niko. It's hard to explain to Payo. He's such a gentle person; even Niko can't stand the thought of hurting his feelings.

As we walk, Niko leads us to a home and goes to the door.

"Who lives here?" I ask.

"No one—yet," Niko says, entering the home. Payo and I follow him inside. It looks like every other house, including the one where we all stay now.

"There are always plenty of empty houses," Niko says. "When people are ready to start their own family, they simply pick out one that they want to live in. I have had my eye on this one for a while, hoping no one else chooses it before I'm ready. I like that it's close to Papa and Ana."

I wonder if my cheeks are red. I know I must be blushing.

"Are you and Ari going to get married and move here, Niko?" Payo asks.

I laugh as now Niko's face turns red. Thank goodness Ari is out of the picture. But I can see also how many of the young people in the province stare at Niko. I understand. Niko is a very talented hunter, a very well-mannered person, and, as I have come to realize, a very handsome young man. But I am confident that his heart is taken, as is mine. And even though Payo doesn't understand why Niko is showing me this house, I do, and I am moved deeply by it. I look down at my necklace and picture our own table with a vase of fresh Kablooms on it. I lie awake many nights now, thinking of becoming Niko's mate and having a home of our own.

Payo sticks with us all the way back to Vet's house. Niko reminds him that tomorrow is egg day. He finally takes the hint and leaves us. As we stand at the door, Niko suddenly leans in and places his lips on mine. I have seen couples at the Market and even in the forest make this gesture but was unsure of the meaning. I am also frightened since my one experience with Tag was hardly an enjoyable one. But as our lips meet, I am overwhelmed by his gentleness and fully understand the meaning. My heart races. As he pulls away, my lips follow, not wanting the moment to end, and we embrace again. Ash is whimpering inside the door, which opens abruptly as we step apart.

"There you are," Ana says. "What are you doing?"

Niko smiles. "We were just saying buenas noches to Payo and about to come in. Is that okay?"

She ignores him, takes me by the hand and leads me to the table. She sits in her chair and asks me to brush her hair, a task I never tire of doing, even though I am ready to go to bed. I still look forward to breakfast each morning and although I still don't eat the meat, the fresh fruits and berries are much better than the ones that have been stored all winter.

The next morning we sit and eat at the table as usual. "This is a big day," Vet says.

Niko nods his agreement. "This is the last day to gather fruits and berries, and it's the only day we have to gather eggs. The lizards will be laying eggs for about a month, but tomorrow is the first day of harvest and that lasts several months."

"You're not allowed to pick fruits or gather eggs during harvest?"

"It's not that we're not allowed," Vet says. "It's just we get home too late every day. It will be near dark and too dangerous to go into the forest at that time."

After we finish eating, we go outside. I am surprised to see a huge crowd of people walking toward the forest. "Does everyone go to the forest today?"

"No, not everyone," Ana says with a grouchy tone.

Vet laughs. "About half of the population goes since it's the last chance before the cold days come. You kids go ahead. I'll drop off Ana and catch up."

"I don't understand," I say. "If so many people are going, why can't Ana go?"

Ana smiles at me.

Niko shakes his head. "Because today a lot of us go past the forest into Scav territory, so it's a little riskier and we're more spread out."

That makes me a little nervous. Although some of the people will be after the fruits and berries, Niko and I, along with many of the young men and women, the stronger ones and ones who are good with weapons, will be going beyond the forest into Scav territory to hunt for lizard nests.

Halfway through the forest, Vet catches up with us. Like the path to the lake, this one is also worn and quite visible. Many people are on both sides of us and Ash and other dogs walk in front and behind sniffing the air. We walk fast to make up the long distance.

Groups of people break off to search for fruits but we continue on, for hours. Finally we reach the other side of the forest and, looking out over the desert-like terrain devoid of plant life, my stomach churns as I remember my first day here on the surface. I follow along as half the group begins searching the rocky areas while the other half stand guard with bows loaded. We hear someone call out.

"Found one."

Niko and a few others close by go to assist. As we walk up, I see the hole tunneled under a large boulder. The boy who found the hole holds his spear. On the end is a loop made from leather. He nods to Niko, who takes his spear and starts tapping the front of the entrance. Suddenly a large lizard rushes out of the hole and attacks Niko's spear. I almost scream. The other boy drapes the loop around its neck and pulls it away from the hole. He holds it as it struggles to free itself.

"Aren't you going to kill it?" I ask.

Niko shakes his head. "No. We will only take half the eggs and let her go back and raise them."

I understand. That is the same system applied to everything on the surface. Take only a portion of the eggs, only a portion of the fruits and berries, only a portion of the fish, and only a portion of the trees, but resist the boundless fields of ripe crops while many starve to death.

I watch as one of the girls crawls down and digs through the opening until she begins to pull out round eggs. Another girl behind her stuffs them into a bag. When half of the eggs are gathered, we walk away as the first boy leads the lizard back and releases it, making sure it goes into the hole. The lizards are very large, and I have learned that one bite can cripple a full-grown man and possibly kill a woman or child.

Suddenly I hear a strange noise, a buzzing sound, as if it went right by my ear. I first think I am hearing things, but I hear it again then again. Then I see it—a flying creature. "What is that?" I scream as I wave my hand frantically in the air.

Everyone around me laughs.

"It's just a flying bug," Niko explains. "Remember Maren talking about them at the market? I guess you've never seen one."

I shake my head. "These are the things that make that wonderful golden stuff?"

Niko laughs. "No, that stuff is made by the flying bugs with stingers." He points to one of the red areas still vaguely visible on his face. "Bugs get much worse as the weather gets hotter. They are really bad in the fields when the crops are ripe."

It's as if I have been wearing a blindfold. But once I noticed one bug, I saw hundreds. Some of them fly, some walk, some seem more to slither. They are everywhere. Then I see one that seems to be floating in the air on beautiful red and yellow wings. I am mesmerized by its beauty and follow the dancing up and down motions as it flutters across the sky.

"Watch out!" someone screams.

I snap out of my trance and scan the horizon for Scavs. I have wandered off a distance from Niko without realizing it. I see him running toward me, fear on his face. I turn and look the other way expecting to see the horrible Scav creatures, but I only see others running toward me from that direction with the same expression as Niko's. Then the movement catches my eyes. A huge lizard has gotten away from someone and is charging directly at me. I know I can't move fast enough to get out of the way. And even if I could, I find I can't move at all. I am frozen. I see the foaming jaws of the giant lizard, its sharp teeth glistening in the light, its talons kicking up stones and dirt as its legs thrust hard to propel its body at me. Ana flashes in my mind.

The lizard leaps, and I can't even look away. Suddenly everything goes dark as something rushes in front of me. It is one of the boys gathering eggs with us, one of the Children. He intercepts the lizard in midair and they fall to the ground, the boy holding the giant reptile in a bear hug as it fights to free itself. Niko is the first one to reach us and swiftly thrusts his spear into the lizard's chin, ramming the entire tip through its head. It lies motionless.

The boy is still holding onto the lizard with all his strength. The lizard is as long as the boy is tall. Niko squats down and reaches out to the boy.

"It's okay It's dead. You can let go now," Niko says.

The boy finally releases his grip and slides away from the lizard as the others catch up to us. One boy is holding a spear with a broken loop. He stares as me with sad eyes as if to apologize. I smile to let him know that it's okay.

I look back at my savior as Niko helps him off the ground. I can't help but smile when I see who it is.

"Are you okay, Piri?" he asks, still shaking.

I am still shaking, too. "Sí, Payo. I am okay. Gracias."

CHAPTER SIXTEEN

Niko was right. The flying bugs are thick in the air as I drag my sack through the rows of crops. The heat is unbearable, and they say it will get hotter. The plants are over eight feet tall now and full of giant yellow balls. I pluck one from its stem and hold the yellow ball, which is almost as big as my head, to my nose. I take a big whiff. The smell is so sweet that water forms instantly under my tongue. I want to take a bite. But even though I don't believe the farfetched precognitions of The Book, I know everyone else does. If others were to see me, I'm not sure how they would react. I let the ripe melon fall into my bag, brush away several flying bugs, wipe away the hair that has adhered to my sticky forehead, and continue onward.

It is relentless. After two weeks, I now look forward to worship, something I didn't think possible. I can't see very far through the stalks, but I know I'm walking in the direction of the carrier, my third trip this day. Much more than physical exertion, this entire concept weighs on my mind. I find that my brain thinks about everything as I work, possibly to keep distracted from what is really happening.

I think about Ana's ninth birthday party a month ago, another experience I had never been introduced to. It was very fun. Many of the neighbors came bearing gifts they had made. Payo showed up with the black stuff on his foot again from stepping into one of the pits. He made Ana laugh so hard bumbling around, more than usual, to put on a show for her. With Niko's help, I made her a small trinket to wear in her hair. Like my necklace, it is a miniature of a Kabloom.

She doesn't wear it to the fields, but around home she never takes it off. It was a wonderful day.

In the city, we don't celebrate any events. There are only five birthdays that matter in a boy's life: his tenth, as that is when his sister arrives, his nineteenth, as he is then allowed to visit Level Twelve, his twentieth, as he marries, his fiftieth, as he will retire and raise his grandson, and of course his eightieth, the final one. The only hint of excitement I ever felt was on my nineteenth birthday, arising early for my first visit to Level Twelve. But Adon, my grandfather, was in no hurry, so I sat for hours waiting. Even though he was my grandfather and we lived in the same unit, we had never spoken, much less hugged. That was common.

I think about that day as the tube exploded sending me here to this horrific place filled with all kinds of perils. But the good has far outweighed the bad, for I would have never known the emotions and bonds people could feel for each other.

Niko is much faster than I, so we don't stay together long. He often finishes his row first and helps me finish mine, so we can at least stay in the same area of the fields. I also notice this with the couples who are male and female, while the same-sex couples can normally work at the same speed. But Niko is still much stronger than I.

I see something up ahead, one row over, that doesn't appear right. There is something on the ground but it's not the color of a bag. I pick up the pace a little and pluck the giant fruit off and let it fall as I walk quicker. Then I see an elderly woman who had been picking beside me for the last couple of hours. I think she has the right idea—rest. But when I get to her, I realize she is not resting.

I look up and see Ana bringing me water, her face smudged from wiping it with her dirt-stained hands. The younger children all carry water to the pickers. I drop the open end of the bag and let it fall to the ground so I can rush ahead to meet her. I don't want her to see the woman lying there.

"You must be thirsty," Ana says as I walk up quickly. She smiles, her dirty face making her teeth look brighter than normal.

"Sí," I say. I sink the dipper into the cool water. After I sip and replace the dipper, I look around for Niko. "Where's your brother?"

She turns and points back toward the carrier.

"Will you tell him I need to see him when you go back to the carrier?"

She nods and walks away.

When Niko comes back, I explain what has happened. He looks sad as he goes back to check on it. He calls for another boy to go notify her family. A man and woman and several younger kids come to her. They whisper a few words while looking upward, then take a shovel and bury her right where she lays.

I grab my bag and continue picking. As my bag gets about half full, I drag it toward the carrier. When I get to the track, I see the carrier has moved forward about twenty feet closer to the column. Niko comes out of his row, grabs the end of my bag and pulls both bags toward the carrier. The back gate is in place now, with several people standing around the carrier and some inside it. They have several full bags around them. Niko simply leaves ours amongst the others, grabs two empty bags, and hands me one. "Just give 'er," he says with a smile.

Normally his smile makes me feel alive, but nothing fazes me at the moment. I am too tired, too sore, and too angry. I return to the crops.

By late afternoon, we fill the carrier up for the fifth time. I watch as Niko drives it to the large door and hops off. A minute later, the door opens and the carrier disappears into the darkness, much like it does every seventh day as it carries the Chosen away. I sit down on the dirt, exhausted. Ana sits beside me and lays her head in my lap. Niko sits across from us only a foot away. Others trade their bags for spears and bows.

"You used to never bring your weapons to the field?" I ask.

Niko shakes his head. "No, but Papa don't want to take any chances."

"And you still have no idea why the Scavs are more aggressive this year?"

"No," Niko answers. "Maybe they are running short on food for some reason."

A few minutes later, the carrier is sent back out and we all start toward home. I place Ana in the carrier. She is sound asleep. Niko and I walk, as all the younger, able people do. Vet drives the carrier and hauls the elderly and smaller children that live not too far from the track to benefit from such a ride. It is a long walk, taking many hours, and I am exhausted, but still it's good to be finished for the day.

As we near the end of the track, Vet passes Ana off to Niko. She wakes for only a second and falls back asleep. Payo catches up and walks with us. He is as tired and dirty as the rest of us. He might not be much of a hunter, but he is the hardest worker in the fields, perhaps thinking that will enhance his chances to be one of the Chosen. Still, I don't like to see others making fun of him. Of all the people I have met and became friends with, Payo has become one of my favorites; not just because he saved my life, but his innocence and simple mind, coupled with a gentle nature, makes him hard not to like.

"Hola, lizard fighter," I say as we walk.

Payo grins really big, making the dried dirt on his face crack.

I might not be in the mood to smile, but I never tire of making Payo smile. As he goes toward his own home, we go toward ours. I look at the forest in the distant background, knowing it must be full of ripe fruits wasting away. It doesn't make sense. But it's a good hour walk to the forest, so it would be dark before reaching it, and that is not an option. It will be crawling with Scavs by then.

"Why do people pick on Payo?"

Niko shrugs. "Because they like him."

I don't agree with that. "If they liked him, they could see in his eyes that he doesn't enjoy it."

We walk the rest of the way in silence. Niko washes Ana and puts her in my bed, then comes back to the table. He allows me to use the washroom next. It's nice to be out of the fields where you have to go whenever and wherever the feeling hits. Niko uses the washroom next and then we eat some fruit as we wait on Vet.

"Are all the crops the same?" Niko looks confused, so I clarify. "There are four provinces, so I was wondering if they all picked the same kind of crops as we do."

"No," Niko says. "There are four different types."

I nod and stare at the tabletop, my eyes tracing the grains in the wood running across in front of me. I have memorized these lines and often make images with in my head. Suddenly they take on a new design as I imagine them to be the rows of crops. My mind begins to calculate.

Vet comes in and, like us, takes off his dirt-clogged sandals and goes to the washroom to clean up. He returns and takes his seat and eats some fruit. Had today been the sixth day, we would have made Ana stay awake to eat before the fasting of the seventh.

"Vet," I say as I look at the lines on the table. "I think I can design a new system for picking crops."

He looks confused. "What do you mean?"

I trace along the grain lines with my finger. "As it is now, there is no system at all. People grab a bag and go anywhere. We overlap each other many times and it takes us so long to drag the bags to the end of the rows to add to the carrier. It is very hard on the elderly people, and they are not very productive."

Niko and Vet are staring at me with eyes and mouths open wide. I begin to feel the same way I felt with the bridge idea.

"I just think if we organize, it would work a lot better. If you assign positions for people, and instead of them slowly filling up the bags themselves, you could assign strong runners to go down each row with bags and the pickers could throw the crops in the bags as they pass. I think we could get the same work accomplished in much less time. Maybe it would be so efficient that the elderly wouldn't even have to come to the fields."

Vet shakes his head. "The elderly have to work the fields. The Book commands it."

"Okay," I say, not giving up. "But they could be given easier jobs and we could still finish hours earlier, leaving time to go to the forest."

Niko is staring at Vet, as am I, awaiting his response. Vet doesn't say anything.

"What do you think?" I press.

Vet shakes his head. "We just need to stick to the system and get through it."

I'm shocked. "But it would—"

"No!" Vet says. "You just don't understand our ways. I'm going to bed." He gets up and disappears into his room.

Our ways? Did he really just say that? Once again I feel like a visitor, a feeling I haven't felt for months. I had started thinking of this as my home. I look to Niko for support, but he is concentrating on his food. He seems to sense me staring at him.

"Oh, sorry," he says, putting down the piece of fruit. "Maybe we could—"

"Good night," I say, cutting him off. I am tired and don't want to discuss it, so I go to bed. Very carefully I slide in beside Ana as not to wake her. I am exhausted and usually fall fast asleep after spending all day in the fields, but not tonight. I can't get those two words out of my head—*our ways*. Whatever sense of belonging I once felt has been wiped away. I don't know where I belong anymore.

CHAPTER SEVENTEEN

It is barely light outside as we head to the fields. I walk alongside the track with Niko and Payo. Vet has taken the carrier ahead with Ana. We have been picking the Fathers' crops for almost three months. I look down at my hands, calloused with several liquid-filled blisters. Most have already burst. My hands and feet are so numb I don't even feel them anymore. But this is the last week. I'll be glad when it's over.

We walk in silence. This whole ordeal is an emotional drain, and everyone is ready to go back to their normal lives. We reach the carrier, grab an empty bag, and vanish into the crops. I walk past stalks already picked and get farther and farther away from the carrier. I can hear others nearby but can't see them. I am hardly aware of anything anymore, existing almost like a lifeless machine.

I see a person cross my row in the distance. I don't pay attention. As I continue onward, however, my mind begins to pick up signals from my eyes. Who did I just see? They were large and wearing all black. I freeze, unable to take another step as my mind processes more information. I gasp as the obvious occurs to me—that was not one of the Children I just saw.

Two more large dark figures cross my row in the distance. I know now that my mind is not playing tricks on me. Scavs are in the fields. I turn to go back but see several more dark figures cross the row in that direction. They are everywhere. I start to scream out when I hear a loud explosion. I turn back to look in the direction of the sound. My breathing is short, quick panting, and I still can't move. More screams echo throughout the crops, like the messages at worship whispering back through the crowds. I hear the rustling of stalks as people rush back toward the carrier.

Suddenly it grabs me around the waist, its mighty arms pulling me backward. I turn to try to fight it off, but it is not a Scav.

"Come on," Niko says as he lifts me off the ground and spins around to point me in the right direction.

I run as fast as I can back to the carrier, where I blend in with the huge crowd that awaits me there. Men on the outside of the huge circle of people stand fast, their spears pointed. Behind me the carrier is loaded with men holding bows, scanning the fields. I realize I am shaking uncontrollably. Niko wraps his arms around me for comfort. It helps. I see Ana behind me safe in the crowd and that also makes me feel better.

No one moves for a long time until the word is spread that they are gone. Vet comes up to us to deliver the news.

"Scavs have attacked the fields," he says, his eyes darting from one person to the next. "They are gone now, but they have taken one person from each province. It is unlikely they will come back, so we have to get back to work."

I can't believe it. They still expect us to work after what happened? I can see the worry in everyone's eyes as they slowly dissolve back into the stalks. I am afraid to go. Niko must sense my fears.

"Come on. We'll work together today," he says.

And that's what we do. He stays with me and works even harder than he normally does, helping me keep pace with him. It is hard for me to work. I can't keep from scanning the gaps in the crops, all the way to where light disappears into darkness. I keep expecting to see those creatures any minute, but they never show again.

Once the carrier is sent back out after the fifth load, we start the long walk home, our pace a little faster than usual. The delay costs us time, and it is later than we would have finished, so getting home before dark is not as easy this day. Niko and Payo walk on either side of me, as if guarding me from everything.

"Did you hear who it was from our province?" Payo asks.

Niko nods but doesn't answer. He keeps walking.

"Who was it?" I ask also.

Niko says one word. "Gano."

Payo drops his eyes to the ground and shakes his head. I know who that is as well. I have met him several times. He's a boy who lives close to us, a little younger than me but the same size. He has light hair and light eyes. His hair isn't quite the color of mine, but it's closer than anyone else I've seen here. Ana says we could have been brothers.

We go through the normal routine, getting cleaned up, putting Ana to bed, and sitting at the table awaiting Vet, who comes in much later this time. It is already dark before he gets home. As he sits at the table, Niko and I can't wait any longer to hear the news.

"Well?" Niko asks. "What all happened today?"

Vet looks up with a stern expression. "Scavs attacked every field today. They took one person from every province."

"We already know that news. Girls, boys, or both?" I ask.

Vet exhales deeply. "All boys."

I go to bed that night with tears, thinking of the horror the four boys must have faced at the hands of the Scavs, a fate shared by Niko and Ana's mama. I try not to think about it, but I can't help wondering how it happens. Do the Scavs take their catch back to their tribes? Do they kill them humanely or rip them apart? I try hard to stop letting my mind run wild with these thoughts. The only thing I know for sure is that I don't want to ever find out.

The next day at the fields is an exercise in fear, but the day passes with no incident. The weather, however, is relentless, raining down large drops so hard they sting my face. I have gotten used to rain, something else we never dealt with in the city. I like the rain when it's light, but storms like these make me not want to be outside. I try to huddle under the stalks as much as possible. But it makes the heat more bearable, and the bugs don't like the rain either.

The next day is worship. We get up early and head out. As we arrive in the carrier, I still see the silhouettes of the Scavs on the verge of their territory as they make their own pilgrimage. I am the only one who pays any attention. Regardless of the increase in area and intensity of attacks, no one seems to give any thoughts to the Scavs attacking on the seventh. Still they bring no weapons and still they relax without so much as a glance over their shoulders or a thought to the creatures who have relentlessly hunted them.

One of the Elect holds The Book high over his head, as if he is expecting the Fathers to send down lightning bolts. "As it says in Chapter Eighteen, the Fathers have provided us with everything we need from the fruits and berries in the forest, to the lakes and fish, to the lizards and eggs. They give us rain and warmth and everything we need to have a productive life."

The message whispers back as everyone nods. I still don't buy it. The Fathers take credit for everything and promise impossible punishment. But at least listening to the loco lessons from The Book is far better than picking the crops.

The days march on. Luckily, we suffer no more attacks and finally the last day of harvest arrives. We make sure to pull every crop from the stalks, no matter how large or how small, to make certain we empty the field completely. It is too late in the year for new crops, so after we get through today, there will be no yellow balls left at all. All of the fields of each province will be void of edible substance. There will be nothing left for the Children and, as far as I know, not one person took a single bite out of any of the crops. After all, that is forbidden.

As the carrier is sent back out for the last time, everyone cheers. The walk back home that day takes on an entirely new meaning, as indifference is replaced with jubilation. Although, like the crops, there will no longer be any berries or fruits growing in the forest, there still are many months of fishing and hunting before the cold days. And I am told this is the time for fun as there will be many games and sports in which to participate. I might not have cared for that when I first arrived, but after nine months, especially the last three spent in the fields, I have become much tougher. I still am not proficient with the bow, much to Niko's frustration, but my arms and legs are much stronger than before.

The air even tastes better as I breathe. Vet has taken Ana ahead in the carrier as always, and once again my little trio walks together.

"Payo, when are you going to get a mate?" I ask, knowing this always makes him blush.

He grins and shrugs his shoulder. "I don't think anyone likes me."

"But you're such a great boy," I say. "Right, Niko?"

"Oh, absolutely," Niko says. "They would be loco not to go after you."

Payo grins bigger. Then he looks serious. "I'm not really worried about it. I just want to be chosen so I can see my mama and papa again."

It makes me sad. It's not just the beautiful sentiment, but my deepest fear that The Book is promising things it can't deliver. I decide to lighten the mood. "Okay, boys, I'm thinking of an object in our view. What is it?"

"The track," Payo shouts out quickly.

"The grass," Niko says.

I was indeed thinking of the grass. "You got it right, Payo," I say. "I was thinking of the track. You must have read my mind."

Payo beams with pride. I like his company and enjoy making him feel equal. I watch how the others treat him, and it bothers me. They are not mean; they just talk around him most of the time. When they do talk to him, it's usually in jest. I don't think they understand how it affects him, but I can see it in his eyes. It is something I have become aware of here on the surface. The thing that drew me to the Children was their emotions they display for one another, the love and admiration. But those emotions aren't always positive. Just as we never expressed feelings like love and compassion in the city, neither did we express anger or ridicule.

As we get home, Payo heads to his house.

I look at Niko. "Why do they call him Tonto?"

Niko points to his head. "Because he's a little slow."

I shake my head. I don't like it. We go in and after Vet gets home, we all sit at the table and eat, even Ana. We are all tired, but that doesn't seem to matter tonight. Harvest is over.

"Have you heard about the games?" Vet asks.

I nod. I still think about the words Vet used that one night—*our ways*. I have decided to not let it bother me. I know he was as tired as I was, and I know he cares about all the Children. He doesn't like the elderly having to work any more than I do, but he is hopelessly devoted to the rules of The Book.

"Are you going to play Circle Ball?" Ana asks.

"I don't know about that one," I say. "I've heard it can be rough."

"He's playing," Niko says. "You're as tough as any other person here."

"I'll second that," Vet says.

That darn blushing mechanism activates again. Hopefully no one will notice.

"Your face is all red," Ana says.

We all laugh. We sit around and talk and laugh for another hour before going to bed, and although we are both very tired, Ana and I stay awake and talk and giggle. Even though it is a little warm, she snuggles against me like she always does. I wrap my arms around her and we fall asleep.

CHAPTER EIGHTEEN

After sleeping very late, we all eat and go outside. It's a beautiful day, and the weather is not quite as hot as it was.

"Let's go to the Circle Ball field," Niko says.

We all agree and follow him. Ash takes the lead as usual, his nose in the air. Both Niko and Vet carry a spear. Niko also has his bow on his back. This was common practice before the increased Scav attacks. At least there haven't been any reports of attacks since that day in the fields. I can see a crowd gathered as we approach the area. As I arrive, I see several people I recognize, including San and Payo. There is an area where the ground is packed hard and appears to have been this way for a while. No grass grows there anymore, much like the ground at Market. People either stand or sit along the edge of the circle. Most are there as spectators only.

Payo sees us and quickly walks up. "Hola. You playing today, Piri, eh?"

"I guess so."

"We're going to take a seat," Vet says as he walks away holding Ana's hand. Ana turns and smiles at me and gives me a wave.

San seems to be the ringleader. "Okay, let's get the first game started. Who all is here to play?"

Many raise their hands, including me and Niko. Most are about our age. There are some a little older and some a little younger, but the oldest and youngest seem content just to watch.

"Okay," San says. "We need two pickers." He points at one in the group. "Mari, you're one."

A girl steps forward as people cheer.

"Niko," San says, "You're the other."

Mari and Niko stand beside each other. She smiles at him as I've noticed other girls doing. I now understand the feeling I felt when Ari used to demand Niko's attention. It's called jealousy.

"You know the rules," San says. "Pick eight people to be on your team."

The girl goes first and calls out a boy's name. He walks over and stands beside her. Now it's time for Niko's first pick.

"Piri," he says, which brings laughter and whistles from the crowd. They know he isn't picking me for my skills at this game. I blush and stand beside him.

After the girl chooses again, Niko considers the group of contenders. He looks at me, and I give him a puzzled look as if wondering what he's thinking. He smiles. "Payo," he says.

Payo almost trips over his own feet as he joins us. The look on his face is a combination of pride and disbelief, as if he has never been picked so early. That has already made this a great day for me. This process continues until each picker has selected eight players, forming two nine-person teams. San then puts one hand behind his back and looks at the two pickers.

"Five," the girl says.

"Six," Niko says.

San brings his hand around to reveal four extended fingers. The girl's team all clap. They get the ball first. She chooses one of her players to stand in the middle. Our team must then form a circle eight feet in diameter as we face outward with our legs spread wide. The nine of us stand with a gap of about a foot wide between us. The remaining eight members of the other team form a circle three feet outside of ours. The goal is to pass the ball along the ground and try to get it between two of us, or between our legs, to the middle person. Each successful attempt to do this results in one point. The first team to score ten points wins the game.

San holds the ball, which is a wooden ball covered with strips of cloth to provide padding. "Ready?" he says.

I am not ready. I don't even know what I'm doing, but I say nothing.

"Begin!" San tosses the ball to one of the outer ring players.

The player quickly tosses it to the player opposite me, a boy about the size of Niko, who promptly whips it underhanded, and it goes right between my legs before I can react. The crowd erupts with laughter and yells, "One."

The boy on the inside lobs it back out of the circle to the same player. He whips it again and I close my legs quickly, but he doesn't release it. He fakes it. The huge gap on either side of my legs is his new target.

"Deke!" one of our players yells.

But Niko sees it coming and closes the gap between us, successfully blocking the next attempt.

I breathe a sigh of relief as we trade places. Niko picks one of our boys to take the middle as we become the outer circle, and the other team takes our place. San tosses the ball to Payo to restart the game. Payo quickly pitches it to Niko. The outer circle is allowed to move around however they like. Niko runs behind me and extends the ball for me to take. But he tricks the other team, and me, by keeping it. I see the devious look in his eyes and realize what he's doing. I spin around and make an exaggerated movement, as if I'm rolling the ball directly toward the boy in front of me, the same boy who faked me. He quickly brings his legs together as Niko whizzes the ball past him.

The crowd now yells the word. "Deke, deke, deke..." They erupt with laughter again as they yell, "one-to-one."

The boy laughs and points at me, shaking his finger and nodding, letting me know I got him. I am having so much fun. The game progresses and I start to catch on. Soon I am not the one they single out.

The game is tied nine-to-nine and we have the ball. One more score and we will be victorious. I really want to win. I never knew winning could be so important. We pass the ball around, looking for an opportunity. Niko passes it to Payo, who quickly looks around for someone else to pass it to. I suddenly realize that Payo has never attempted a score. The boy in front of him knows this as well and is not really guarding against him, only expecting Payo to give it to someone else. I see an opportunity and take it. I run behind Payo with my hands outreached. He hands it toward me. I haven't heard the word "deke" before today, but I catch on fast.

Instead of taking the ball, I wink at him and clasp my arms together like I have the ball and continue running. All eyes are on me. Payo understands. He takes the ball and gives it a toss. But his coordination is off. By the time the girl on the inner circle realizes what is happening, she can only spin around in defense of the oncoming, off-angle throw, and the ball hits her right in the backside.

Payo covers his mouth with his hands as the girl jumps up and down in pain. It is mostly exaggerated as everyone in the crowd goes loco with laughter. I am laughing so hard my sides hurt.

San tries hard to regain his composure. "Penalty," he finally announces through his laughter.

"Nice shot, Tonto," the girl says.

I stop laughing, and I walk right up to the girl and poke my finger into her chest. "His name is Payo, not Tonto. Got it?"

Several tense seconds of silence pass as even the crowd grows quiet. The girl looks at me as if wondering what she should do, the smile on her face proving she isn't the least bit afraid of me. And why should she be? She's much larger and stronger. I begin to worry that I am about to experience my first beating until I hear San, who has walked up behind me, clear his throat. The girl looks at San and stops smiling.

"What's the matter with you, Cari? Don't embarrass me," San says.

The girl drops her head. "You're right." She looks over to my friend. "Sorry...*Payo*. Forgive me, por favor."

Payo smiles.

I breathe a sigh of relief. We change circles again. The girl pats Payo on the shoulder to let him know she's okay, and there are no hard feelings. But they quickly score to win the game. They all cheer.

It doesn't matter. It was still more fun than anything I've ever been involved in. Niko and I go and sit beside Vet and Ana.

Payo looks over to us, so I motion for him to come join us. We watch as another team is picked to take on the reigning champions. Watching is almost as fun as playing. Even Ash and a few other dogs around the circle get excited watching the games as their tails wag uncontrollably.

We go to other game events across the province. I play a few more but enjoy watching Niko and sitting with Ana as much as playing. It is an incredible day. As afternoon arrives, the games come to an end and everyone heads back toward their homes. As usual, Niko and I decide to find a place to be alone. Ana still doesn't like it, but she has gotten used to it and doesn't argue anymore. She simply waves and heads off with her papa, Ash leading the way for them. And as always, there's still a third person who isn't quite as perceptive as Ana.

"I had so much fun today. Did you have fun, Piri?"

"Sí, I did, Payo," I say. "My favorite thing today was when you hit that girl with the ball."

Niko laughs as Payo shakes his head. "I felt so bad. I didn't do it on purpose," Payo says.

"Everyone knows that," I say. "You're too nice to do that."

As we walk along, Niko stares as me as if wondering how once again to let Payo know. "So, Payo," Niko says. "I guess we'll see you tomorrow."

Payo smiles. "Sí. I'll go to the games tomorrow, too. What do you want to do now?"

Niko drops his head.

I can't help but laugh. I decide to try a new angle. "Payo, remember when I asked you about having a mate?"

He nods.

"Have you ever thought about that?"

"Sí," he says. "All the time."

We stop walking so I can get his full attention. "When you think about it, do you ever think about spending time with them alone?"

He blushes. "Sí."

I go for the kill. "What if your brother or a friend wanted to hang around you when you wanted to spend time alone with your mate?"

Payo stares upward as if really imagining the scenario. "I'd let them know we wanted to be alone."

I stare into Payo's eyes. They are blank. I reach my hand out to Niko, who takes it in his own. I continue to look Payo in the eyes.

"Oh my goodness," he says. "Oh my goodness. I'm sorry. Oh my goodness. I'll leave you two alone. I'm so dumb. Por favor, don't be mad at me."

I take his hand with my free hand. "We're not mad at you, Payo. Outside of Niko's family, you're my favorite person. We enjoy spending time with you. We just like to spend time with each other also."

Payo grins. "I'm your favorite person?"

"He says so all the time," Niko says.

I nod.

Payo lets go of my hand. "Okay, I'll see you tomorrow." He steps backward right into a pit and his foot sinks into the black stuff. He pulls it out and doesn't even seem to mind. He laughs at himself and turns and walks away.

"You were great," Niko says.

"Thanks," I reply. "But I hated lying to him."

Niko looks confused. "About what?"

"The mate thing. You have never told anyone, not even me, that I am your mate. So I guess I'm not."

Niko doesn't say anything. I can tell by his eyes he is not sure what to say. "I just thought…uh…"

"Si?"

"I mean…" Niko swallows hard. "Well, are you?"

"Do you want me to be?"

He nods. "Sí."

"Then I am."

Niko exhales deeply. "You like making things hard for me, don't you?"

I laugh. "Sí, I do. It's not nice of me. You saved my life and took me into your family and have always looked out for me. You're the best person I've ever known." I raise my feet to lean in to him and we embrace. I love his lips on mine. It awakens feelings in me I never even knew existed, never knew a human was capable of. We pull away, and I can see he shares the feeling. "The truth is, I have been your mate since we met."

He smiles. "And I have been yours. I love you, Piri."

My entire body tingles. "I love you, too, Niko."

CHAPTER NINETEEN

D o you miss your old home at all?" Niko asks.
I am leaning back against him as we sit in the vacant home, the one where Niko wants to live. We have begun calling it "our home." It is the one place where we are sure to be alone. Sitting on the hard floor isn't too comfortable since there is no furniture, but as long as we're together, I'm happy.

"Not really," I say. "Life is much easier for sure, but after being here for nine months, it doesn't even seem like a life at all up there. There is no connection between people, not even between my mama and papa, or between my sister and me. Everything is about following procedure, maintaining the normal routine. I've never seen my mama and papa kiss. I never even knew it was something people did."

"Where did you come from if your mama didn't get pregnant with you?"

I shrug. "I don't know. I never thought about it before. That's another thing I didn't know people did."

"Do you ever want to go back, just to visit?"

I shake my head. "My life is here now."

He wraps his arms around me tighter. "Good."

We sit in silence for a while, just enjoying being together. But I have something pressing on my mind. I don't know if it's safe to broach the subject with him, but I need to talk with someone, and he is, after all, my mate. "There's something I want to talk about, but not if it will make you upset."

"The Book?"

I am surprised and turn my head fully around to look at him. "Sí."

"It's okay. I know you don't believe in it. I can see it in your eyes. You can talk to me about it. I won't say anything to anyone, not even Papa."

I turn around and cross my legs. He does the same, and we are staring at each other. I think of where to begin. "I just don't believe that the Fathers, the people with whom I lived in the city, are capable of the punishments threatened in The Book. We have a much more advanced technology in the city, or technology at all," I say as I look around at the stone walls, "but not the kind it would take to do things like making the oceans rise or making fire rain down. These are things I've never heard of before coming here. I truly believe they are empty threats." I search his face, but I don't see any reaction.

"Go on," he says. "What about the Chosen? You don't believe they go to live in the city, do you?"

"No, I don't. The city is designed to hold an exact amount of people. If we were to take in four hundred new people each seventh day, that's over twenty thousand in a year. And according to The Book, this has been going on for thousands of years."

Niko sighs. "Is it not possible they go to the city just to be servants, maybe on a level you've never visited?"

"Sí, I guess it's possible. But that many people on one level? It just seems like that's something we would be taught. Yet we are not even taught that there are people living on the surface."

"If they don't go to live in the city, where do you think they go?"

"Good question. I don't know."

"What about when we die?" Niko asks.

I look him directly in the eye. "That's even more confusing. I have never seen or heard of one young person coming from the surface to live in the city. I have certainly never seen or heard of dead people from the surface coming to live eternally in the city. There are even more people that die each year than make up the Chosen. You couldn't confine that many people on all twelve levels, much less hide them on one. And the very idea that people can come back to life goes against one of the events of the actual people living in the city. When we become eighty years old, life is over for us. Even the people living in the city are not promised or offered eternal life."

Niko remains silent. I don't know if I've done the right thing by telling him this.

"I'm not saying these things to make you feel bad or to question your own beliefs. I just needed to tell you."

"I know," he says. "What you say makes sense. That's what worries me the most. You're the smartest person I've ever known. I didn't know people could be smart like you. These are things I've never thought about before and never would have thought to question. I have always accepted everything in The Book because we are taught to do that. It never occurred to me to think about the real possibility of the things in The Book. I just don't know how to feel."

"I don't know, either. I know things have been the same for a very long time. This is where I want to be, so I'll live life as you do. I'll never say anything to anyone else about my feelings, only you."

Niko smiles. "Do you want to know the worst part of it?"

"What?"

"I believe you."

I almost cry as I lean in and kiss him. "It only matters that we're together," I say as I lay my head on his chest.

Then I hear a noise outside the house. Niko hears it too as we stand up. We have the door locked, but someone is definitely trying to get in. We can hear regular voices, so Niko opens the door. San is standing there with a surprised look.

"What's going on?" he asks. He smiles at both of us. "Am I interrupting something?"

"What are you doing?" Niko asks.

"We were going to look at this house." San steps aside and I see Cari, the girl from the Circle Ball games. "We just got married and were looking for a place to live."

"Oh my goodness," I say. I understand now why San told Cari she was embarrassing him at the games. I walk out and hug Cari. "Congratulations."

"Gracias," she replies with a big smile.

"Where's your gift?" I ask.

Cari proudly displays an intricately hand-woven necklace.

"It's beautiful," I say. "And where's yours?"

San reaches into his pouch and pulls out three arrow tips made from bone.

"Those are nice," Niko says. He takes them and examines them closely. "Very nice. You did good, Cari."

Cari smiles.

"So, what were you doing?" San asks again.

"We were looking at this place, too," Niko says. "We've been looking at it for a while now."

"Did you get married?" Cari asks.

"No, not yet," I reply. "We were just planning for the future."

Niko nods.

"So, the place is still available, then?" San asks.

"Oh yeah," Niko says. I can see he is torn to give that answer.

"I'm joking with you, Niko," San says. "We have other places we're going to look at."

"Sí," Cari says. "Will you come with us to look at a few other places?"

"We would love to," I say.

Niko agrees. I know he is relieved.

We spend the rest of the afternoon with San and Cari visiting three other homes, all of which look identical. They pick out one and declare it theirs. As the news is delivered throughout the area, people come bearing gifts, some in the form of furniture. I am so happy for them.

Niko and I finally bid good-bye to the new couple and head back home. It is such a good feeling seeing them so happy. I am already happy but find myself looking forward to our day as well and moving into our home. Hopefully it will still be available.

"We better hurry and marry and claim our home," I say as we walk.

"You're so right," Niko replies.

"I hope to receive a gift as nice as this one," I say, holding out my Kabloom necklace.

"Thanks for the pressure."

I smile. Then I see Payo running toward us, smiling as always. He stops about ten feet away, and his smile disappears. "Is this alone time?" he asks.

I laugh. "You're fine. What's going on?"

"Did you hear about San and Cari?"

Niko explains that we not only heard, but helped them pick out a house.

"What were their gifts?"

I tell him about the necklace and arrow tips. He thinks those are great gifts. I do, too.

It's getting late so we go home and get ready for bed. Ana and I tell funny stories and giggle until she falls asleep. Afterward, I lie there thinking about San and Cari. I know Niko and I were being funny, but that day for us will come soon, I think. I suddenly realize I don't know how the gift exchange goes, but I don't have anything for him. The Book says that marriage means the exchange of gifts between two people eighteen years old or older and the acceptance of said gifts.

Ana and I get up the next morning and go to the table. Only Vet is there.

"Where's Niko?" I ask.

Vet looks at me strangely. "Uh…he went hunting, I think."

That's odd. He has always told me when he goes hunting.

"Can I take Ash outside?" Ana asks.

"Sure," Vet says. "There are lots of people out today, but stay right in front of the house. Okay?"

She jumps up and runs to the door. Ash follows.

Then it dawns on me. "Why didn't Niko take Ash hunting with him? He always does."

Vet shrugs.

I know something is wrong. Vet never acts this way, and Niko never keeps anything from me. "Vet, you've never lied to me before."

Vet turns around with a silly grin. "I know, but I've never lied to Niko either and he made me promise not to tell you what he's doing. But I assure you, it's a wonderful thing."

My face stretches into a smile as I understand what's going on. "Okay, I won't ask. But I do have something else to ask of you."

"What's that?"

"I understand what The Book says about gifts and marriage," I say, "and I saw the gifts yesterday that San and Cari gave one another, but I don't know how that works. How did they know to have a gift ready?"

Vet can't hold back his smile, revealing to me that I am correct in assuming what Niko is up to. "Okay, here's how it works. Most girls have their gift ready for years, saving it until that special day. Boys usually create their gift once they find someone they want to marry. When they present the gifts to one another and both accept them, they are officially married."

"Oh my goodness," I say. "I am behind, then, aren't I?"

He nods.

"Is it normal for boys to get a weapons-related gift?"

"Not always," Vet says. "It is usually a safe gift, though."

"What did your wife get you?" I ask, forgetting that I shouldn't mention her.

Luckily, Vet smiles. "Come," he says.

I follow him into his bedroom. I've never been in here before. In fact, I've never even been in Niko or Ana's bedroom. He walks over to the bed and points behind it to the back wall. There is a stone structure stuck on the wall. The stones are black and chiseled away to form the letter V-E-T.

"It's beautiful."

Vet nods. "She was a unique person."

I remember what he said about girls having gifts for a long

time. "This is not something she had for years. This was designed just for you."

He smiles. "Sí. I think she did have a regular gift, but she decided to make this. I was so impressed. Everyone was. She was very good at making things and painting things."

"What did you give her?"

He smiles again. "A woven bracelet. Took me weeks to make it."

"I need your help. I have an idea. I saw something at the Market that Niko was looking at it, but I don't know how to find the people now. Do you know anyone who can make something out of metal?"

Vet scratches his head and looks up at the ceiling. "I know one person who doesn't live too far away. But he's not what I would call a stable person."

"What do you mean?"

"Well," Vet says, "he's very old and his mind has gotten a little off. And to be honest, he never was that stable even when he was younger. He doesn't really like people. But he's the best metal worker I know."

I'm not sure I like the sound of that. "Does he set up at Market?"

Vet shakes his head very fast. "Oh no. Like I said, he doesn't like people. But I don't know where the metal workers from the Market live. That's the only one I know. Maybe you should think of something else."

"No," I say. "I'll do it."

CHAPTER TWENTY

"Well, I got to go meet some boys to go hunting," Niko says as he gets up from the table.

"Good luck," I tell him. "We sure know you need it. This is your fourth trip, and you haven't brought home anything."

"Sí," Niko says. "I don't know what's happening. I can't seem to find any lizards." He walks to the door and grabs his spear and bow. "No, Ash, you stay here."

"Maybe that's the problem. You used to always take Ash hunting."

"Yeah, maybe." Niko goes out the door.

Vet and Ana laugh. "Payo should be here soon. He will take you to the old man's place," Vet says.

"Can I go with Piri?" Ana asks.

"Sure," Vet says. "But I'm pretty sure this old man cooks and eats little girls."

Ana's eyes get real big and she swallows hard. "I better stay here and look after Papa."

I nod. "That's a good idea, Chiquita, and very brave of you."

She smiles.

Thirty minutes later, Payo arrives and enters. "I'm here. I'm glad you need my help. What can I do?"

Vet explains.

Payo doesn't say anything for several seconds. "You want me to take Piri to old man Curz. Wh...what...what if he kills us?"

Vet laughs. "He has never killed anyone." Then he looks at

Ana. "Well, just little girls mostly. You'll be fine. Can you take Piri or not?"

Payo nods nervously. "Sí. Of course I'll take Piri."

We set out for a long walk. We talk along the way, and that puts Payo's mind at ease. I only wish I could put my own mind at ease. I'm not sure if I'm doing the right thing, but I'm sure of what I want Niko's gift to be. An hour later, we come to the old man's house. There are no other houses around it. I've never seen a place like this. There are all kinds of junk items around the house, pieces of wood and metal. There are several large drums behind the house, and the whole place smells awful.

"Are you sure you want to do this?" Payo asks.

"No, I'm not sure." I walk down the steps to the front door. Payo follows and stands beside me. I knock on the door.

Nothing.

I knock harder. "Hola?"

Suddenly the door swings open wide, and a man rushes out so fast that Payo jumps back and falls onto the steps. The man is old and his hair is pure white, like Maren the Elect, but it is wild and unmanaged. Coarse white whiskers grow from his face and bushy white eyebrows adorn his brow. They cover half of his eyes, which are almost as pale as mine. He glares at Payo as if he did something wrong. Payo is afraid to move. The man stands so close to me I can smell his breath, but he still hasn't looked at me.

"Hola, I'm Piri. Are you…"

"What do you want?" he yells, turning his glare at me.

I swallow hard. "I'm told you are the best metal worker around. I need to make a gift for my mate."

He looks me over as if I'm from another world. I guess in a sense I am. He leans forward until his face is only inches from mine. He stares into my eyes without blinking. I don't flinch. "You think just because The Book says not to kill one another," he says, "that I won't cook you two and eat you for dinner?"

Payo stands and walks backward up the steps. I ignore the threat. "Will you help me or not?" I ask.

"No, I won't!" he yells. "Now get away from my house before I put my attack lizards on you."

Payo continues to walk backward.

But it is not fear I am feeling at the moment. "You loco old man. What's the matter with you? Of all the people I have met on the surface, you are the most vile, rude, obnoxious person by far." I give back his stare as good as he gives it.

He stands up straight. "What's obnoxious mean?" he asks in a gentle tone.

It catches me off guard. "Uh...it means annoying and offensive."

He looks upward and smiles. "Yeah, I like that word. That's a first. What do you have to trade?'

I didn't even think of that. "I don't really have anything."

He laughs. "And you call me obnoxious."

"Tell me what you need and I'll try to get it for you."

He smiles deviously. "Come inside." He looks out at Payo. "You stay right there and don't move, boy, or I'll release my attack lizards."

I follow him inside and he shuts the door. He walks into the kitchen and sits at the table. I do likewise. "You don't really have attack lizards, do you?" I ask.

He winks. "Of course not. Who does?"

I laugh.

"Tell me what you need, and I'll tell you what I expect in return," he says.

I explain it to him.

"Sí, I can do that. Very simple really. But I need you to get me measurements. Can you do that?"

I nod. "Sí, I can. Now, as much as I'm afraid to ask, what is the payment you expect?"

He smiles a wry smile. "Tell me what it's like in the city in the sky."

I am shocked. "You know?"

"I'm loco," he says, "not dumb."

I laugh and stick out my hand, a custom I know they do here when they make a deal. He shakes it gently. "When do we start?"

"As soon as you can get me the measurements, my dear Piri. Then come every day, and, as I work, you talk."

I smile, get up, and walk toward the door.

"Oh," he says as I look back. "Not a word about my attack lizards."

I hold my finger up to my lips, the first gesture I learned from Niko. I walk out to see Payo standing exactly in the same spot, afraid to move. I walk up to him. "Okay, we can go now." I continue back the way we came, and Payo walks alongside me.

"I thought he was going to kill you or feed you to his lizards," Payo says.

I shake my head and continue walking. Payo is happy to talk about other things. I know he was very scared back at the old man's house. I wish I could tell him the truth, but that would feel like I was betraying my word. The old man obviously enjoys his privacy, and if the scary old man routine helps him maintain it, who am I to destroy that?

Later that afternoon, Niko returns from yet another game-free hunt. Vet, Ana, and I tease him about it as we sit around the table and eat. I think of how to get the information I need. I decide on my plan of action. I take my middle finger and thumb on my right hand and wrap them around the wrist of my left hand. I do this several times until I get Niko's attention.

"What are you doing?" he asks.

I look up at him as I continue. "I'm just surprised at how large my arms have gotten. I think they're bigger than yours." My fingers actually wrap all the way around my wrist and overlap.

Niko laughs. "You're kidding, right? Your arms are not near as big as mine."

"Let me see," I say. I hold my hand out, fingers outstretched. Niko shakes his head and laughs again, but hands his arm over. I wrap my fingers around the wrist. My middle finger and thumb don't reach, not by an inch. "Wait," I say and slide my fingers up his arm four inches and measure again. My fingers leave a one-and-a-half-inch gap. "I guess you're right."

Niko looks at me like I'm loco and continues eating. I wink at Ana, who giggles. Vet is trying hard to maintain composure.

The next day, Payo again walks me to Curz's house, but he waits a longer distance away this time.

"Good morning, young man," Curz says when he opens the door.

I smile and follow him inside.

"Did you get the measurements?" he asks.

I hold up my fingers and he laughs.

"Perfect." He motions for me to follow him outside and we walk around back to his work area. There is a table with a stick of wood, like from a limb or small tree, the bark already removed. It is slimmer on one end and gets slightly larger as it goes in the other direction. He holds the wooden shaft out to me. "Okay, show me."

I smile. I take the piece of wood and slide my hand along until I find the exact circumference of Niko's wrist. "Here's the lower part."

Curz scrapes the spot with a black rock, which leaves a thin line. "See how the upper part looks."

I slide my hand up the shaft about four inches and the gap looks perfect, about one and a half inches wide. I smile and nod as he marks that spot as well.

He takes the piece of wood and slides it into a vise of sorts and proceeds to whittle away the areas on each side of the lines. "So, tell me about the food in the city."

I smile and begin to tell him about the food tablets. "In the kitchen area, there is a dispenser with a button above it. When you push the button, a square tablet comes out. It's only about this thick." I hold my finger up to show him. "We chew on the tablet with water. One can actually fill you up once it gets in your stomach." I talk about other parts of life in the city. He continues working, looking up occasionally to make eye contact. I talk about whatever comes to mind, from the city Central Link where we get all our information, to Level Twelve's entertainment venue.

Once he has the wood neatly trimmed away, leaving a perfect mold of Niko's wrist, he walks over to a fire pit constructed of rocks. "Now we need a very hot fire," he says. He builds a fire using small pieces of wood. As the fire burns, he walks over to one of the drums and dips a bucket of the black stuff out and walks back to the fire.

I walk up to watch.

"No, step back," he says.

I obey.

He dips a wooden spoon into the bucket and throws a small amount of the black stuff into the fire. WHOOSH! The flames jump high into the air and continue to burn. I jump back and scream making Curz laugh. "Sorry, didn't mean to frighten you."

He walks over and holds a thin flat piece of metal over the fire with a long gripping rod. In only a minute, the thin metal is completely red. He carries it over to the wooden mold and uses a hammer to pound it and shape it around the form. As the metal cools, it becomes harder to shape. He goes back to the fire, throws another spoonful of black stuff on it, and as it roars once again, places the metal piece in the fire and waits.

"What is that stuff?" I ask.

He smiles. "It comes from the pits."

"It doesn't look like the stuff from the pits I've seen. And it doesn't burn like that."

He nods. "I boil the stuff from the pits for a long time and then add some stuff I make from plants."

"Plants?"

"Sí. I let plants sit in a drum of water for months, then boil off the burnable part, then mix that with the boiled-down black stuff from the pits. It makes the fire ten times stronger, as you can see."

I laugh. "You really aren't dumb for a loco old man." I look around the area and count fifteen large drums. "Are all those filled with your special mix?"

He nods.

"Do you do that much metal work?"

"No," he says, looking around. "I just kept thinking I would figure out a new use for it. Never did, though. It's enough to drive a man loco."

I laugh.

He winks, then takes the metal piece from the fire again and returns to pounding it on the form. I watch as the metal begins to take on the curved shape. He looks up at me and smiles. "So, tell me more about the tubes and transports."

CHAPTER TWENTY-ONE

It's the fifth straight day of going to the loco man's home to work on Niko's gift. I had feared that Niko would finish before me, and I wouldn't have his gift ready before he presented his. But that has not been the case. Niko comes home a little flustered sometimes and always explains the bad fortune on the hunting trip. It continues to make me smile. I'm sure he knows that I know.

The air is starting to get a little cooler as Payo walks with me again, as he has done every day.

"Can I ask you a question, Piri?"

I never tire of Payo's questions. They are innocent and honest. "Sure. Go ahead."

"Why do you not want to go back and live in the city in the sky?"

This question was a little different. "I like it here. I like the people—Niko, Chiquita, and you."

He looks confused. "But if you stay here until you die, you hope to go back to the city, right?"

I'm not sure how to answer, so I simply nod.

"I really want to get to the city. I only have two months left before I can no longer put my name in."

I try to prepare him for the possibility that he might never be chosen. "But if you don't make it, you still enjoy living here, don't you?"

He looks at me and smiles. "I didn't so much before, but now that you're here, I like it fine."

I smile. "Then you're in a better position than anyone else. You will be lucky to be chosen, and you will be lucky *not* to be chosen. You're in a win-win situation."

His head shifts to the left then to the right as he ponders my analogy. Then he grins. "Sí, you're right. I never thought about it that way."

As we get close to Curz's home, Payo still stays back out of sight. I go on without him as usual.

Curz walks around back with me and shows me the four pieces he has constructed. "Just need to add the finishing touches today. Then your mate will be the envy of the province."

He's right. The ones we saw at market are nothing compared to these. They are amazing. I watch as he chisels away at the edges to add the locking clasps that will hold them together. As usual, I tell him stories about the city, stories I have already told but can think of no more information to provide. He doesn't seem to mind.

"I wish you had more stories," he said. "I wish you knew what it was like on Level Twelve."

I nod. I wish I could explain it to him also. "Can I ask you a question?"

He stops working and glares at me. "I'm sensing this is a personal question."

I nod.

He smiles. "Sure, go ahead."

I giggle. "Were you ever married?"

"Yep."

I wait but nothing else comes. "Por favor, don't elaborate."

He laughs then frowns. "What does that mean?"

"It means por favor don't give me too many details."

He concentrates on his work. Finally he looks back up. "I married when I was about your age, but I had been in love with her since she was about twelve years old. Her name was Anore. She was so beautiful…and smart. We moved into this very house many years ago. And like you, I spent a long time on her gift, wanting it to be right before I presented it to her."

"What was it?"

He smiles as his mind wanders back in time. "It was a necklace made of these clear stones I had found when I was a kid. Something told me to save them, and I did. I polished them to a smooth finish. You should have seen them. When the light hit them, they would shine outward in bright colors of red, blue, yellow, and green. She loved them. She would sit sometimes and just watch the colors dance on the wall."

I worry about my next question but I need to know. "What happened to Anore?"

His smile disappears, and he concentrates on his work once again. "She died."

"I'm sorry."

He keeps working without looking up. "It was a long time ago. She was pregnant with our first child. We knew it was getting close to time to have the baby, but we weren't sure how close. It was the first day of harvest, and I told her she should stay home. But she was afraid. What if she wasn't about to have the baby and broke the rules of The Book? That was her thinking. Halfway through the day, she collapsed. They weren't able to save her or the baby."

I feel like someone kicked me in the stomach.

"You're the first person I've told this in over fifty years."

I don't believe what I'm about to say, but I say it anyway. "Do you look forward to seeing her again in the city in the sky?"

He smiles. "I told you, I'm loco, not dumb. I believe in metal, in wood, in fire, and these hands." He holds his hands up to show them to me. "But I don't believe in magic."

I smile and nod.

"You want to know what else?"

"What?"

He looks around almost to make sure no one hears him, although there is not even another house visible to his. "I ain't been to worship or to harvest in fifty years."

I laugh. "Wow. And you haven't caused the deaths of everyone on earth."

He laughs.

We talk for another hour until he is finished. "Let's try them out," he says.

I hold the original wooden form as he gently takes two of the curved metal pieces and presses them together. The edges have an intricate groove design and as he presses them firmly, they snap and join together, a perfect fit around the form. The metal has been polished, and you can see your reflection in them. There are even intricate designs chiseled into the metal. I've never seen anything like them, not even in the city.

"They are beautiful," I say. "I feel as though I have cheated you. All the conversation in the world isn't worth what you have created here." I can see the look of pride in his face.

"I'll let you in on a little secret," he says. "It wasn't just the conversation; it was the company." He takes the four pieces and places one inside the other. They stack up neatly. He wraps them in a cloth and hands them to me.

I am at a loss for words.

"There you go," he says. We walk around to the front of the house. "I hope you'll come back and visit."

"Sí, I will." I turn to leave, then stop and turn back around. I walk up to him and tiptoe to kiss him on the cheek. "Muchas gracias."

A single tear rolls down his face. "You're welcome. Now, get out of here before I release my attack lizards."

I laugh. As Payo and I walk home, I don't know what has brought me more enjoyment: the great gift or the new friendship. As we walk, the clouds get dark. It rains a lot here, and I can now smell it when it's in the air before it reaches the ground.

"Oh no," Payo says, looking upward.

I see a vacant home. You can tell they're empty because the grass is not worn in the front. I rush up and knock on the door just in case. No one answers, so we go inside just as the rain comes down hard. Most of the rains are like this: hard, fast, and short-lived. The light is on in the home, so we close the door and sit against the wall. Even though I have never forgotten my experience with Tag, I feel completely safe with Payo. It was one thing adapting to emotions, yet another to learn to listen to my feelings. Vet explained to me that it's called "instincts," something I wish I had understood with Tag.

"What happened to your mama and papa?" I ask, hoping it isn't a tender subject.

"I didn't really know my mama," he says. "She died before I was born."

I smile and wait for him to see the error of that statement. He doesn't. "I don't think she could have died before you were born, Payo."

"Oh sí," he says. "I think maybe she died right when I was born. I think I did something wrong. My papa was really sad and upset with me. He would beat me most days. I have three brothers, and they would try to make him stop."

I swallow hard. "And what happened to your papa?"

"Uh...I was about seven and one day he said he was going hunting. He took his bow and went to the forest. My brothers were worried because it was already close to dark. But he never came back."

That sends chills down my spine. "And that's when you went to live with one of your brothers?"

He shakes his head. "No, they weren't a lot older than me, so we were sent to live with a like couple who couldn't have kids. That's what they do if someone doesn't have parents anymore and they don't have family to live with; they are sent to live with a like couple. But when my oldest brother got married, I went to stay with them. But they have four kids now, so it's really crowded."

I look around the empty home. "Why don't you get your own place? There are plenty of them."

He smiles. "You know why. The Book says you have to be married to have your own home."

That's right. I forgot. The rain subsides, and we continue onward. When I get home, I hide the wrist bands in my bedroom.

Things go back to normal. Niko returns with lizards and fish, distributing some of them to the elderly people in the area. I go with him and recognize a lot of the people from the Market. I'm glad

Niko is building up his credit and look forward to going to Market to cash it in. Along with more torches, I should make out well.

A few days later after we eat breakfast, I know something is happening.

"Chiquita and I are going to see if there are any games going on. Right, Chiquita?" Vet says.

Ana can't hide her devious smile. "Sí, Papa, that's what we're going to do."

They get up and leave the house, taking Ash with them. I turn to look at Niko. He looks pale and is sweating. It's a strange sight considering it is a little cold in the house. He searches for words but can't begin.

"What's up?"

"Wait here," he says and goes into his bedroom. He returns with a tunic wrapped around something. "This is my gift to you. Uh...this is *the* gift, if you'll have me as your spouse."

My palms are sweating now. I wasn't expecting something so large. "I think this bracelet will be too large for me."

He laughs a nervous laugh.

As I remove the tunic, I stare at my gift. I'm not sure what it is. "It's a little bow with arrows?"

"Sí," he says, still sweating. He lifts it up. I thought it was just resting on a block of wood, but the wood is attached. There is a groove cut into the top of the long block of wood that the little bow is mounted on. Niko pulls back the string and it locks in place and points to one of the short arrows and then to the groove. "You put the arrow in here. Then all you have to do is pull this lever." He turns it over and points to the lever. He pulls it and the string releases so hard that it makes me jump. "I just worry about you so much, and since you never learned to use the bow, I thought this would be easier for you. It's actually stronger than my bow, and very light. Try it."

I take it from his hands. It is indeed very light. "How did you come up with this design?"

"I didn't," he says. "It was your idea. Remember one day as we were practicing, you said the bow was too big for you, and I should make you a smaller one that was easier to use?"

I smile. I do remember that.

"It was a dumb gift, wasn't it?" he asks. "If you give me another day, I can make you something else."

As I look over the clever design and think about the tedious hours of labor he must have put into it and the reason for it, it suddenly makes all others seem like cheap gifts. My eyes begin to water. "No, it's the most perfect gift I've ever heard of. I love it. And I accept your gift—and you."

Niko drops to his knees in front of my chair as if exhausted— mentally exhausted. I rub the back of his head as he lays it across my legs. I was so taken with the gift, I forgot about his. "Let me up. I have to get your gift."

He smiles as he stands, placing my bow on the table. He takes my hand to help me out of the chair. I run into my bedroom and come back with the cloth. I hand it to him. He unwraps it and stares with the same confusion I displayed as I saw my gift.

I smile and raise his arm up. He holds it there, and I take two of the curved pieces of metal and position them around his wrists. I see the light in his eyes as I press them firmly and lock them into place. He quickly lifts his other arm, and I join the other two pieces together. He stands there staring in amazement with both arms raised.

"Oh my goodness," he says. "These are incredible. I don't think I'll ever take them off. They fit perfectly. How did you do this?"

"That's my secret," I say.

"Fair enough. I love them. I love you. Do you realize we are officially married?"

It hadn't occurred to me at all. "Oh my, you're right. You're stuck with me from now on."

"And you with me," he says with a big smile. He leans in and kisses me for the first time as my spouse. "Let's go claim our house."

CHAPTER TWENTY-TWO

As we near our house, we are surprised to see a large crowd of people. As they recognize us, some pull away from the group to walk our way. I see Ana running toward me, so I get down on my knees. She throws her arm around my neck.

"I love you, Piri. I'm so happy," she says.

"Me, too, Chiquita. Me, too."

Payo, San and other friends of Niko's gather around to admire his metal wrist bands. Vet also joins in.

"Look at those," Vet says. "You look like a super warrior."

Niko puts his fists on his hips and sticks out his chest. "I am." Then he looks at his papa. "What's going on here?"

Vet smiles. "We knew this was going to be your home, so we started early. Come on inside."

We walk through the crowd of people, mostly the same ones I saw at San and Cari's new home celebration. The men pat us on the shoulder as we pass, smiling and nodding; the women lean in to hug us. We enter the house and I am surprised to see it is already fully decorated with donations from other families. There is already a bench in the front room and a table in the kitchen. We are led into one bedroom and see a new bed already stuffed and padded for the sleep area. There are new clothes and sandals as well. I am speechless. Several have followed us into the house and, as I turn around with tears streaming down my face, they all laugh and cheer.

We go back outside where the celebration is under way with plenty of cooked fish. Unfortunately, this time of year, we can't spare the stored fruits and berries for the celebration, so I nibble on a few pieces I keep in my pouch alongside my two flat stones, which I continue to carry.

"I'm so happy for you, friend."

I turn and smile at Payo. I give him a big hug. "Gracias, friend." I point to all the young people. "You might be next."

He grins and blushes.

The day continues in the same fun manner, but I am getting exhausted from celebrating. I sit on the grass with several younger people around me, including Ana. I think most of them are laughing inside about my gift, but to their credit, they only tell me how great it is.

Afternoon comes. As much as I enjoy everyone being here and appreciate all they have done to start me and Niko off in life, I am hoping the festivities will be over soon, and I can be alone with my spouse. I think to myself what an odd feeling that is for someone from the city. Marrying is more of a duty in the city, one that you give no more thought to than going to work. I have never heard my mama or papa speak of each other this way, the way Niko and I feel. I realize I would not be married yet up there, not for another two months or so. I am glad I am not there. But still I hope the people leave soon.

I scan the crowd and stop as I see Payo sitting away from the others. I smile at him. He is looking at me funny, as if wondering what I am thinking. Maybe he can read my mind. I laugh at the thought. Payo can hardly understand my words. But I have underestimated him. He gets up and walks to the area between the house and the crowd.

"Hola. Listen up, everyone," he yells loudly to get their attention. He raises his hands up high in the air, a formidable posture for someone his height. "Listen up," he yells louder.

I don't know what he is doing, nor does anyone else, but they all stop moving and talking and turn to face him.

Once he has everyone's attention, he continues. "This is a great day. My two best friends got married…to each other. It's great that you have all come here, but now is alone time."

I search out my spouse, and we begin laughing right away. It takes a few seconds for the rest of them to understand Payo's words, but everyone joins us in laughter. I hop up and run over and hug Payo. This is twice he has saved me. Niko walks over and pats Payo on the back.

People line up to give us one last word of congratulations and head to their own homes. Payo smiles and waves and follows them. Soon it is just me, Niko, Ana, and Vet. Vet hugs Niko hard and Ana runs up and hugs his leg, much like they did the first time I met them. They hug me again and then turn to follow the crowd. We stand there until everyone is out of sight.

"Good old Payo," Niko says.

I turn to smile at my spouse. I still tingle at the very thought of that concept. I realize that I have not had him to myself since early this morning. We go inside our new house and lock the door behind us. I am nervous as we enter the bedroom. All of the sensations of having a mate and now a spouse are new to me, and I know this will be no different. I am even a little scared. Not of Niko, of course, since he's not only the one person who would never hurt me, but he would do anything within his power to make sure no one else does either.

"Let's just lie here a while," he says as if sensing my reticence.

I smile and join him on the bed. As I stare into his eyes, I fully understand happiness and what life is supposed to be. Happiness is not something we even aspire to achieve in the city, but I know now that is no way to live. As Niko begins to caress me, I melt into his arms.

The next few days are magical as we never leave the house. Most of the time, I don't even know if it's daytime or nighttime. And I don't care. All that matters is we're together. The brave man who took me into his arms the very first time we met and has never put me down. The man I have loved since that day and didn't even know it. My spouse.

Finally, we venture outside and decide to go visit Vet and Ana. I take my new bow, although I have not yet tried it. Niko is dying for me to learn to use it. He still wears his wrist bands with pride.

We walk to his papa's house, which is only fifteen minutes away. Vet and Ana are outside as we walk up, along with a few other boys. I worry that something is wrong, but everyone is smiling. Vet and Ana greet us with a hug.

"What's going on?" Niko asks.

"Big hunting and fishing party today," one of the boys explains.

Niko smiles. "Great. We need to go to the forest to practice." He looks at me and smiles. "Ready?"

I hold up my bow and smile. "Sí, I am. What day is this anyway?"

Everyone laughs. "It's the sixth day," Vet says. "Worship tomorrow."

Moments later, a huge group of people is ready to go, most of them I recognize from the previous fishing trips. Ash and several other dogs happily tag along. This is what makes it safer to venture into the forest. We all walk together until we enter beneath the canopy of the trees. They spread out and take their new positions as we travel through the forest. I am no longer afraid.

Niko and I stop at our practice area as the others go on to the lake. Ash stays with us. We stand at the shooter's area facing the large tree in which Niko had carved out a large flat area for a target. There is a red dot in the center he made with the same paint Ana and I use at the column. We are about thirty feet away. Niko nods to me, but I sit on the ground. "What are you doing?" he asks.

"I have to prepare myself," I say and grin. Niko looks confused, so I explain. I look around the forest. "We're alone."

Niko smiles and sits beside me and we embrace, falling back onto the ground. Ash rushes up and licks our faces, making us both laugh. I don't even mind. I am so happy. "How long do you think we have?" I ask.

Niko smiles. "Not long enough. We would have if you hadn't built the bridge and made fishing so easy."

I cover my eyes with one hand as I laugh. "Oh my goodness. You're right. What a stupid invention that was." With my eyes still covered, I feel Niko's lips on mine. I wrap my arms around him and kiss for what seems like an eternity. Then he stands and reaches down with his hand.

I don't want to move, but I give in. He pulls me up and hands me my bow.

"Give it a try," he says.

I shake my head. "You go first."

Niko takes an arrow from the long pouch strapped around him. He pulls the string back and releases. The arrow sticks into the tree mere inches from the red dot.

"Not bad," I say. I pull the string back on my bow until it locks. I take one of the arrows from the side and place it into the groove. I raise the bow to aim, but I'm not sure how to hold it.

Niko sees my dilemma. "Try holding it to one side and tilting your head over to look down the arrow."

I do that and it makes sense. I stare down the arrow at the red dot. I pull the lever and the arrow disappears. I look up. "Where did it go?"

Niko laughs. "I don't know."

He walks to the tree and looks around the ground.

"Are you sure it even went that way?" I ask.

"I think so."

I look around the shooter's area just in case. I don't see it anywhere.

"It's okay," Niko says. "I can make more."

I am frustrated. I load another arrow and keep it pointed at the ground. Niko goes to the target to retrieve his arrow. He pulls it from the tree, then stops. He turns to look at me with a strange look.

"What?"

"I found your arrow," he says.

"Where?"

He points to the center of the red dot. I walk up to see what he's pointing at. When I see it, I can't believe it. My arrow is buried in the tree up to the back tip. Even the strips of lizard skin that are attached to the arrow to make it fly straight are completely submerged in the soft wood of the tree. I start to laugh.

"Who's the master now?"

Niko rolls his eyes. "There'll be no living with you now. Let me see if I can dig it out."

"You didn't answer the question," I say.

He laughs. "Okay, you're the master."

I laugh and turn to go back to the shooter's spot. But his next words make me freeze.

"Where is Ash?" he asks.

I turn to see him scanning the forest. I stop breathing so I can listen. Ash never leaves our sight. I also search through the trees.

"Ash?" Niko yells.

I turn again to look at Niko and I see him. Entirely on reflex, I raise the bow and aim it at Niko and pull the lever. Once again the speed of the arrow makes it impossible to follow. Only the loud grunt as the arrow soars over Niko's head and penetrates the face of the Scav coming up from behind Niko verifies the accuracy of my aim. The creature falls back dead, its body hitting the ground hard.

"Let's go," I scream and turn to run but stop in my tracks. There stands another Scav, his bright red eyes shining at me, his arm already in motion, the clear bubble already flying through the air toward me. My reflexes react again, and I do the only thing I can think to do. I run directly toward him. The bubble explodes, making my ears ring, and the force pushes me right into the arms of the Scav. He doesn't even budge, only wraps his massive arms around me. I stare up at his face, his jagged teeth smiling at me. Then I see Niko's arrow appear as if it just materialized, at least half of it. The other half is sunken into the creature's forehead. He falls, but his arms drag me down with him.

Niko grabs me and pulls me away. "Come on."

We start to run but suddenly the sky is filled with several bubbles, all coming from different directions and flying in the air directly above our heads. That's the last thing I remember.

CHAPTER TWENTY-THREE

My eyes open halfway. Everything is blurry, but I can see the canopy of the forest above me. It seems to be moving. My head is hurting, and the ringing is still in my ears. I close my eyes hard and open them again, hoping my vision will clear. It helps a little. I can see the tops of the trees a little better, and I can tell it is I who am moving. I can feel strong arms cradling me and think they must be Niko's, but then I see the black hands coming up around my side. I look in the other direction and my heart races as I realize I'm being carried by a Scav.

I fight to free myself from his grip. He lifts me like a toy and puts me over his shoulder. I can see at least six more Scavs now. I pound on his back but my fists make no impression on his large muscles. My hands begin to turn dark as the blackness rubs off on them. There's nothing I can do. I think about all the times I had wondered what happened to those taken by the Scavs. Now it would appear I would learn firsthand.

Then I think of Niko. I shut my eyes tight as the tears roll down. What did they do to him?

Soon we are clear of the forest and are in the barren lands, the Scavs' territory. They form a single line as we continue onward through the rocky terrain. Two hours later, I can smell something in the air and hear the sounds of water. He carries me down a trail cut into the side of a cliff. When we reach the bottom, he sits me on a large cloth and walks away.

I look around. There are hundreds of Scavs going about their day and, other than an occasional glance, paying me no attention.

The one who carried me, as well as the six others, remove the belts in which they carry the clear bubble explosives, and they place them on a short wooden fence. Judging by the other belts draped over it, I assume this is its only purpose. None of the Scavs wear them here. I guess it is the same as Niko and the Children's weapons. They only use them when they leave home.

I see my first female Scav and even children. The children seem to be the ones most taken with me as they stop their games to stare. I see more Scavs who appear from the cliffs themselves. I see no actual structures to signify a house, so I assume these creatures dwell in caves in the cliffs. But the most incredible sight is the ocean, of which I had only learned from Niko and the map in The Book. That is what is producing the smell and the sounds as the water seems to have a life of its own, pushing inward then rushing out again. I stare out over it in awe. It goes on forever.

There is also a large container, larger than the carriers, full of the clear bubbles, only bigger. I watch as two Scavs carry several into the side of the cliff and then come out. Several other Scavs appear from the cliff. Suddenly I hear a large explosion, which makes me jump. Dust fills the air where the Scavs are standing, and then they disappear into the cliff again. Maybe it isn't where they live. I don't know.

I am not bound in any way, nor am I guarded. Two Scavs stand at the entrance of the trail at the base of the cliff. It appears to be the only way back. I could make a run for it down the edge of the water, through the sand, but Scavs are everywhere. They are very tall and muscular, so I'm certain I could not outrun them. But I decide to test my boundaries.

I rise and walk off the cloth. My sandals sink into the sand as I stride, the grainy stuff sliding between the bottom of my feet and my sandals and sticking between my toes. Several of the adults now turn their attention to me. One of them walks toward me, pointing at me, his black crooked finger waving back and forth. I stand fast, waiting for him to kill me. He strolls up and gently places his hand on my shoulder and guides me back to my spot. I sit again as he walks away.

What are they waiting for? I sit for hours. The light of the short day begins to wane. A female comes up and sits on the cloth across from me. Her hair is black like the males', only longer, cascading down her back. She is wearing the same kind of cloth around her waist as the males, but nothing covers her top area except the dirty black paint. She reaches out with a wooden bowl. I can see it is filled with dried fruit. I don't move. She smiles and sits it in front of me then reaches out with a slimmer, taller container. She tilts it forward, and water spills over the top. I take it and smell it. She smiles and nods. I turn it up and drink. I am very thirsty.

I hand the empty container back to her, and she smiles again. Then she points back behind the cloth to a small clearing at the base of the cliff. She motions with her fingers in that direction. I conclude that she wants me to walk back there, so I do. I wonder if this is where she will kill me. As I reach the rock wall, I turn to see she has followed me. Then she turns around and just stands there. I'm not sure what is happening, but she appears to be blocking me from everyone else. Then it dawns on me. I can't believe it, but I don't pass up the opportunity. I raise my tunic and relieve myself.

She leads me back to my cloth. It is entirely dark now, and the air blowing off the water is very cold. It doesn't seem to affect them, but I am shivering. As I take my place on the cloth, she walks away. Several large fires burn across the camp. The female Scav returns with two younger girls, each carrying a large blanket. They wrap me in one and lay the other behind me. I decide they are not going to eat me tonight, so I lie back on the makeshift bed. It is strangely comfortable, and I am exhausted from the day's events. I assume I will be breakfast. I think of Niko and drift off to sleep.

The female Scav wakes me early in the morning. She has slept with me all night. It is barely daylight. She motions toward the cliff, and we repeat the process of her guarding me while I take advantage of it. She holds out her hand for me to take. For some reason, she doesn't appear to be a threat, so I take her hand as she walks with me onto the sand. I see every Scav is walking up the sandy areas alongside the water's edge. They are all heading west. Then I realize it is the seventh day. They are all going to worship. I wonder why they didn't eat me last night because I don't think they are allowed to on the seventh. That is the only rule they have kept during the last year as attacks were escalated.

I now see the entrance to the cave. It is not a natural cave, however. The entrance is perfectly square and looks to be the exact size of the roofs and walls of the homes of the Children, of mine and Niko's home. I see many huge lizards going in and out of the cave.

I struggle to walk in the sand. The Scavs seem to have no trouble with their large feet, but it is hard for me to keep up with my small feet and short legs. She sees this and motions to another younger but fully grown Scav, who walks over to us and smiles. She motions for him to turn around, which he does. She picks me up with ease and puts me on his back. I wrap my arms around his neck as he holds my legs. I feel like a traitor letting someone— or something—do this other than Niko. I feel like a traitor for not fighting them. I don't know why I'm not. Even though I wouldn't stand a chance against these creatures, a part of me still thinks I should go out fighting. But I do nothing. Maybe it is the human gestures of food, water, providing privacy when needed, and even the smiles that have me confused. I am also surprised to discover that I am not afraid anymore. Maybe I'm just numb.

As we continue to the west, I see many more square caves and many more huge lizards. They seem to coexist with the Scavs. I also see more containers filled with the large bubbles. The Scav children run along playfully without a care in the world. The adults keep a watchful eye on the children but don't interrupt their play. These creatures are so different than how I had always imagined them. But still, they are murderers who kill and eat the Children. That's something I can't forget.

We walk for many hours. Like Niko, the young Scav doesn't seem to tire as he carries me. I wonder what their worship is like. Will it be like the worship of the Children? No one carries The Book. Of course not. These are mindless animals. What am I thinking?

I stare out over the remarkable view of the ocean. I see movement. Is there something alive in the water? Suddenly a huge school of thousands of large fish breaks the surface. I think of how the Children always make sure to leave plenty of fish for the future, but here is enough to feed an entire province. I'm certain the ocean must be full of fish.

Many hours later, we finally reach our destination. There are thousands and thousands of Scavs. All greet each other like the Children do, with hugs and pats as the tribes all come together for this day. I can no longer see the ocean, and the land seems to go on far to the north. This means the map isn't accurate, showing nothing past the north but water. I can even see a forest in the far distance. There are several fires burning in different locations. I see a large white structure, which seems to be our destination.

The female Scav leads us to the structure. The walls are made of a thin material I've never seen. It sways in the wind like cloth but is much thinner and smoother. She pulls aside the material, and I am carried inside. She helps me down from the young Scav's back and motions for him to leave. She leads me to a large wooden chair and has me sit. Then she leaves.

Outside the structure is another square cave, only this one is much larger with a track running a hundred feet out of the front of it. It is the same kind of track the carriers back home run on, only larger.

I look around. I can see all the Scavs outside through the material. But the light is darker in here, and that's why I couldn't see through from the outside. It is a simple wooden structure consisting of large poles to form the framework. It is about twenty feet wide and forty feet long. The white material is draped over the top and hangs all the way to the ground on the sides. There seems to be an adjoining room at the far end.

Suddenly a young girl Scav appears from the other room, slipping through a division in the material, which closes behind her. She is almost my height but considerably younger, I think. She is entirely white. She is carrying a wooden bowl, much like the one in which the fruit was offered to me last night. She sits the bowl on the ground in front of my chair.

She reaches into the bowl and takes out a cloth and squeezes it to remove the excess water. Then she reaches for my hand. I don't move. She looks into my eyes and I into hers. Her eyes are big and red, and she smiles. She seems very gentle, so I extend my hand. She washes the dirt from my arms and the black smudges still visible from pounding on the Scav's back. After she cleans both my hands and arms, she kneels down and removes my sandals. I let her. She scrubs my feet until they are clean. Next she cleans the cloth again and begins to gently stroke my face.

Her lips are parted, and I see the sharp jagged teeth. Still, I think she is beautiful. Without realizing what I'm doing, I wrap my arms around her and hold her close to me. I begin to cry. To my surprise, she holds me tight and caresses my hair. I don't know what I'm doing but I needed someone to hold me. Even my enemy.

I pull back and look again at the girl. She is now crying as well. I smile and wipe away her tears. She turns and goes back into the other room. I realize my hands are shaking. I was prepared to be killed, eaten, maybe even tortured, but I was not prepared for this.

I sit there for several minutes until I see the material separating again. I think my new friend is returning, but it is not her. It is another female, an adult. She is remarkable, taller and more muscular than the males. She is also white with the same long black hair, but her hair is longer and moves like water. Her body is covered in the same white material, which hangs to the ground, making her seem to glide rather than walk. I can see her muscular midsection through the material as well as the large breasts. She is so masculine, yet amazingly feminine. What happens next takes my breath away.

"Hello, Piri."

CHAPTER TWENTY-FOUR

Y ou can talk?" Not to mention she knows my name.
The female smiles. "Of course. All Spirit People can talk. They just might prefer not to talk to everyone they meet."

"Or eat," I say.

She smiles as she keeps getting closer to me. "My name is Lucent," she says.

"Who are the Spirit People?"

She continues to walk until she is in front of me. She motions toward the outside. "We are the Spirit People. I believe the Children call us Scavs."

"Why are you and the little girl white?"

"All Spirit People are white," she explains. "The workers, soldiers, and children cover their bodies with the black substance from the pits to protect against the elements."

"Is this where the two tribes meet? Are there only two tribes?"

"No," she says. "There is a third. It lives a mile north of here where the gap is less wide between the oceans, just before the forest. The northern tribe is the largest of our tribes, largest by far, yet there are no miners, only soldiers."

"I can see the edge of the forest," I say. "So, it's green land, with trees and plants, like where the Children live? How far does the forest go?"

"The forest goes all the way across to the northern ocean, hundreds of miles of forest."

This is incredible. But of course it doesn't really help the Children since the Scavs live between them and the forest. "That's why the northern tribe stays there? And that is why it is only soldiers, to keep the Children from being able to use the land and resources there? We have to keep that balance, don't we?"

She looks out to the north then back at me, almost as if she's deciding if she should tell me something, or maybe deciding what to tell me. "My sweet, sweet child," she says. "I would love for the Children to be able to utilize the land to the north, but it is not possible. The northern tribe is not there to keep the Children from going to the forest; it is there to keep the forest from coming to the Children."

"What do you mean?"

"There are worse things than Spirit People in this world."

"You're lying,"

She stands motionless, still staring into my eyes. I don't know if she really believes what she is saying or has learned a few tricks from the Fathers. The Book is, after all, full of empty threats, fear harnessed as a means of control.

"Admit it, the northern tribe exists to kill the Children," I say.

"Not kill, Piri—protect. And not just the Children, but our other tribes as well."

"Protect the Children? What does that mean? Protect the Children from what?"

She doesn't answer.

"But you all come together here at this spot to worship every seventh day?"

"We do not gather to worship," she says. "We come together every seventh day to celebrate. This is our day of harvest. This is why the three tribes meet here on this sacred land."

I don't know what that means. I understand the words, but why call it sacred if it's not about worshipping? "Is that why you don't attack on the seventh, not because of the rules in The Book, but because you have better things to do?"

She nods. "Today we feast and stock up until next week."

"Are you going to eat me?"

Lucent shakes her head. "No, my dear. We want to send you home where you belong."

"My home is with the Children."

Her large red eyes stare at me with real compassion. "I am sorry, Piri. The balance must be maintained. You must go back to the city in the sky." She reaches into her clothing and pulls out several cloths and hands them to me. "We have been looking for you for a long time."

I take the cloths from her hand, and my heart drops. How can this be possible? I don't understand what is happening as I stare at the notes that Vet wrote back when I first came to the surface, the notes he sent each week with the Chosen Ones. "Where did you get these?"

She ignores the question. "The Fathers need you back. We told them we would find you and send you home."

I suddenly feel dizzy as I realize I was the cause. It was me. It was my fault. The Children couldn't understand the reason behind the increase in Scav attacks, but I brought it upon them. I think about poor little Gano, the young boy who Ana always said looked like me. That's why he was taken. That's why he is dead now. I feel sick, then I realize what she just said. "What do you mean? How do you know what the Fathers want?"

"The Children are not the only ones who have an agreement with the Fathers. We also have an arrangement," she says.

I feel my anger returning. "I don't care about you or your arrangement. I don't care if you can talk. You're still animals, vile creatures that attack the Children for no reason. Look around you. You have more resources than anyone. You have unlimited fish and lizards, and still you attack and kill many Children each year. Why? Why do you do that?"

"I know you are upset," she says.

Her calm tone makes me angrier. "You know nothing. You haven't the capacity. You're just a reject of evolution—a talking lizard!" I figure my intellect is my only weapon against her, but my words seem to have no effect.

"Look out there," Lucent says.

I turn to look at the crowd of Scavs.

"We have evolved," she says, "but not from lizards. I know

you were taken in by the feelings the Children have for one another. I know the Fathers display no such emotions. They considered it a weakness a long time ago, and over the years it was weeded out. But we embrace it even more than the Children. Look at the adults as they interact with the young ones. It is pure love."

I watch as both male and female adults play with the children, encouraging, caressing, and watching over them. But I don't want to admit how I feel about it. "Any parents would do that with their children."

"Yes," she says, "but these are not the children's parents and still they provide love and guidance as if they were."

"I don't understand."

Lucent smiles. "Like the Fathers, we maintain the balance in population. Most of the males are made unproductive at birth. Only a select few remain capable of siring offspring, and they mate with only select females. But the devotion to our species is still stronger than any other."

"Are you the leader?" I ask.

Lucent nods. "I am the queen. Our way of life has ensured our survival. This is how it has been for tens of thousands of years, back to the beginning of the city in the sky, back to the arrangement with the Fathers. The city is older than you know." She turns to point to the large cave. "This tunnel here was constructed at the same time as your great city. It is exactly the same distance in length as the column that supports the city in the sky is high. This is how we barter with the Fathers. Just as the Children provide you with food, we provide you with other needed resources."

"What resources?"

"We are miners by nature," she says. "We live in the earth and mine the precious metals that your city needs to maintain its structure. We also provide certain plants from the forest to make the robes you wear, and we separate the pure air from the ocean water. We send you this air, and your city mixes it with the air they take from up there to provide the city with the air you breathe. You could not breathe the air that high on its own, so without our contributions, life could not exist in the city."

I can't believe what I'm hearing.

Lucent continues. "The element left over from separating the pure air from the water is what the clear balls are filled with. It is highly explosive. We use this for mining, and the soldiers use it as well."

"Sí, I know that from firsthand experience," I say. "I don't care about your deal. I don't care that you are the ones who provide the city with air and metals. That is all I care about—your soldiers using these things against the Children. Why? Like I said, you have plenty of meat available. I know that's all you eat, but you have it in abundance."

Lucent looks me in the eye before answering. "We do not eat fish or lizards."

"What?"

"I am afraid our diets have evolved into a specific need," she says.

"No!"

Lucent nods.

The pit of my stomach churns as her words sink in. "You only eat the Children?"

She neither nods nor speaks, but her eyes confirm.

"What kind of creatures are you? Why would the Fathers deal with animals like you?"

She reaches over to caress my hair, but I jerk back. "My dear," she says. "We are not animals. We are you."

I don't know if I can take anymore. I think of jumping up and running away. I think I would rather die than hear what she's saying, but I am frozen. "You are not like us. You are not like the Fathers. You are not even like the Children."

She turns and walks away several feet before turning back. "We are all the same. Before the city was constructed, we all lived on the surface together. You do not have to believe me, but it is true."

I am not angry because I don't believe her; I am angry because I don't know what to believe. Then something else dawns on me. "Wait. If you only eat the Children, how do you survive? There are what, twenty people taken from the Children each year? That's not enough by far."

"It is not supported, these random attacks, nor is it necessary," she explains. "But we do not force our people to refrain from it. It is more of a sport really."

"Not necessary?" I ask. "What does that mean?"

The queen doesn't answer. She sits on a bench and stares out the side wall toward the tunnel.

I try again to spark her anger to get her to talk. "Come on. You're a talking animal, aren't you? Answer my question. How can the three tribes live off a mere twenty people a year? I doubt that would last you dirty Scavs one month."

Lucent turns her head to me and places her finger to her lips.

I am furious. I want answers. Think, Piri. You can figure this out. I begin to speak aloud, but for my own benefit. "You provide the Fathers with valuable air and metals. You have an arrangement, a deal with the Fathers to provide them these things. You meet here every seventh day not to worship, but to celebrate, to harvest, to feast. You only eat the Children. You don't attack and steal enough Children to fulfill your needs, and you say those are more for sport and are not even needed."

The ground begins to vibrate. I stare outside and see this has excited the entire crowd of Scavs. Thousands of them stop what they're doing and turn to stare at the tunnel.

I see the queen still staring at the tunnel as the vibrations intensify. Suddenly, like a blast of hot air, it hits me as every piece of the puzzle flashes before my eyes. All of the evidence comes crashing down in my mind. Everything that didn't make sense before now does, not just with the queen's words, but with everything I have been told since arriving on the surface. All the craziness about the Children coming to live in the city when I knew the population never changes is all perfectly clear now. The sheer horror of the truth rushes through my body like hot coals. I jump and run toward the see-through wall. Suddenly I am grabbed from behind by a large male soldier Scav. He holds me tight as I fight to free myself to no avail. He drags me back into the center of the structure beside the queen who sits motionless.

"No!" I scream. "No, you can't."

The vibrations escalate until the entire ground shakes. The Scavs yell in excitement. I continue to struggle to get away, as if I could stop what I know is about to happen. I don't want to watch. I try to turn away, but the Scav forces me to face in the direction of the tunnel.

The ground shakes so hard that I would probably fall if I wasn't being held. Then it subsides, and I know what is coming. It all fits into place now, but the knowledge makes me so sick I can hardly breathe.

As the vibrations weaken, the excitement builds. Then I see the large carrier coming into view as it slowly exits the tunnel. I see the atrocity behind the alliance between these creatures and the people in the city in the sky. I see the horrified faces, all four hundred of them.

I see the Chosen Ones.

CHAPTER TWENTY-FIVE

I cough and retch. The Scav must think I'm going to vomit, so he lets me go. I collapse and fall to my hands and knees. The queen still sits motionless beside me. I stare out the wall at the huge metal cage carrying four hundred of my people. I want to rush to them, but I can't move. Their screams fill the air as they find themselves not in the paradise in the sky like they were promised, but surrounded by their mortal enemies.

"You're animals," I whisper.

"No, my dear boy," she says. "We are the true Chosen Ones. We are the ones favored by the Fathers. This is how it has always been."

I tilt my head to stare at her, my veins burning with every pulse of my heartbeat. I wish I had my bow. I would not hesitate.

The queen looks down at me and sees my expression. She smiles. "Who is the animal now, my love?"

I smile back, not at her words, but at the rock I see two feet from my hand. It is a nice rock, about half the size of one of the crops from the fields. The large male Scav is still standing over me. I take my tunic and wipe my mouth. I nod as if to display my acceptance, my acceptance of the world as it has to be. I slowly begin to rise, my knees straightening as they push my body upward, my hands walking backward along the ground to better position myself to stand.

But I do not stand. Instead, from this lower position beneath the monstrous arms of the creature behind me, I dart toward the queen, grabbing the rock in one motion. I bring my arm back to deliver my blow, but my guard has had time to react. He grabs me again with his muscled limbs and pulls me back. In an instant of intuition, I change my weapon from a club to a projectile and throw the rock with all my might. My aim is good, and the large rock strikes the queen on the temple as red lines quickly dart down her face like lightning bolts.

She jumps from her bench and towers above me, her arrogance and smugness nowhere to be seen, only rage. She raises her hefty paw high in the air, bringing around her long limb, and the back of her hand connects with the side of my face, the force literally knocking me out of the big soldier Scav's grip. I fall hard to the ground, my entire head throbbing from the impact. The stinging rushes over my entire body, but I laugh as I realize every gush of pain represents my first victory.

I rise to my hands and knees again and stare up at the queen. My continued laughing is having exactly the effect I want it to have. She is still fuming. "What's the matter, Your Highness? For all your big talk, you can't disguise what you really are. Where are your pompous words now? Your instincts give you away. You're one level above the stinking lizards. You are the garbage of this world."

The queen laughs. She wipes the blood from her face with one long, bony finger, and then slides the bloody appendage across her lips. She grins at me, her mouth open to display those horrible teeth, now stained with blood. She regains her composure and returns to her bench. "I do hope you enjoy the festivities, my dear."

I look back outside at the carrier. I watch as four Scavs approach the cage with long metal rods. On the ends of the rods are loops made of metal rope. They look almost exactly like the devices the Children use to harness the lizards as they search for eggs. The Scavs open a locked door on the end of the cage as the Children crowd toward the back. Each of them removes one person, who is then led to the middle of the crowd.

Still on my hands and knees, I turn to follow with my eyes to where the four Chosen are taken. The other Scavs cheer as the Children are laid upon four table tops. I lie down on the cold ground and close my eyes. I can't watch. But my ears record the event as I hear the screams, which are silenced almost immediately. I keep my eyes closed. I can hear the cheers fade from the Scavs, and I know that means they are busy, busy with the feast.

I'm glad now that the Chosen Ones, the Children in the cage, can't see into this structure. I couldn't bear them seeing me here doing nothing, only hiding like a coward. I sit up but stay faced away from the carnage. But it comes to me. Motion catches my eye on the other side of the queen, and I see the little girl who washed me. I can't take my eyes off her. She's staring straight at me as she bites into…I can't even say it. Her perfectly white face is now bright red around her mouth.

Another Scav brings the queen a treat. I don't care to watch that either. I stare out at the cage and see the young ones from our provinces as some cry, some fight to free themselves, and some pray. It's all in vain. Throughout the rest of the afternoon, Scavs continue to approach the cage with the rods, taking fresh meat to the tables for the feast. It becomes so surreal that I don't think of it as really happening.

"How many do you eat today?" I ask unexpectedly calmly.

The queen wipes the blood from her mouth. "We feast on forty today, then the tribes each take their shares to their own camps."

I laugh. "Sí, just divide them right up, eh? Well, at least that's only one more trip to the cage. I have counted nine trips already."

The queen smiles. "I am glad to see you taking this better. There are customs of the Children and the Fathers that seem just as odd to us."

"Oh, I'm sure," I say. "Like *not* killing and eating people, I assume."

"It will be over soon," she says.

I slowly rise and walk toward the queen. The soldier holds out his arm, and the queen waves her hand. He allows me to pass. I walk over and sit on the bench beside the queen. "Do you have a mate?" I ask.

Lucent looks down at me and shakes her head. "No, my dear. I have only one heart's desire, and that is for the happiness of my people."

"It isn't fair," I say.

She shakes her head. "No, is it not fair. Life is not fair. It never was nor will it ever be. It is not fair to the Children." She points out to the cage. "It is not fair for the Spirit People. It is not even fair for the Fathers in their great city. But life is still what guides us, motivates us, and makes us carry on. I suspect it has always been that way from the beginning."

"Do you know about the beginning? Do you know how it all came to pass?"

Lucent shakes her head. "I only know what little the Fathers have told me. I only know we all came from the same place. I only know where we are now. I only know what it takes for everyone to survive."

I look up at her red-stained lips. "Why? Why the balance? You're the strongest species. The strongest species should always be at the top, not the bottom. Why do you accept the scraps the Fathers send you? You could take over all of Canus and control The Garden."

She looks at me as if she never thought of that before, but seems to quickly brush the idea aside.

I stare out over the sacred area at the thousands of Scavs scattered about. I see lots of children, even small children, but no newborns. "Where are all the babies?"

Lucent smiles. "We do not have babies this close to the cold days. It is not safe for them. We control our breeding."

"Where are the females who have the children, and the males who are capable of helping them?"

She seems surprised at my questions. "They are here in their own structure. They are kept away from the population. But we are all here."

I'm not sure why I'm asking either, but just sitting here doing nothing is bothering me. I figure the least I can do is learn as much as I can about my enemy. "How long have you been their queen?" I ask.

"Almost thirty years."

"How long do you live?"

"The same as the Children and the same as the Fathers," she says. "Like I said, we are the same."

"What happens when you die?" I ask. "Do you believe you will have a life after death?"

She smiles. "No. I believe this life is what I have been privileged with. When I die, another queen will take my place, one that has already been selected and prepared. She will fully understand the importance of maintaining the balance."

The balance? How can life hang on that one stupid word? I have had enough of learning, so I sit there quietly.

"You will be back home soon," she says, "safe and sound."

"I don't care. There's nothing more you can do to me. If you would kill me, you'd be doing me a favor. If you want to send me back to the city, that's fine. At least you'll be out of my sight. Nothing matters anymore."

I see the Scavs going back to the cage, but I am numb. Even the pain from where the queen hit me is gone, as if my very nerve endings are severed. I feel nothing physically, mentally, or emotionally. But as the Scavs bring out the last four Chosen, I can't believe what I see as all my numbness quickly vanishes. Like a second wind doused with adrenaline, the pain once again ignites every fiber of my body and mind. I leap to my feet and run out through the see-through wall. A Scav tries to grab me, but I duck his massive arms and continue running toward the cage. "No!" I scream. "No! No! No!" The sand and rocks hurt my bare feet as I run. I realize only now that I have not put my sandals back on. I look to where I'm running. A younger Scav tries to grab me, but I knock him down as my hatred seems to have boosted my strength. Nothing will stop me from reaching my destination as I near the cage and fly into Payo's arms.

"I was chosen, Piri. I was chosen." He looks around with a confused expression. "But, but…"

"I know. I'm sorry. I'm so sorry."

"I don't know what's happening," he says.

The Scav jerks the rod to shake me free, and I watch Payo gasp for air. But I cling tight. I grab the metal rope and pull, freeing enough space for Payo to breathe. Another Scav comes up behind me and grabs around my waist, pulling me, but I don't let go. "I'm so sorry, Payo. I'm so sorry."

The Scav continues to pull me. I remember my training. I can't use my arms, so I bring my leg up hard between his legs. He doubles over either in pain or from reflexes. Payo reaches back, grabs the Scav by the hair, and yanks him so hard that the creature falls to the ground.

"Leave Piri alone!" he yells.

Tears are streaming down my face. With all that's going on, Payo is still trying to protect me. The Scav with the rod yanks hard and we both go down, me on top of Payo. I am still pulling at the metal rope around his neck. I turn back to look at the queen. She has walked outside of the structure to watch, the blood still visible on her lips and her head.

"Let him go!" I yell. "He's harmless. He's my best friend. Por favor, let him go. I'll do anything you want. But por favor, just let this one go home."

The Scav stops pulling. I watch the queen, waiting for her to give the order to release him. She stares at us for several seconds but says nothing, only turns and walks back inside. Another Scav grabs my legs, and the one with the rod yanks Payo free from my grasp. I try to go after him, but the creature has his strong arms wrapped all the way around me and locked tight. "Payo!" I scream.

He is being dragged on the ground, kicking, choking, dying. He slides his fingers underneath the metal rope and pulls it with what little strength he has left, and frees it enough for one last breath.

"I love you, Piri."

CHAPTER TWENTY-SIX

I give up, and the Scav lets me fall to the ground. I am completely defeated. I watch as they attach a metal rope to the collars and lead the rest of the Chosen away. The queen orders the Scav to bring me back. He picks me up, carrying my limp body back inside and sitting me in the chair. I remain motionless.

When the cage is empty, they load it with large canisters of air and containers of raw metal. It is almost dark by the time they finish.

"This is for the best," the queen says. "I wish you could see that. It is sad that you ever fell from the sky. Once you are home, you will understand."

I don't even look at her.

When the cage is loaded, they carry me out, put me inside the door, and sit me on a small box. That's the only room left available. The door closes and locks. The carrier slowly moves back into the tunnel. That's when I see it—my Kabloom necklace on the ground where I had struggled to hold on to Payo. Other than my dirty tunic, that would have been the only evidence of my life here. Soon I'm in darkness, the only light coming from the fires outside the tunnel entrance. That light gets smaller and smaller as the carrier picks up speed. Then it's gone and only darkness remains, darkness in the tunnel and in my heart. I hate the Scavs. I hate the Fathers. I have lost my spouse and my best friend. I have lost everything.

The wind whistles as the cage zips through the void. I think of Ana. How I long to be sleeping right now with her curled up in my arms. I can see her face so plainly. I have to get back to her. That's the only purpose I have in life, my only goal. All that's left to me. I take deep breaths to prepare myself. Inside the column, there will be no menacing Scavs, only people from the city, people as small and weak as I used to be. They will be no match for me now. I'll overpower the first one I see and run back down the tunnel, back toward home. They'll be too afraid to follow.

The carrier slows, and I can see the sides of the tunnel being illuminated from a light farther down the track. The light gets brighter as the carrier enters a large open area. I can tell I'm inside the column. I see the massive interior walls disappearing high into the darkness, and I hear voices. The carrier comes to a stop.

Several men from the city rush around and unlock the door. "Piri? Are you Piri?" one asks.

My muscles tense as I wait for the door to open. "Ouch!" I feel a sharp pain in my arm. I look down and see the man as he removes a shiny object from the cage. "What was that?" I yell.

The man simply stands there…waiting. Then he opens the cage door. I lunge, but my legs don't move and I fall forward. The man motions for the others, and they drag me from the cage and place me in a metal chair. I don't know what's happening.

"Let us get you home," the man says.

The metal chair has wheels, and as he rolls me away, the others turn their attention to the shipment. He pushes me around to a large round shaft running up in the middle of the column. I can see the four other tracks that come in from the other provinces, and all of them end at the base of the shaft. There are about ten workers around the room's perimeter. I see more of the air canisters like the ones that made this trip with me. Everyone goes about their job without a glance of curiosity. I see a room high up with a glass front. My eyesight is getting dim.

The man pushes a button, which opens a sliding door. He rolls me inside a small elevator and the door closes behind us. There are three buttons labeled *Ground*, *Control*, and *Lower Level*. He pushes the Lower Level button, and the elevator rises, picking up speed. Soon, it's going so fast I can feel the pressure on my face.

"Do not worry," he says. "It is airtight."

I'm not worried about the elevator; I'm worried about why I can't move my arms and legs, and why I'm finding it hard to stay awake.

Just like the large carrier, the elevator begins to slow. When it comes to a stop, the door opens and I see another large room. The man pushes the chair out and I smell a familiar odor. It's the crops. This must be the processing area. There are many workers here. Through my blurry vision, I see very large vats mounted to the floors. They are at least twenty feet high, thirty feet long, and ten feet across. Some of the workers are walking along the top edge, looking into the huge containers.

The man rolls me across the room to another door, another elevator. We go inside and I see the buttons on the wall, starting at Lower Level and then the numbers count upward from one to twelve. The man pushes number one, and the door closes. I never knew this Lower Level existed. I wonder what the Control floor is. The door opens, and we exit onto Level One—my level. I black out.

After that, I have only brief moments of semi-consciousness. I always seem to be lying in a cot. I hear the word "quarantine." I see people wearing masks. I experience more sharp pains in my arm. I hear the word "clean" and the word "sterilize."

I wake and look around me. I try to clear the fogginess from my mind and eyes. As my vision focuses, there is a strange familiarity to my surroundings: bed, covers, walls. It's my room. I sit up and look around. I look down at my clean night clothes and wonder if it was all a dream. I scoot down to the edge of the bed.

The door opens, and my mama enters. I jump up and run to hug her. "Hola, Mama."

She struggles to free herself. "Let go of me."

I step back and see the look in her eyes. I remember that physical contact is not normal here, but I must get back to where it is. "Mama, I have to get back."

She's still in shock. "Yes, you have to get back to work. Do you know how far behind you are? You have to declare your position with Maintenance and get started on training."

She points beside my bed as she leaves. I see the chair sitting in front of the rectangular area imprinted on the wall displaying where I always sat to activate the city Central Link. I walk over and take a seat and touch the wall. The screen illuminates. The menu is the same as I remember, but now there is the added icon regarding my profession, which I would have already chosen had the accident with the lightning not have happened. But it did happen. I did not dream any of it. I was there, and I was married, and I have to get back. But how?

I try searching for anything to do with the surface: the Children, Scavs, crops—anything. Nothing. No wonder I never knew of these things before. I search for information on the food production. I find a link, but it's classified and requires a Government access code. I try to find a layout of the city, but only the parts I already know about are available. But I'm certain I was wheeled through a lower level where the crops are somehow converted into the food tablets we eat.

I notice a flashing dot in the bottom right of the screen, signifying the screen in the main room has been activated. That would be my mama. I touch the flashing dot, and my screen is divided between my mama and my papa. I listen close to hear her.

"I told you I did not like it," she is saying. "Something is not right. He spoke to me in a foreign tongue and attacked me. I thought he was going to kill me. I am…I do not know what I am. I am so uncomfortable right now. You have to come home right away."

I turn off the screen. "It's called fear, Mama." I lie back down and try to go to sleep, but my mind is racing, trying to figure out how to get home. The walls are making breathing hard for me. I miss being able to see the sky. I think of going to the tube, but I think my papa is on his way home to deal with me. Although I'm not sure if the results will be any different in trying to communicate with him, I know I have to try.

I finally drift off to sleep.

My papa is gently shaking me. I wake and see him and sit up. I resist the urge to hug him.

"How are you feeling?" he asks.

I nod. "Much better."

"You surprised and confused your mother."

I smile. "I know. I'm sorry. I only hugged her to let her know I was glad to see her."

My papa looks relieved. "Okay then. I need to get back to work."

"No, Papa," I plead. "Por favor, let us talk."

He looks confused but stays. "About what?"

I let it all out. "I know about the Children. I know about The Book. I know about the crops. I know about the Chosen Ones. I know about the Spirit People. I know about the arrangements."

"These are not things you should know about," he says without a hint of expression.

"I didn't read about them, Papa. I have seen it with my eyes."

He continues to look at me but doesn't say anything. Maybe he doesn't know what to say.

"We got to do something, Papa."

Now he shows expression. He is confused. "About what?"

I shake my head in disbelief. "About everything I just mentioned. We have a deal with the Spirit People to provide them with four hundred of the Children every week. Do you know what they do with them?"

He nods. "Of course. That deal has been the basis of our survival for countless centuries."

"It's not right," I say and begin sobbing.

"Piri, you are home now. Get on with your life."

"Didn't you hear me? It's not right."

"Yes, I heard you," he says. "But it is not about being right or wrong, it is about survival. It is about maintaining the balance."

I'm so tired of hearing that word. "Disguise it how you want, but it is murder—cold-blooded murder."

He is confused again. "Is this really how you feel about it?"

I nod and wipe my eyes. "Sí. And I'll do anything to make it stop."

He doesn't say anything.

"You are my papa. I'm not sure you realize it or not, but because you are my papa, you got to help me. You got to."

He stands up. "I have to get back to work." He walks to the door.

I drop my head as the tears build up again.

"I will see you when I get home from work. Get some rest. Tomorrow morning you are going to work with me. We are going to explain everything to my superior, and we are going to figure out the best thing to do."

I look up and smile. I taste the salty tears as I open my mouth to speak. "Gracias, Papa."

CHAPTER TWENTY-SEVEN

I stare out through the clear walls of the cylindrical transport, through the clear walls of the tube, hoping to find one opening in the clouds that will give me a glimpse of the world below. I have made five complete trips. I had to get out of our living quarters after my papa went back to work. The walls seemed to be closing in on me, and I felt like the air was stale. The sunlight warms my face as I lean over and peer out the side. I wish Niko could have seen the sunshine. I wish all the Children could. I pass the spot again where the lightning struck and sent me spiraling toward the surface. I wish it would happen again, but that was a fluke. Now I'm not sure how to get home, but at least my papa is going to help.

People get on and off the transport as it zips around the perimeter of the great city. No one speaks or even makes eye contact. Such is the norm. I'm restless but don't know what to do. I'm angry for all that has happened and angry at myself for not figuring out a way to get back. I know there must be a way. I know I'm smart enough to discover it. I'll see what my papa and his superior come up with first. In the meantime, I don't know what to do. Then it dawns on me. There is something I need to do before I get back to the surface.

I leave the transport and get into the elevator. I push the button for Level Twelve. A screen appears and instructs me to put my hand on the screen for age verification, which I do. The elevator begins to rise. It comes to a stop and the door opens. What I see takes my breath away. The ceiling is at least fifty feet high and painted to look like the sky, complete with an illusion of the sun. The room is completely open as far as I can see. Living quarters for the Level Twelve inhabitants are positioned around the perimeter. But what grabs my attention first and foremost is the resemblance to the Market back on the surface.

The people of Level Twelve look like everyone else, but most are dressed in fancier clothing. And even though they are the same height with the same eyes and hair, I can see their bodies are like mine, more defined. I stroll through the walkways, which are made of the same soft materials as the floors of my level. There are little booths set up everywhere with entertainers. I see jugglers like I saw at the Market. There are stages for shows. I see one that is about to begin, and I take a seat on a padded bench along with a few other people.

I think of the play I watched with Ana at the Market. But this show is not a comedy; it's serious and sad. I feel my eyes tearing up as the performers enact the storyline. No one else seems to be affected. I get up and continue through the area. I pass a large booth and a woman asks me if I want a massage. I don't know what it means but I go inside. She removes my robe and has me lay face-first on a padded cot. She begins to rub my back muscles deeply.

"You are very tense, young one," she says, "and very strong. You should have been one of us."

I don't say anything. All I can think of is Niko on our wedding day and how he caressed me. I get off the cot, throw on my robe, and leave. I did not come here to enjoy myself; I came to find out what it was all about. That's all.

I leave and go back home. I go to the kitchen and push a button. It dispenses a food tablet. I push it two more times and get two more. I take a container and put it under a dispenser and watch as it fills with water. I take these to my room and get on the city Link again. I take all three tablets. I remember only taking one at a time before, but they don't fill me up. I would give anything for some fresh fruit or lizard eggs. Eating the tablets again feels like the seventh day and fasting like we did back home.

Later, I hear my papa when he comes home from work, but he

doesn't come to check on me. I know it is still early, but I go to bed. At least I have some direction in the morning. I can only hope my papa's superior will be able to help.

I set the alarm on the Link and go to sleep. I assume my papa will wake me, but I don't want to take any chances. I take my pillow and pull it into my chest, curling up around it. I run my hands across the soft material, stroking it gently. "It's okay, Chiquita. I'm going to come back to you." I drift off into an unnerving sleep filled with more nightmares about Scavs.

The alarm sounds, and I get up and get ready. I'm sitting by the front door when my papa comes out of his room already dressed for work, his robe pressed neatly. He looks surprised to see me.

"I see you are ready," he says. "Come with me."

I follow him out into the hall. He walks without looking back, but I stay close behind him. We walk for a long time. Others are coming out of their quarters to begin their days as well. No one speaks.

We finally come to a door, and I follow my papa inside. Several people are sitting in padded chairs, all positioned by the wall as they concentrate on the screens in front of them. No one looks up as we pass. We come to another door and go inside. A man sits behind a desk and motions for us to take the two chairs. We sit across the desk from him. His screen is illuminated on the wall beside him. He looks older than my papa, but still has the same appearance.

"Hello, Piri," he says. "My name is Eraph. Thank you for coming in today."

"Gracias," I say. "I'm glad you could take the time to meet with me."

He nods. "I have been looking over your file. Your scores are very high. I am surprised to see you have not selected your profession yet. You are cleared for a Maintenance position. That is very impressive."

I look at my papa. He's staring straight ahead. I look back to Eraph. "Gracias. But I didn't think that's what we were here to discuss."

"Of course. Your father told me about your conversation yesterday. That is the condition of this conference." He looks at me as if waiting for me to say something. I don't know what to say. He continues. "This is an unprecedented circumstance. No one has ever fallen to the surface. I cannot fathom what that was like for you. It must have been very dramatic."

I sit motionless and silent.

"This means we have no idea what to expect," he says. "But the Link has provided us with possibilities. It says that ten months on the surface could have a profound impact on a person's thinking, attitude, and conformity. That has already been witnessed. That is why your father reported you."

"Reported me?" I turn again to look at my papa, but he continues to avoid eye contact. "I thought you were going to try to help the situation."

"What situation is that, Piri?" he asks.

"We're killing innocent people." I look him straight in the eye. "We're making deals with the Scavs to provide them with innocent kids and young adults so they can tear them limb from limb and eat them. That is the situation I speak of. It's got to be stopped."

He ignores me and looks back at the screen. "I am afraid we will have to go with the recommendation of the Link."

My papa finally speaks. "And what is that?"

Eraph reads directly from the screen. "Piri will turn twenty in two months. At that point, he would have been matched with a wife from his profession and delivered his own son. He and his wife would have gone to work while her parents watched the son for ten years until their daughter came along. But it is deemed that Piri would not accept this role. This makes him a threat to our way of life, a way of life that has existed for a very long time to ensure our survival."

I feel my cheeks turning red as they talk about me as if I'm not sitting here.

"Hence, this is the recommendation," he continues. "Piri will be assigned a wife but will not live with her or go to work. The wife's parents will raise the son for ten years as is expected. Piri, however, will take his grandfather's place. Since Adon passed away before his normal time, Piri will be confined to his grandmother's quarters for ten years, until it would have been time for his grandmother to report for the end. At that point, Piri will have the option to assume his role in society again or report to the end along with his grandmother."

I laugh. "You think a twenty-year-old girl will not want to have her new husband living with her?"

Eraph's face displays indifference. "I do not see why it will matter."

He's right. It wouldn't matter. A spouse is nothing more than an object. There's no emotional tie. I've got to act before I end up locked away. Use your brain, Piri. You're smarter than these Level One men. Think. Think. I drop my head. "Whatever you think is best for the city."

Eraph sits up a little straighter. "Exactly. That is all that matters. I am glad you see that."

"I do," I say. "I apologize for all the trouble I have caused you and my father. I know that what happens on the surface is best for us. But like you said, it was quite dramatic seeing it in person." I can see the doubt in Eraph's eyes. I continue. "It is logical. The balance must be maintained."

Eraph nods. "Explain it to me."

I hold my head up high. "If we did not deliver four hundred of the Children every week, their population would become uncontrollable. In one year, there would be over twenty thousand more. In just fifty years, their population would double. If they are starving now, what would happen then? They would have to go after our crops."

Both he and my papa are nodding. "Very good, Piri," Eraph says. "And what would happen if the Spirit People did not receive that on which they rely?"

"Chaos," I say. "They would hunt the Children at will with nothing to control their actions or their numbers."

Eraph smiles. "That is correct. It would cause the downfall of every faction of people in the world, especially ours."

"I see it now," I say. "I do not know what I was thinking. I apologize again." My own words are making me sick to my stomach.

"Very good," Eraph says. "We can wait before making a decision about your wife and grandmother's quarters. I think we just need to see if you can get back into a regular routine."

I smile. "Gracias. I mean, thank you."

"But you are behind with training," he says. "Let us get you signed up for Maintenance so you can begin learning that field."

"No."

He looks at me with shock. "No?"

"No," I repeat. "I want to go into Government."

He laughs. "Piri, your scores are very high. Maintenance is the most respected profession. They are highly regarded in the city."

I nod. "I know that. But do those people know everything you know?"

"Well…no," he says.

"Exactly." I look around at my papa then back at Eraph. "One thing I know is that knowledge is power. After I have learned so much, I can't walk away. Sure, I know you pretend to be lowly Government workers, but you know more than any other segment of the population. You know the secrets of every aspect of our history and existence. You have the real power and are the true leaders of our great city."

Eraph's cheeks are red. I turn to see the same in my papa's face. "Well, your son is very smart."

My papa is still blushing. "He always has been."

That's something I learned on the surface. No amount of evolution can squash the one element of humanity that truly controls us—ego.

"Well," Eraph says, "you certainly qualify. Are you sure that is what you want to do?"

"Absolutely."

He turns his attention back to the screen. "Okay. I can enter that information here. You can begin training tomorrow."

"Very good," I say. "There is one place I would like to start while it is still going on."

"What is that?" he asks.

"The food production."

"Very good idea."

"Yes," my papa confirms. "A very good idea."

CHAPTER TWENTY-EIGHT

The crops come up through this large open shaft here." My trainer points to the guardrails around the large closed door in the floor. "The small elevator to the right is for personnel."

I nod. He was just introduced to me an hour ago, and I can't remember his name. I don't care to remember. He appears to be much older than I am.

"The crops are carried along the large beams," he says, pointing toward the ceiling, "and deposited into the first vats here for washing. They are thoroughly cleansed before processing. We can only imagine what kind of filth and disease exists on the surface."

Then it dawns on me, the room I saw at the bottom of the column; the one that is high up with the glass front. That must be the control room. That must be what the Control button in the elevator stood for. They stay up there to direct the Chosen Ones onto the large carrier. Of course. They don't want to get too close to those filthy surface people. That's why the notes were never delivered, although I'm sure the Chosen Ones were waving them in the air. But the Fathers in the control room didn't care; they only needed to get the next shipment off to their Scav buddies.

"Do you have any questions?"

I smile and nod. "At what time of the day do they stop working?"

"It does not stop," he says, "until it is complete. It takes several months to convert the raw crops into the food tablets from the time we receive the last shipment. Now over here—"

"How do they turn on the power for the processing area?"

He stares at me. "I do not see that as being important."

"Really? But after the food processing is over, we only use this room every seventh day. Is that not correct?"

"Yes."

"Does the power stay on all that time?"

He shakes his head. "Of course not. Very well, come this way." I follow him to the far side of the giant room. He points to several large metal boxes on the wall. "These control the power to the entire city. The first box is the one that powers this room."

"Got it," I say.

We walk back to where we were. "After the food is cleansed, it is transferred to these grinding machines and from there it goes into these giant ovens for dehydration."

We walk to another section.

"Here," he says pointing to other large containers, "is where the food is compressed into sheets."

We walk over to a conveyor, and a four-feet-square sheet of our food slides out of the machine, then makes its way along the conveyor track. It's only a half-inch thick.

"When it moves under this section, the lasers will cut the sheet into strips."

I watch as it does what he says. The lasers fire as the sheet slides under it, leaving perfect lines across one direction. Only the light dust from the food sheet makes the laser beams visible. As the sheet passes all the way through, the track turns clockwise and pushes it back through in reverse. The lasers activate again and create the same lines perpendicular to the first cuts, leaving the perfect squares I have eaten most of my life.

My trainer picks up one of the squares and holds it out for me to see.

"That is very interesting," I say.

He shrugs and tosses the square back onto the dissected sheet. The bottom opens up, and the pieces fall onto another conveyor and are zipped away.

"That is it," he says. "Those will be added to the city's food source."

But I'm not paying attention. I'm looking at the lasers. They're only two inches long and an inch in diameter. "So, this bar depresses the button on the end of the laser as the sheet passes underneath? That is what activates them?"

He looks at the lasers as if wondering why that matters. "Yes."

"I see that each is mounted in place by a single bolt. So, if one malfunctions or stops working, you have replacements nearby?"

I must be the weirdest trainee he has ever dealt with. "Of course not. They rarely stop working, but we call Maintenance if they do."

I nod. "Of course."

He continues to show me around the processing area. Then we go over the air processing. The rear of the area is where the canisters are connected, the canisters of pure air that the Scavs extract from the ocean water.

In total, I spend three days with this trainer learning the operation of the Lower Level. And what I learn is invaluable. I know that the only access to the surface is here. I know that this room is full of people until all the crops are processed. And I know how to activate the power to this room.

After this training is complete, I'm paired with other trainers who explain other facets of the city. I'm given tours of almost every level. I already knew of Levels One, Eleven, and Twelve. Level Two is General Labor, like the guys working in the food processing area. Level Three is manufacturing, where they utilize the raw materials sent from the Scavs. Level Four is recycling. Level Five is the Central Link. Level Six is Solar, whose only job is to keep the giant panels atop the city providing power. Level Seven is Programming. Levels Eight, Nine, and Ten are the most shocking.

Level Eight is called Defense, but I'm not allowed in there, so I have no idea what it means. I know there is not a transport around that level, but the floor and walls extend out to the edge of the tubes. This I noticed as I took the tube on Level Seven.

Level Nine is the Morgue, where citizens report for the end.

They are placed in tubes that put them to sleep, and then the bodies are liquefied and pumped underneath the fields on the surface to keep the soil rich, the same reason The Book instructs the Children to bury the dead there. Watching people report for this with no more thought or emotion than drinking a glass of water was disturbing. It saddens me. On the surface, people fight with every ounce of their being to preserve life.

But it is Level Ten that upsets me the most—Nursery. I watch as babies are grown in test tubes. The DNA used is from the very ones reporting for the end. There are literally one hundred and forty-four thousand DNA samples as each inhabitant of the city is re-grown over and over and sent randomly to new families. They are even given the same names. I shuddered to think of how many boys named Piri with identical DNA have lived in the city before I came along. I hate it all.

When I return each night, I go to my room and try to learn more. I've been given a trainee's code so I can now access more information on the Link. Although I'm still not allowed to research anything pertaining to the Children, Scavs, or anything to do with past cultures or civilizations, I can at least learn about the natural disasters. I read about the shrinking of the land known as Canus. It was much larger at one time, like The Book says. But it was the heating of the atmosphere that caused the water to rise, not someone eating the forbidden crops. I read about earthquakes and volcanoes and other disasters the Fathers take credit for to manipulate the Children with fear. It disgusts me.

I can find no information about the northern forest, the area past the camp of the soldier Scavs, but it doesn't matter. I have my plan worked out. The only problem is I have to wait until the food processing is over, and I'm not sure when that will be.

I have now been back in the city for six weeks, and although I play the role of devoted city boy, I can't stand being here. I eat more tablets than I used to, and I'm still hungry. Often I visit the kitchen area to push the button to dispense a tablet. I hit the button several times to collect four and five each visit. There is no kitchen table since families here don't dine together. I miss that. I miss sitting around the table, and I miss the taste of everything on the surface. I'm not used to these tablets anymore. I stay hungry all the time.

I lie in bed tonight thinking of what I must do. I get up and pull my pack from underneath my bed. I'm almost ready. I have clothes, a handheld light, and food supplies. Now I need only to add the last item.

My mama and papa are fast asleep, and I've never seen my grandmother leave her quarters. The main room is dark, and I leave the lights off. Only the glow from a small green light in the kitchen provides any illumination at all. I carry the chair from my room with me. Once I am underneath one of the main ceiling lights, I stand on the chair. I don't want to shine any light for fear that it will wake someone and I'll be discovered. I take a small metal object, the only one I could find, and begin tapping away at the edge of the flat round disc. There is a divider between them to keep them from interacting and I'm hoping it will buffer the noise as well. Finally I notice a chip in the stone.

The next morning is an off-day for me and my papa. Besides the food processing, most citizens work four days in a row and are off three days in a row. I normally spend these days in my room or traveling around the city in the tubes, but not today.

As my papa and mama get up, they notice my handiwork. "There is a light out," my papa says.

"I will call Maintenance," my mama replies. She opens the screen in the main room and punches a few buttons.

I go back to my room and wait. A few minutes later, I hear the front doorbell. I walk out and see my papa as he motions for the Maintenance person to come inside. She's a young woman, which makes me believe she has not been working very long. My papa points to the light not working, so she places a stepstool underneath and climbs up to take a look at it.

I look at the small box on the floor and walk over and open it.

"What are you doing? Leave that alone."

I look up and see her glaring down at me. "Sorry. I was just admiring your tools. You Maintenance people are awesome. You keep the entire city working. I bet you had really high scores."

Her cheeks blush, and a smile makes its way across her face. She replaces the stone, then steps back onto the floor.

"You already fixed it?"

She nods. "It was just chipped."

"Wow. You are good."

She blushes again, grabs her toolbox, and leaves.

I walk back into my bedroom. Sitting on the edge of the bed, I reach under my arm and pull out the vise-like tool I just stole. I open and close it to see how it works, then pull out my pack and add it to the mix. I have everything I need.

"Good news."

I see my papa, who just entered my bedroom. I fake a smile. "What is it?"

"The city Central Link has assigned your wife."

"That is good news, Father," I say. But that's not what I want to say. I want to say that I had a spouse before you killed him. I want to say I had a best friend before you killed him. I want to say that I had a life before you killed me. I want to say these things, but I don't. I have to stick to the plan.

"It is an important day for you," my papa continues. "You will be twenty in three days. You will have a wife, daughter, new home, and new job."

I punch some tabs on the screen for effect. "I cannot find her, Father."

"Who?"

"My wife," I say. "I want to see what she looks like and read her name."

"You cannot access that," he says. "Not yet anyway."

"But you can."

"Very well." He walks over and punches several numbers very fast and pulls up the data.

I stare at the screen. "Okay, looks like she will be a fine wife."

"Very good," he says. "Now concentrate on your studies."

I nod. "I will. I am learning a lot in training. How many more days until the food processing will be completed?"

"I do not know. Why?"

I look at him and smile. "I was just curious. Those people work hard and have such an important job."

He shrugs and leaves.

I look at the screen. My wife-to-be looks like everyone else. I quickly delete the information and try to access the files regarding our history. I find such a file. When it calls for the access code, I try to remember the numbers my papa entered. I remembered them perfectly. The screen comes to life with more information than I could hope for. I begin to read.

Most of the records of Canus were destroyed by wars and floods. What is known is that the land was much larger consisting of thousands of species of animals"

I scan through many pictures of all kinds of animals. I continue reading.

There were countless rivers and lakes including five giant lakes. These are all dry now. They were two large mountain ranges to the east and west of Canus. It is unknown if life exists there now, but it is believed that these areas might still be rich with life. There are many other areas like The Garden spread throughout Canus, and some on other land masses across the planet.

I knew it. There are other areas of life. I read on.

After the great wars, the cities were left in ruins. The poor had no means to leave, nor anywhere to go, so they were forced to reside in those contaminated ruins with very little to eat. They became scavengers, living off anything they could find. Over time, this rugged existence took its toll and they changed physically, as well as in other ways. They became larger, stronger, and more daring as their food sources were depleted. Finally they found a new source, as unthinkable as it was, and the citizens with the most wealth knew they would not be safe for long. It was predicted that the warm air would cause the seas to rise, driving the scavengers into their territory, so they began constructing the great city.

When it was completed, the Fathers made deals with the surface dwellers to aid in the areas of food production and mining.

I can't believe it. Lucent was right. We *are* the same; at least we were. Then I see a link that gets my attention—*The Book*. I click on it.

Many of the surface people still clung to the hope their sacred book instilled in them. Although eventually all copies of the book had long decayed, and electronic technology no longer existed on the surface, the stories were still told amongst the people. The Fathers used this to their advantage, printing copies of The Book to distribute to the surface people. These books would not decay and were rewritten to provide new rules. It was decided that the promise of punishment and reward after a person dies was not enough to ensure compliance, because even though the majority of the people believed in the book, most did not follow the rules. So it was rewritten to provide the premise of instant punishment, and not just for the offender, but for many people. Rewards also were made more real in the form of the Chosen Ones program. Thus the balance has always been maintained.

I sit back and stare at the screen. It disgusts me. Then I see a link to the food production and click on that. The word I see takes my breath away—"Completed."

CHAPTER TWENTY-NINE

I turn off the screen. The life back then doesn't seem any better than life now. In fact, it seems worse. All that matters to me is the Children. I'm very nervous, but I know what I have to do. And now I know when—tonight. I go about my day as if nothing is different. I try to keep my mind occupied, but it isn't easy. I keep going over the plan in my head, hoping I won't get caught. I know that if I am discovered, I'll be locked away in my grandmother's quarters for a decade at least.

The day passes. I go to bed that night but can't sleep. It's just as well. I didn't want to set the alarm to wake me. Many hours pass, and I know the time is now or never. I have to go. I take my pack, slide it onto my back, and fasten the straps in front of me. I quietly walk out of my room and out the front door. The hallways are illuminated, but barely. I walk quickly, staring ahead into the dim light to make sure the path is clear. Soon, I'm at my destination. I push the button for the elevator and take it to the Lower Level.

It's completely dark as I enter the giant room at the bottom of our city, the room where the crops are processed. I take my handheld light and shine it along the floor. I don't want to turn on the power until I have to. I walk over to the conveyor belts and shine my light on the lasers. I sit the light on the top of the bar so it shines on the first laser unit. I take off my pack and set it on the floor to retrieve the tool I borrowed from the Maintenance woman. I place it on the bolt holding the laser in place and try to turn it. It doesn't budge. I try harder. Nothing. I think of going on without it but decide to try one more time. I take a deep breath and squeeze the tool and pull down with all my might. It gives.

"Sí," I say aloud.

I twist it until the laser becomes loose. I slide it out and place it into my pack. Next I go to the power box. I remember my trainer saying it was the first one. It is the only one not locked. I open it and see one large handle that I flip upward. All the lights on the machines come on, and the room is flooded with bright light. I run to the personnel elevator and push the button. The door opens and I step inside and push the bottom button. The elevator begins to descend.

I can't believe it's working. The elevator picks up speed. I'm so worried that the lights will set off an alarm, and the elevator will stop any second. But it doesn't. I make it all the way to the bottom. I exit the elevator and step out into the large dark room at the base of the column. I shine the light and see the other tracks, each rising on an incline. Oh how I want to follow the eastern track that leads to home. But I can't squeeze under the giant door. I go around to the northern track, the only track I know that will take me out. It's the track that leads to the sacred area where the Scavs gather every seventh day, and I don't even know what day it is on the surface.

I run until my lungs are burning, and I have to walk. Suddenly I think I see movement. I disregard it as paranoia or simply my mind and eyes playing tricks on me. That is, until I see it again. I shine the light to the far sides of the tunnel and I see many sets of dots reflecting back in my direction. My heart races but I continue walking. I finally see what it is. The tunnel is filled with huge lizards. They are everywhere. I think back to the day when Payo saved me and I start breathing hard. I know they are dangerous, but I also know that one attacked me to protect her nest. As they dart out of my way, I realize they are as afraid of me as I am of them.

But that is not my main fear. I keep listening in the darkness for the telltale signs of the carrier. I worry that they will discover what's happened and come for me. But I never feel the vibrations.

I walk on for hours. It was probably already early morning by the time I reached the bottom of the column, and it's taking me longer than I expected to walk the distance of the tunnel. And of course I don't know what I'll find once I do get there.

I finally see a pinpoint of light in the far distance and know it's the end of the tunnel. I push onward as the spot grows larger in my view. Finally I reach the end and walk slowly and quietly out and look around. There's no one there. Thank goodness it's not the seventh day.

I exit the tunnel and look up the jagged, steep cliff behind it. There's no path cut into the side like at the Scav camp where I was first taken. I tighten my straps and climb. The rocks are sharp and painful to my bare feet. I keep climbing, slowly, making sure I have a firm grip or footrest before making my next move. It's taking a long time, but I have to be careful or I'll fall. My muscles are becoming very fatigued. As I rest, I have to let my arms fall to my side and shake them to rejuvenate the circulation. I press on.

I'm near the top, and I can feel the warm fluid on the bottom of my feet. They are bleeding. But I can't stop now. I reach the top, and I can see the column in the distance. I walk over the rocks trying to find any semblance of a path. Although the weather is cool, my robe is soaked with sweat.

I stop and sit on a rock. I remove my pack and withdraw a container of water. I'm very thirsty. I drink the entire container and drop it on the ground. I make my way around large boulders and over jagged ground.

Suddenly I freeze. I hear noises. I don't move for several minutes as the noises become clearer. I recognize the sound. It's Scavs. I look around the rocks to find the source and see three soldier Scavs standing in a small circle. I wonder if I should try to circle far around them. I know I'm not far from the edge of the barren land. From there it's not far to the base of the column. I know if they see me, I'll be killed or sent back.

I peer out again. I have a plan, but it requires me to get closer. To do that, I would have to make myself visible for a few seconds. They are looking at each other and conversing. They don't speak like the queen. Their communication consists more of grunts and growls.

I watch as one of them points off into the distance. The others look that way as well. I slide around the rock and walk toward them with my back bent over and head down low, carrying my pack in my hand. I see another large rock ahead and ease up behind it. I don't know if they saw me, but I don't hear them anymore. I stand there and wait. Nothing.

Finally I hear them conversing again and peek around. They're still in the same place. I reach into the pack and pull out the laser. I see the belts with the clear bubbles of explosives around their waists. I point the laser and push the button in the back. I can't see the line, but I can see the reflection on one of the bubbles. If it will just make it explode...I know they're much tougher and stronger than the Children, but at that range an explosion should render them unconscious long enough for me to get around them. I hold the laser in place, but nothing's happening.

I hear a loud grunt and look up to see the Scav pointing at me. The others quickly turn and see me too. I don't move, but it doesn't matter. They have discovered me. I close my eyes.

Suddenly the ground shakes as I hear not one explosion, but a series of loud booms. I drop the laser and fall back behind the rock. My ears are ringing. I clear my head and rise. I forget my pack, which carries extra food, water, and clothing and I run. I look to make sure they're unconscious as I pass, but the point is moot. From the huge circle of blood, I realize that the bubble exploded and set off the rest of the bubbles. There are only a few pieces large enough to even identify.

I run with all my might over the rocky terrain, leaving a blood trail of my own. Finally I am free of the barren wasteland, and the ground is covered with tall grass.

I run as fast as I can toward the column, which is still a good distance from me. I turn my head to look back over my shoulder, but the horizon is clear. It's already getting dark when I run past the column and go to the track that leads home. It's smoother and feels better on my feet, though both of them are hurting and bleeding profusely. The fields are once again dull and lifeless, and the brown stalks sway back and forth in the strong wind.

It's darker when I reach the edge of the fields. I can see a house in the distance. I look back over my shoulder again, and the wind knocks me off the track. I go down hard but jump back up. I stare back at the horizon behind me. Like back in the tunnel when I thought my mind was playing tricks on me, it seems to be doing it again. I think I see black outlines far away moving in the darkness, but I'm not sure if they're real.

I see the first house, the light shining underneath the thick wooden door. I also see a torch planted in the ground. I see others in the distance—white dots scattered throughout the darkness, and realize they have implemented my idea. I'd smile if I wasn't so scared. I run down the steps and bang on the door. "Help. Let me in."

The door opens, and a man looks at me in shock. "Are you okay?"

"Por favor," I beg. "Can I come in?"

He reaches out, grabs my arms and pulls me inside. "Sí. Of course. Come in. What's happened?" He closes the door behind me, and I collapse on the floor. A woman, boy, and girl stare at me in wonderment. A dog resembling Ash rushes to me and licks my face.

"What's going on?" the woman asks.

"Por favor," I say. "Por favor lock the door."

The man looks at me funny as if that's a loco thing to ask. But then the dog points to the door and growls. Everyone in the room stares at each other with eyes full of fear. The man takes the large brace and bars the door with it. He turns to look at his family with confusion.

The son rushes to his room and comes back with two spears. I can sense their fear and it's warranted. Scavs have never ventured into the home areas before, never past the fields. The dog continues to growl, shifting its attention from one wall to the next, sometimes whimpering and lying down to rest its head on its legs as its eyes dart around nervously. I believe the house is completely surrounded.

I suddenly feel guilty for bringing this upon the family. They did not deserve this. I try to stand but everything goes black.

CHAPTER THIRTY

My eyes slowly open, and I try to focus. I see the woman and girl sitting on each side of me. They are both staring at me as if they have been waiting for me to wake. I'm on a bed with covers pulled halfway up my chest and exposing my legs and feet. I can see my feet are bandaged. The door is open and I see the man and boy sitting on the bench by the front door, gripping the spears tightly in front of them. The dog is lying on the floor in front of the door, his nose in the air. I remember the Scavs. I try to sit up, but I am too weak.

The woman pushes me softly back down. "Just rest now."

I can't rest until I know. "Is everybody okay? They didn't get in, did they?"

"No, they didn't. Drink this," the woman says.

I drink and hand her back the container. I look at the little girl and smile. She's about Ana's age. "Gracias," I say.

The man must hear my voice and know I'm awake. He walks into the bedroom. "Are you feeling better?"

"Sí. Gracias. Muchas gracias."

"Who are you?"

"My name is Piri."

"Well, Piri, I'm Lon. This is my wife, Dera, my daughter, Risa, and my son, Keb, in the other room."

I look and see the young boy, younger than Niko by many years. He still sits by the door with spear in hand, but he's stretching his neck to try to see what's going on in here.

The papa looks at me and shakes his head. "What were you doing out there, and why were Scavs after you? And what are you wearing? Where did you come from?"

I laugh at all the questions and ignore them. "I'm sorry if I have caused you trouble."

He smiles then repeats the last question. "Where did you come from?"

"The barren land."

He looks at me as if in disbelief. "I'm not sure what you were doing out there in Scav territory with no footwear or cloak, but it's not safe out there."

I laugh. It's not the first time I've been told those very words.

"Why were you there?" the wife asks.

I smile. "It's a long story. I'm just glad nothing happened to you guys."

He shakes his head. "We're all okay. We're glad you're okay, too. But I still don't know what's going on."

"I have to get to Vet," I say. "You know the Elect named Vet, eh?"

"Of course," he says. Then his eyes open wide. "Oh, my. You're Piri that lives with Vet and his family, the one from the city in the sky. We heard you were taken by the Scavs. Did you escape? That's why they were after you, eh?"

That's not the real reason, but I nod. I look around the room to see their expressions, even the son who has forsaken his post by the door to peek into the room. They are all shocked.

"How did you get away from them?" Dera asks.

There is too much to explain, and I don't have the energy. I am thankful that they took me in, but I just want to get home.

"You're the one who made the light, eh?" the little girl asks.

I am confused.

Her mama explains. "The poles that we use to light the outside at night, and the sticks we use to carry light with us."

I smile. "Yes, I invented those."

"And the bridges," the boy shouts from the front room.

I nod. I'm glad they know who I am, but that doesn't help me. "I just need to get to Vet."

The papa nods. "Yes, we will get you home. But we can't go anywhere tonight. I don't know why, but there are Scavs in our land. I know they have been sighted in the fields, but I've never known of them coming this far. I don't believe they're still outside. It's too dangerous to check, though. In the morning, I'll send Keb to get Vet. You can't go anywhere on those feet."

"Yes, Piri," the wife says in a gentle tone as she pulls the cover up to my chin. "You just rest and we'll take care of everything."

I nod as tears run down my cheeks. I'm just happy to be back. "Whose room am I in?"

The little girl smiles and raises her hand. "I can sleep with Mama and Papa tonight."

I smile. "You can stay with me if you like."

She grins. Apparently she likes that idea, but her papa isn't sure. "No, you have this bed to yourself tonight. You look exhausted and need to rest."

I agree. I am exhausted. After they leave the room, I fall fast asleep, but it isn't sound rest. I'm not even sure you can call it sleep. I seem to exist halfway between consciousness and subconsciousness, in a twilight zone of sorts, as visions of the cage full of the Chosen keep coming out of that tunnel. In this dreamlike state of mind, I keep trying to run away from it, but the screams chase me down and grab around me like the Scavs did, as if the very sound of fear had grown arms and fingers. Sometimes my eyes open, and I can clearly see the room, the flat stones in the ceiling putting out their murky illumination. I try hard to open my eyes fully, to wake and rid myself of these images, but my eyelids do not obey my commands, and I drift again into awful hallucinations.

In one dream I see my father and he is smiling, but he is not alone. Someone is in the dark behind him. I can see the shape of the shadow, and it is much larger than my father. Then it comes forward, and I can first see the crimson eyes followed by the snow white skin. It is Lucent. She is holding hands with my father and kissing him. I can see now they are sitting on the grass, leaning up against one of the homes of the children. I recognize this place. Then I see that it is not Lucent, it is Tag. And it is not my father, it is me. I struggle to get away, but he is too strong. I can't breathe. I can't move.

"Piri. Piri. Wake up."

I scream as I jolt awake. My entire body hurts. My feet are pulsating with pain. I sit up and wipe my eyes. It's Dera, the wife.

"It was just a dream, Piri. You're safe. It's daylight out," she says. "Keb has already gone to get Vet."

I sit up and try again to clear the drowsiness from my thoughts. "What about Vet?"

Dera smiles. "Keb has gone to get Vet. He'll come back with the carrier, so you can wait here."

"No, I can't," I say. I slide off the bed and stand on my tender feet. "I got to go and meet them on the way."

She can see in my eyes that I'm adamant about it, so she doesn't say anything. She helps me to the other room while she explains to her husband what's going on. He grabs his spear and bow. He and little Risa both join me and Dera as we go outside and start walking alongside the track toward the east, toward home.

The bandages become thick with dirt mixed with blood as we walk. I don't care. I'm going home; that's all that matters. I'm going to see my little Chiquita again. I can't help but periodically check behind us, scanning the horizon back toward the column. This makes Lon nervous as he too keeps checking behind us.

The pain in my feet escalates, but I don't care. Nothing matters anymore except going home, going to see my little Ana. I don't know how things will be without Niko, but I can't live without any of my family. Ana is all that matters now. I will dedicate my life to helping Vet raise her to be the most wonderful person she can be.

We walk for over an hour making painstakingly slow progress but at least in the right direction. Then I see it. In the distance I see the carrier. It grows larger as it speeds toward us. I try to walk faster. It slows as it gets close. I can see Vet at the controls and Keb standing beside him. Vet shouts out my name. Then I see her. Little Ana's head pops up on the other side of her papa. She sees me and screams. She begins pounding the top of the rail of the carrier with both hands, the excitement overwhelming her innocent soul. Tears are streaming down both sides of her face as she cries uncontrollably. She continues pounding the side of the carrier as it pulls up beside me and comes to a stop. I walk around to the back and she follows, still crying, still screaming; still pounding the carrier. We meet at the back and she jumps into my arms. She is heavy, but I don't flinch. I squeeze her tight.

"I love you, Piri," she shouts between the sobs. "I love you."

"I love you, too, Chiquita. I love you, too."

We stand there for a long time, neither ready to let go of that first embrace. I hug her so tight I fear I will hurt her. But I can't let go of the moment. Everything feels right now: her warm body, the smell of her clothing, the feel of her messy hair on my cheek. Every night in the city I went to sleep with one thought, the thought of holding Ana again. Now it's real, and I'm afraid to let go for fear I'm still dreaming. Finally I drop to my knees as Ana steps back to look into my eyes. I look into her bloodshot eyes as well.

"I knew you'd come back," she says.

"Of course I came back. I can't be without my best friend."

We hug each other again.

I look up and see Vet still standing on the carrier, tears running down his face as well. I look over and see Lon and his family, all smiling and crying. It seems almost surreal.

Vet thanks Lon and his family, and they walk back toward their home. He helps me up into the carrier. "Are you okay?" he asks. "Are your feet okay?"

I sink down on the side of the carrier and Ana sits in my lap, facing me, her arms once again tight around my neck. "I'm okay now." I squeeze my arms tighter.

Vet manages the controls and the carrier glides along the track. I turn my head to face the direction we are going and let the cool air blow in my face. I close my eyes and finally breathe a huge sigh of relief. I'm going home. I think about everything I went through to get here, to get away from those horrible people. Not just the Scavs, but the emotionless zombies in the city who cater to the Scavs.

"You're not going to leave again, are you?" Ana asks with her face still buried in my shoulder.

"No, Chiquita, never."

"Promise?"

I smile and nod. "Promise."

I look up and see Vet. He is studying my attire and looking confused. "That's the same thing you were wearing when we first met you. I thought you were taken by Scavs. But it looks as if you were back in the city."

"I was."

"How did you get back? How did you get up there?"

I shake my head to let him know I don't feel like answering questions right now. "I'll tell you everything. I promise. But now I just want to go home."

"Okay," he says. "We'll take you straight to your house, Piri."

"No," I say. "Por favor, let me come home with you. I don't think I can bear to be alone right now."

Ana pulls back and looks me in the eye with a curious expression. "But Niko will want to see you."

CHAPTER THIRTY-ONE

When the carrier comes to the end of the track, I kiss Ana and jump off and run. My head has not stopped spinning since the revelation that Niko is still alive. Soon I see my house and go as fast as I can, leaving Ana and Vet behind. I don't even feel my feet as the bandages unravel and sprawl out on the ground, leaving a dirty white and red trail of cloth blowing in the wind with the grass.

"Niko!" I yell. "Niko!"

I'm still thirty feet away when the door opens and Niko appears with his spear. Our eyes meet as if we both just saw something impossible to exist. He throws the spear aside and rushes to meet me, his eyes now spilling tears as fast as mine. We come together as our arms circle each other and our lips meet. We fall to our knees as our lips never part. He runs his hands all over my head and face as if making sure I'm real.

I pull back and stare into his eyes. "I thought you were dead."

He cries even more. "I thought *you* were dead."

We embrace again. Everything feels right from his strong arms to his smell. I know I am home. I realize that Vet and Ana are standing beside us.

"Come, Chiquita," Vet says. "Let's leave them alone."

"No!" I yell. I stand and Niko stands also. "No, we have much to talk about." I look straight at Vet. "Take Chiquita to your friends. Niko needs to send the message for the Elect to meet tomorrow."

Vet doesn't question me. He nods to Niko and leaves with Ana.

It breaks my heart to watch her walk away. Niko kisses me again and goes with them to retrieve the flag to send the signal.

I walk into my house and look around. I remember how happy I was to move in here. I remember how happy I was to be married to Niko. I wish I could be happy now, but unfortunately that's not easy knowing the reality that awaits the Children and the Chosen. I take off my robe and put on one of my tunics then sit at our table. I think about all that has happened and I cry. Then I stop. No! I'm not going to cry anymore. I need to be strong, and crying will not help.

When Niko and Vet return, I have them sit at the table and take a seat myself. I take a deep breath and think of where to begin. "All the Scav attacks that began to increase once I came to live here were because of me." I see the confusion in their eyes. "It's true. The Scavs were looking for me. They were not running short of food or anything else. The escalation in attacks had nothing to do with that." I look at Niko. "That's apparently why they left you alive when they attacked us in the forest that day."

"Why?" Niko asks.

I look at him and then at Vet. "To send me home. To send me back to the city in the sky."

Vet shakes his head. "I don't understand. How did they know you were even here?"

"We told them."

They look at each other, then back at me. I know they have many questions.

"Let me tell you everything. I knew something was not right from the first time I came here, but I said nothing. I knew the population of the city never changes. I knew in my gut something was not right with the promises in The Book. And now I have seen it with my own eyes."

"I don't understand, Piri," Vet says. "What have you seen?"

I swallow hard. "I know Payo was chosen."

They stare at me as if wondering how I could know that.

I continue. "The Fathers don't just deal with the Children; they deal with the Scavs as well. And the arrangement they have with the Scavs is unthinkable but exists nonetheless. The Scavs provide the Fathers with valuable minerals, metals, plants, and air. And in return, the Fathers provide them with food."

"From the crops," Vet asks.

I look at the floor for several seconds, then take a deep breath and look back up. "The Scavs don't eat crops. They don't eat fish or lizards. They only eat one thing and you know what that is." I can see their breathing has increased like mine as what I am saying sinks home. I keep going. "And the Fathers have a deal with them to provide them with a fresh batch of food every seventh day, a batch numbering four hundred, to be exact."

Vet jumps up so quickly that it causes his chair to fall over backward. "No. It's not true, Piri. Por favor, I beg you. Tell me it's not true."

I look at Niko, but he is silent, his eyes looking longingly at me as if wishing I would also tell him it's not true.

"The Scavs took me to where they meet on the seventh day. But they don't meet to worship; they meet to feast. I saw the Chosen Ones delivered directly to them. I saw some of them torn limb from limb and eaten." My eyes begin to well up again, but I fight it off. "I saw Payo." I grit my teeth as I relive that day, as I have done so many times in my dreams; Payo being so happy he was finally chosen but not understanding what was going on. It is burned into my memory how he tried to protect me before being dragged away to his death. Like a demon, it has been summoned too many times in my nightmares. But I won't cry.

Niko puts his arm around me to comfort me. He apparently recognizes that my look of anger is to overpower my thoughts of grief. I see Vet leaning over the table, his head in his arms, his whole body shaking. It surprises me and apparently Niko, too.

"Papa?"

Vet looks up with bloodshot eyes and whispers one word. "Bren."

I feel sick again. I'd forgotten about Niko's older brother who was chosen. Now I've just explained to them that Bren is not living in a paradise in the sky, but was instead brutally murdered and eaten.

But Vet is taking it very hard. He suddenly retches and puts his hand over his mouth and runs outside. We can hear him vomiting. I look at Niko as if to say I'm sorry. He looks back at me. I can see he is sad, but I'm glad that I can still see his eyes full of love.

Vet comes back in and sits at the table. I knew he would be distraught, but I didn't expect this. He stares at Niko as his eyes begin to fill again. "He was so lonely after his mate left. You remember how sad he was?"

Niko nods and tries to maintain his composure. "I remember, Papa. It's okay."

Vet puts his head down and shakes it. "He was feeling so lost. All he wanted was to go."

I gasp as I realize what he is saying. "Oh no," I whisper.

"What?" Niko asks. He looks at me, then his papa. "What is it?"

Vet stares up at me as if wanting me to say it so he doesn't have to. I oblige. "You cheated."

"Papa?" Niko asks, his eyes watering again.

Vet puts both hands over his face. "I wanted him to be happy. I kept his cloth in my hand as I drew the names. I did it because I loved him. But I killed him."

"No!" I yell so loudly that Vet opens his hands to look at me. "You didn't. The Fathers and the Scavs killed him. And it's going to keep happening unless we stop it."

Vet nods. "Okay. We're going to meet with the Elect tomorrow and figure out what to do." Without saying another word, Vet gets up and leaves the house.

It is only midafternoon when he leaves, but I am emotionally and physically drained. Niko helps me up, and I walk into our bedroom and sit on the side of the bed. I see my bow propped against the wall, reach over to get it, and sit back down. I smile as I look over the construction, remembering how much time Niko spent making it, how he kept spinning those loco hunting stories to cover his actions. I'm so glad that we are together again. I see him standing at the door, smiling.

"Put your feet off the bed so I can tend to your wounds."

I do as he instructs. I sit on the bed with my feet sticking off the edge.

He takes water and a cloth and begins to gently wash the dried blood from my feet. Once again I am taken back to my first day here when Vet did this very thing.

"What happened the day I was taken? Were there others hurt that day?"

Niko shakes his head. "No. We were the only ones attacked. Most people didn't even know anything was happening. A few close to us heard the explosions and came running. They found me knocked out, and you were gone." He stops washing my feet and looks up. "I thought I had lost you forever. It almost killed me. I tried to put together a rescue party, but it was dark and everyone was afraid. I went around asking everybody I knew."

"No one volunteered?"

"Well," Niko says sheepishly, "just one."

I stare at him as I await the name.

"Tag."

I am confused. "Tag? Are you serious? Why?"

Niko shrugs. "I think he wants to be certain he does right by you, to go by the rules of The Book. I was glad to have someone along. We went out that night and found our way to a Scav camp, but it was almost completely dark outside. I could see them below the cliffs. There were several fires. I could see a trail that went down the cliff, and I could see two guards at the bottom. But I couldn't tell if you were there."

I feel the lump in my throat, but I'm glad to hear this story. "That's where I was. I was at the base of the cliff. I'm glad you didn't try to come down the trail, or they would have killed you. The only reason they didn't kill me was because they were trying to get me back to the city."

"I wanted to wait until daylight," he says. "That way I could see better. But I knew the next day was worship and we had to go to that."

Our eyes lock for several seconds before we both start laughing.

"Okay," he says, "I thought we had to go to that."

It feels good to laugh with all that's going on. "We're together now—for good. That's all that matters."

He nods as he begins to add fresh bandages to my feet.

"What about Ash?"

He does not look up. "They killed him."

"I'm sorry," I say. "He was a great dog."

Niko nods and continues working.

"I still remember when I first fell to the surface. I thought for sure he was going to eat me. How long had you had him?"

"About six years. I got him from a friend when he was just a puppy."

"Maybe we can go to Market and pick out a young one and name him Ash," I say.

Niko looks up and smiles. "I think that's a great idea." He finishes wrapping my feet and walks up and pulls me close to him. He kisses my forehead. I have missed that. "I love you, Piri. I always will."

I don't want this moment to end. I don't want to think about the Elect. I don't want to think about the Chosen Ones. I don't want to think about the Scavs and the Fathers. I only want this moment to last forever. But of course it cannot.

"Get some sleep," he says. I slide up fully onto the bed. Niko walks to the door to leave.

"What are you doing?" I ask.

He shrugs. "I know you're tired, and you've been through a lot. I'll stay in here and let you rest."

"No, my love," I say and hold out my arms. "I need you now more than ever."

CHAPTER THIRTY-TWO

I walk out of the washroom still feeling tired and sore. Vet is already there, and he and Niko are ready to go, just waiting for me.

"Are you okay?" Vet asks.

"Sí," I say. "It's just been a rough couple of days."

Niko grabs his spear and bow, and I take my bow. I have on sandals now, but my feet are still bandaged. I think I'm okay to walk, but I don't complain when Niko offers to carry me. It makes me think of the first time we met. We walk to the carrier. It's a very cold morning, and we wear thick cloaks over our tunics. We stop and pick up the other two Elect, who, like us, have brought ten guards each, all with spears and bows.

We arrive at the column, and the guards take their positions. The other two Elect walk with me, Niko, and Vet as we follow the column around the south side walking due west. The meeting is always in the same place. We cross the track that goes into the southeastern province and continue until we reach the southernmost point of the column.

All the other Elect are already there. I recognize them all. There is a large fire burning in the center of the circle to provide warmth. Maren meets us and throws her arms around me.

"I thought we had lost you, Piri. I'm so happy to see you."

The others smile and wave to display their happiness as well. It is short-lived.

I tell them everything. I tell them of being captured and taken to the first campsite. I tell of the female and children Scavs. I tell of the mines and the lizards. I tell of the large bubbles with explosives. I tell of the voyage on the seventh day and meeting the queen. I tell of her being white and of her intelligence. I tell them everything she said, except the part about the Scavs guarding the Children from whatever lives in the northern forest. We have too much to worry about right now, and I'm not sure the queen was telling the truth.

All eyes are fixed on me, unblinking, unwavering, all mouths open. Getting detailed information from a person who has been captured by the Scavs has never happened, and the revelation that news carries is earth-shattering.

I tell them of the purpose of the Scavs gathering on the seventh, and I see the looks of horror in their eyes. When I finish, I scan their faces, waiting for a response. None comes. Just silence.

Finally one speaks. "I can't believe it. The Book says the Chosen Ones are delivered to the city. I can't believe that's not true."

"How can you not believe it?" Maren asks. "Piri saw it all with his own eyes."

"Did he?" another Elect asks.

Another chimes in. "Sí, how do we know this is true? Maybe he dreamed it."

Soon a heated discussion takes place, mostly accusing me of lying or simply in error. I did not expect this.

"Stop it! All of you!" Niko shouts. They all stop and turn to look at him. "Think about what you're saying. We all know Piri. We know he wouldn't lie to us. He risked his life to get back so he could warn us. He deserves a lot more respect than you are showing him right now."

I smile and look lovingly at my spouse. When I look back at the circle of Elects, I see some heads nodding and others hung in shame.

"I'm sorry, Piri," one says. "It's hard to suddenly hear that your entire world is not what you have been taught."

I nod. "I understand. I know it's not easy to hear."

"What do we do?" Vet asks. "We can't send four hundred more to their deaths on the seventh."

Shon, the youngest of the Elect, steps forward again. He holds up The Book. "We have to follow the rules. They will punish us if we don't."

I shake my head. "No, it's not true. All the punishments they mention in the book were not caused by the Fathers. They were caused by natural events. The water rising was caused by lots of ice melting. The raining of fire was caused by a mountain erupting, something that used to happen more frequently when the land was much larger. None of the punishments mentioned in The Book are possible for the Fathers to do."

"Are you sure about this?" Shon asks.

"Sí. I read it in their own history in the files they keep in the city."

Shon shakes his head and holds The Book up again. "But we have always followed the rules and never have been punished. If we deviate at all, we could be destroyed."

I know he is afraid. I know they all are. Then I remember something. "I know a man who lives in our province. He has not been to worship or to harvest in fifty years."

They are all stunned.

"It's true," I say. "His name is Curz. He made the wrist bands for Niko. He told me this himself. And nothing has happened to him or to the people of our province. Don't you see? The Fathers created The Book to control you. They use fear to keep you picking the crops and sending the Chosen to the Scavs."

Shon still doesn't believe. "But The Book—"

I grab The Book from his hands, my cheeks burning with anger, and throw it into the fire. "Your book is a lie!"

Everyone freezes as they stare at the fire, now spitting fresh cinders high into the air. Some look to the sky as if expecting immediate retribution.

"You see?" I say, holding my arms out wide. "Nothing happened. But The Book says you are not allowed to destroy it without the Fathers raining down fire. Where is the fire? It's all a lie."

A few minutes pass and nothing happens. Along with the story about Curz, it starts to sink in. I think they are beginning to believe me.

Maren steps forward into the middle of the circle. "Let's assume we don't send the Chosen Ones on the seventh. It's not just the Fathers we would need to fear. What would the Scavs do?"

All eyes turn to me. "Without their needed food, they would come after it," I say.

Murmurs erupt as everyone looks around at each other. "They will slaughter us," one says.

"They already slaughter us," Niko corrects. "If four hundred of us have to die, I say we fight. At least we can take some of them with us."

"They're too strong and too fast," another says. "And they have explosives."

The discussion becomes heated again, some vowing to fight; others saying it would be pointless.

Maren speaks again and they all stop talking to listen. "I, for one, can't send any more of our young people to them. I don't care if I'm killed, but I just can't do it. I say we prepare; we defend ourselves."

"No," I say, as all eyes shift their focus to me. "We don't defend ourselves. We attack them."

Silence. Finally Vet speaks. "How?"

I look at each face before continuing. "They all meet on the seventh. Every one of them. And they carry no weapons with them. Why would they? They've never been attacked. The area where they meet has a large cliff overlooking it. We gather together every man, boy, woman, and girl with a bow, and we take the high ground and surprise them."

"Will our arrows reach them from that point?" Shon asks.

I honestly don't know the answer. "I'm not sure." I look to Niko, who takes his bow from his back, loads an arrow, and points it into the air to the south and releases it. I watch as it speeds through the air with a slight wobble. It carries a distance and falls to the earth. I think about the mob of Scavs and how far they stay from the cliff. I drop my head. Everyone knows what this means and they look defeated.

I think of the queen sitting in her cloth-covered structure. "It will reach their leader. If we take out the queen, they might not know what to do." A part of me thinks this is true. The other part of me just wants revenge.

"It is the soldiers you mention that pose the greatest threat," one says.

"I can design weapons that will work better." I hold up my own bow. "Niko designed this for me. It shoots farther and more accurately than regular bows. We can build thousands of them."

Maren looks at me with a logical expression. "In two days time, Piri?"

I shake my head.

"We have much to discuss," Maren continues as she looks around the circle. "The Elect must work this out amongst ourselves and decide the best course of action."

Niko and I take our cue and walk back around to the eastern track where the guards are spaced out across the fields, bows at the ready. I lean my bow against the column and sit on the very track that takes the Chosen Ones to their demise. Niko sits in front of me.

"They will decide what's best," he says.

"I don't know," I say. "They're all afraid."

"Me, too," he says.

I laugh. "Me, too. But if they'd witnessed what I saw, they'd all be ready to fight."

Niko looks down at the track before asking his next questions. "What if we did fight? What if we could continue to fight? What if we somehow kill every Scav? You say they provide the city with minerals they need to survive. Would that not hurt the people in the city? Would we still send them crops?"

I'm mentally drained. I don't answer. I don't know the answer.

Niko continues. "It just seems anything we do will put us in the middle of the Fathers and the Scavs."

I look him in the eyes. "You're not suggesting we continue with the Chosen Ones program, are you?"

"Of course not," he says firmly. "But I'm thinking about what the Elect are most likely discussing right now. They're probably wondering what will actually happen if we change even one little thing. Our actions will certainly have a reaction, both from those in the city and the Scavs."

I realize now that I hadn't thought past not sending four hundred people to the Scavs. After seeing the heartlessness and barbarianism, after seeing what happened to Payo, all I cared about was stopping it. Hours pass as we speak of other things. I tell Niko of my return to the city and my escape. Finally we see Vet approaching, so we stand.

"Well?" I ask.

Vet shakes his head. "We're still discussing it. We just decided to take a break."

"Discussing what? Are you trying to decide how best to fight the Scavs?"

"That has not been the focus of the discussion yet," he says.

"What does that mean? What have you been talking about?"

Vet takes a deep breath. "The first thing we're trying to decide is if we make any changes or not."

I stare at him in disbelief. "Are you joking? How can that be the topic of discussion?"

"They're afraid," he says.

"They're cowards," I shout.

Niko speaks up. "Papa, what's your argument?"

Vet looks at Niko. "You know where I stand. I can't send any more kids to their death."

I feel a little better, but I still can't believe that not every one of them feel that way. "How many of them agree with you?"

Vet turns his attention to me but drops his head.

"How many?"

He holds up two fingers.

I can't believe it. "Just you and Maren, right?"

He nods. "It's not that they want to continue it forever; they just want time to figure out how best to deal with the aftermath of not sending the Chosen. They trust that you can come with the ideas and weapons needed to make this stand successful, but they're afraid of what will happen to more innocent people if we attempt it unprepared. I'm sorry. I have to get back." He turns and walks away.

I can feel the anger welling up inside me. I take off running around the northern side of the column. Niko runs after me. "Piri, don't," he yells.

I run until my lungs are burning before I stop. I lean over and place my hands on the column to catch my breath. Niko comes up behind me and puts his hand on my back. I see a large rock at the base of the column. I pick it up and begin hitting the column with all my strength. A large chunk breaks away and falls to the ground. I look at the hole that remains; a portion of one of Niko's mama's painting has been destroyed. I pick up the chunk and try to put it back to make the painting whole again.

"I'm sorry," I say.

"It's okay," my spouse says. "I know you're upset."

I look at the painting again. I step back and look at all the paintings, Kabloom flowers as far as the eye can see to the right and left. I stare upward to where the great column disappears into the clouds, then look to the north. I look at Niko. "We got to get back to the Elect. I got an idea."

He stares at me for a second, then nods.

We hurry back, and I walk right into the middle of the circle and all talking stops. I convey my plan in intricate detail as every member of the Elect looks on. I rotate in circles as my eyes seek out each one individually. No one speaks or even looks around as I explain everything. Niko stands beside me, his chest protruding with pride as I lay it all out. When I finish, I search for expressions of doubt and fear, but there are only looks of wonderment. Only now do they flinch and each seems to draw a deep breath, each looking at his neighbor as if deciding if it's possible, as if wondering if it could really work.

"Let us discuss it," one says.

"No," I say. "Vote now. And I want to see how you all vote."

"He's right," Maren says. "He deserves that much. Let us vote now. All those in favor of Piri's plan, raise your hands."

I can't believe it. I drop to my knees and begin to sob. Niko puts his hand on my shoulder. I stare up again to make sure it wasn't a dream. But there they are—twelve hands raised high in the air.

CHAPTER THIRTY-THREE

News of the Elects' decision spreads throughout The Garden like the strong winds that are forever present as tens of thousands of volunteers show up to help. Twenty people are chosen by the Elect as supervisors to report directly to me.

"Okay," I say as I stare at the faces of the twenty people circled around me. "The first thing you need to do is take as many buckets as you can find and fill them with the black stuff from the pits. Be sure to stay in large groups with plenty of armed guards. Take the filled buckets and line them up across the northern side of the column."

They nod their understanding and rush off to pass the instructions to their teams of volunteers.

I turn and smile at Niko. "There's someone you need to meet."

"Where are we going?" Niko asks after we have been walking for thirty minutes.

I smile and keep walking along the path I know so well. "You'll see."

Finally we come to the house, and I run down the steps and knock on the door. A few seconds later it opens, and Curz smiles as he sees me. I fly into his arms.

"I knew you'd come back to visit," he says, a big grin on his face. Then he looks at Niko, and his smile disappears. "And who is this? Shall I release my attack lizards?"

"I'm Niko." He extends his hand, ignoring the lizard threat.

I forgot to warn Niko about Curz's favorite way to keep his

privacy, but it's just as well. Niko would not be frightened by lizards.

Curz accepts the handshake and looks at the wrist bands. "That's some beautiful work. But I don't take returns."

I laugh. "Everybody loves them."

Niko nods to confirm. "That's true. If you were to take these to Market, you could have anything you want."

"All I want is privacy. Can I trade for that?" Niko doesn't know how to answer, which makes Curz laugh. He looks at me and taps his head. "Obnoxious, eh?"

I laugh. "Sí. You have it perfected." Then I look at Curz as my smile goes away. "We need to talk."

He nods. "Then come in, by all means." He leads us to the table, and Niko and I take a seat. He brings us a container of water and sits with us. He looks at Niko. "You're a lucky man, my friend."

Niko nods. "Sí. I know that. Can I ask you something?" Curz neither nods nor shakes his head, so Niko continues. "Is it true that you ain't been to worship or harvest in a long time?"

Curz just looks at Niko for several seconds with no expression. Then a smile snakes across one side of his face, then the other. He nods slowly. "Sí, Niko. Sí. It's the truth."

Niko takes a deep breath. "Wow."

Time to get down to business. "Curz," I begin, "I believe you have a gift. Remember how you never threw the stones away that you found when you were a young boy?"

He nods.

"You saved them all that time without knowing why. But it turns out it was for a great cause."

"Sí, it was," he says.

I reach over and squeeze his hands. "I think the same is true for your magic mix. You have fifteen huge drums behind your house, but you weren't even sure why you made so much."

He smiles and pats my hands. "And you, Piri? Do you know why?"

"Sí, I do," I say. "I do know why." I tell him my plan.

He laughs. "And they call me loco."

That makes Niko laugh.

Curz sits back in his chair and scratches his wooly head. "I don't know. I like your plan. I hope it works. But that's valuable stuff and you came empty-handed. What possibly could you offer to barter for such a treasure?"

I lean in and speak softly. "I've been to Level Twelve."

Another crooked grin appears on his scraggly face. "You got a deal."

Niko goes off to find volunteers as I stay with Curz. We go to the back and make sure all the canisters are sealed tight. He even puts a lid on the one he is using.

"You want to hold on to that one?"

He shakes his head. "No, I think this is too important. And I can always make more."

When Niko returns, he comes with around forty other people and fifteen carts. We instruct them to handle the drums with care as they load them onto the carts.

I say good-bye to Curz, promising to return when it's all over. "Once we're gone, you can unleash your attack lizards."

Everyone in the group stares back at the house with fear in their eyes. Curz laughs.

We take the drums to the carrier and carefully load them. I send Niko with them and instruct them to also place the drums along the northern side of the column, spaced three hundred feet apart, so they go from our track on the eastern side all the way to the track on the western side. I watch the carrier glide away. I wanted to go with them, but there's something I feel I must do before we implement the plan.

A little while later I knock on the door. Vet answers and motions me inside.

"Where is she?"

He points to my old bedroom. "She's taking a nap."

I walk in quietly and see her sleeping, facing away from me. I slip off my sandals and slide in bed beside her. She doesn't wake.

I wrap my arm around her, and she instinctively turns to cuddle in my arms.

"Piri?" she says as she opens her eyes.

I smile. "Sí. It's me."

She snuggles closer. "Tomorrow is the seventh day, ain't it?"

I nod.

"I'm scared, Piri."

I hold her closer. "Me, too, Chiquita. Me, too."

She begins to cry. "I want to stay with you tomorrow."

"Okay."

She stops crying and looks up at me. "Really?"

"Sure," I say. "We can find someone else for the important job."

It takes a second for it to sink in. "Wait. What important job?"

I caress her hair. "The job the Elect wanted me to assign to you. But I can find someone else, so don't worry."

"What was the job?"

I try to think quickly to figure that out myself. "Well, when the warriors form the first and second lines of defense, your papa will be where everyone else is gathered in secret. His job is to keep everyone calm, so he will be going up and down to talk with the men and women. But there will be a lot of kids there as well, and we didn't have anyone who could talk with them. That's what we wanted you to do, let them know that everything was going to be fine. We figured it would be best coming from you since you're my best friend. But we can find someone else."

"No," she says. "I can do it. After all, they'll listen to me better since I'm your best friend."

I hear a slight noise and turn to see Vet smiling and closing the door.

"Piri?" she asks. "What will it be like after tomorrow?"

"It'll be like it was long ago. Did I ever tell you what it was like long ago?"

She shakes her head.

"Oh, my," I say. "Long ago before the city in the sky ever existed, everyone lived on the surface. There were so many people, a thousand times more than now, and some lived on other lands around the entire world."

"Wow. Were they starving?"

"Are you joking? There were so many animals that you could hunt every day and never run out of them. Some of them were fluffy and bounced around, some of them flew through the air, and some had no legs at all, just slid along the ground like the carrier does on the track. There were more animals than anyone could hunt. And there were more fish than land animals. And some lands had huge fields of all kinds of crops. They shared their crops with all the poor lands because everyone loved one another in those days."

"Really?"

"Sí," I say. "There were no weapons because no one attacked others. They all lived in peace. That's how it's going to be again. We'll all live in peace and love one another. There'll be lots of animals to hunt and lots of fish to catch. There'll be plenty of eggs and fruits and berries for everyone. We can go to the ocean every day if we like. We can stay in the forest all night. No one will ever be hungry again and most importantly, no one will ever be hunted again. It's going to be a new world. You believe me, don't you?"

Ana doesn't answer. I look down and see her sleeping soundly. I gently get out of bed and wrap the cover over her. I walk into the kitchen where Vet is sitting at the table.

"Gracias," he whispers.

"For what?"

He smiles. "For giving her something to do tomorrow."

I nod. "I love her so much."

Vet slides a bowl of dried fruit over to me and I eat. I hadn't realized how hungry I was.

"It's going to work," he says.

I look down at the fruit. I wish I had that confidence. I get up to leave.

"Where are you going?" he asks.

"I want to be home when Niko gets there. We have to get up very early. I'll see you tomorrow." I get up and head toward my own house, my unique bow resting across my shoulder as I think about tomorrow and then beyond tomorrow. When I get home, I set out some fruits and meat for Niko. He comes home, washes up, and we sit at the table.

"Everything's ready," he says as he bites into a piece of dried meat.

I nod.

"Don't worry," he says, apparently reading my mind. "It's going to work."

I smile. "Whatever happens tomorrow, our lives will be very different from that point."

He nods.

It's only late afternoon when we go to bed. We'll be starting in the morning several hours before daylight and want to be ready. I snuggle up to my spouse as we pull the covers over us. He kisses me on the forehead, something he does every night.

"I can't believe how right I was," he says.

"About what?" I ask.

He smiles. "The first time we met, I thought you were a gift from the Fathers. I was so right."

CHAPTER THIRTY-FOUR

Niko wakes me. "It's time."
Those words strike fear in me as much as anything else has on the surface. I rise and make myself ready. We go outside. It's still dark, but a full moon above the clouds provides faint context to the landscape. We are joined by others and together we walk toward the northeast corner of the forest. Although I can't see any faces, I know everyone is as nervous as I am. Our group builds to an incredible number as we reach the edge of the forest. The subdued glow from the sky is completely absent in the forest as our path is now in total darkness.

Niko leads the way since he's been through here many times. The massive crowd follows single file, each holding on to the person in front of them. As we get deep into the forest, the line is over a mile long. We have brought no dogs, no light, nothing to give our presence away.

I think about the Children of the western province on their similar journey to the ocean on that side.

We continue for hours. Eventually, I can see the first hint of tree trunks as the green canopy above us filters through the first rays of daylight. I feel safer now as I know that all the Scavs are well on their way to their sacred meeting place.

We're able to let go of each other as the trees become more visible. We know we are going the right direction when we see a worn path stomped hard by Scavs' feet pointing the way. We clear the forest, and I lead them over the rocky terrain.

We come to the cliff, and I point to the campsite below. "See that huge container with the large bubbles?"

Niko and several others beside me nod.

I point westward along the coast. "There's another just up the sand. You all know what to do. I have to get back to the carrier."

Niko kisses me and begins to descend the trail cut into the cliff.

I remember something. "Niko?"

He turns around.

"Make sure to bring back two belts with the smaller bubbles," I say "You'll find them on a fence down there."

He nods and waves.

I turn to make the long walk back, walking as fast as I can and passing the entire line as I retrace the path. Young and old faces smile at me, all of them carrying a bag like the ones we use to collect the fish. Most of them pat me on the shoulder or touch my arm as I pass. So many of their faces are filled with fear, but there's something there I've never seen before—hope.

Hours later, I clear the forest and make my way to the carrier. It is already getting close to midday, so I know time is short. I reach the carrier and see Vet and Ana waiting for me. I run to Ana and drop to my knees and hug her.

"Are you ready to do your job?"

She nods and smiles.

Vet hugs me, then takes Ana by the hand and begins the long walk to the end of the next track over.

I take a deep breath and wait. I feel sick to my stomach, but I fight it off. Soon I see the first line of volunteers returning from the ocean. Niko is with them. Each carries a bag full of the large bubbles. Niko gets into the carrier and they hand the bags up to him. He stacks them neatly and gently.

More people come until the carrier is full. I stay here as he uses the carrier to deliver the bubbles to the column. I instruct everyone to sit their bags on the ground and wait. The bags are soon everywhere along the ground.

Niko returns, and we fill the carrier a second time with another load to go. I ride with him this time. I stare to the south and see people still walking in that direction, to the meeting place. I think of Ana going around to all the kids to comfort them, and it makes me smile.

I get to the column and thousands of volunteers are there. That's a good thing as I stare at the horizon and see a few black dots heading along the north. There are so many people here; it should resemble worship from that distance.

Niko drops me off and goes back for the last load.

"After you get them all loaded, send everyone south," I say.

He nods, and the carrier takes him away.

"What do we do, Piri?"

I turn and see San and a little farther back is his wife, Cari.

"Follow me." I walk around the column and get everyone's attention, at least those in hearing range. "Okay, everyone, here's what we need to do." I take a large bubble from a bag and dip it into the bucket holding the raw black stuff from the pits. I pull it away, and a glob adheres to the bubble. I walk over to the column and press. It sticks to the wall. "We need to cover the entire northern wall with these."

San tells a younger boy to go inform the other side and the boy takes off running.

I walk in that direction myself. I am too tired and sick to my stomach to run. I keep an eye on everyone to make sure they're doing it properly, although I can't imagine how you could do it wrong. I smile as I think of Payo. Well, maybe my friend could have found a way.

Before I even reach the other side of the column, I see the bubbles adorning the outer wall. "Let's keep them close together," I say.

The few places where the bubbles were a little wide apart are quickly filled. I turn and walk back toward the other side. When I get back to our track, Niko has returned with the last shipment of bubbles, and we join in gluing them to the column. Finally all the bubbles are attached to the column, and there is a wall of bubbles beginning at the ground and extending upward ranging from five to seven feet, uniformly distributed all the way across the northern wall.

I send seven of my supervisors to lead all the volunteers south. I keep thirteen with Niko and me and show them the next step. I take one of the buckets that had held the black stuff and take it over to one of the drums, which are compliments of Curz. I remove the lid and fill the bucket. I go over to the wall of bubbles and splash it on. The black liquid instantly covers a huge area and runs down the wall, dripping from bubble to bubble.

I nod to them, and they all rush off to take their own drums. Niko takes the one nearest me, but still three hundred feet away. I continue to fill the bucket and work my way toward Niko. It's harder than I thought and requires much more physical exertion. I sweat profusely and remove my thick cloak. The smell of Curz' magic liquid is strong, making me sicker to my stomach. I stop to vomit, then continue. The day is getting late, and I'm starting to get worried. But we finish, and I stare at the bottom of the column, which is now completely black.

I lead them over to our track and take one of the belts Niko brought back, the ones the Scavs wear around their waist, the ones with the smaller bubbles they use to attack the Children. I coat the inside of the belt with raw material from the pits and stick it hard to the giant door, the one that receives the crops and Chosen Ones. But not after today. I glue the belt right on the edge of the door. Then I glue the first bubble to the column beside the door.

I look up at the two designated supervisors. "Go to the other door on the western side and do the same thing. Make sure you glue them well. Glue every bubble to the column. When the door lifts, it will pull the plugs from the tip of the bubbles."

They turn and run as fast as they can to the other side, carrying the second belt with them.

After I glue the last bubble from the belt to the column, Niko helps me up. I am dizzy. He puts me on his back, and we head toward the second track over, the other eleven supervisors following. We reach the carrier, and he lifts me up. I sit on the floor with my back against the side, much like I always have. The other supervisors pick a spot. The carrier begins to move, then moves faster. I watch as we get farther away from the column. My tunic is soaked with sweat, and the cold air actually feels good as it hits me. I know the other two supervisors are probably on the next carrier over, already on the way to where everyone will be waiting for us.

I stand beside Niko and let the wind hit me in the face. It makes me feel better. We reach the end of the track, and there are people as far as my eyes can see. It's an amazing sight. At worship, the same people would be there, but because the crowds curve around the column, they are never all visible. The crowd goes on for miles and miles.

The carrier stops, and we all get off. Niko helps me down. We walk toward the crowd, pass the line of men with bows loaded with arrows, pass the second row of men with spears, all poised and ready in case things go wrong.

I see Ana. She rushes to meet me. I take her hand as she guides me back to the front of the crowd. Vet is there waiting as well. I'm too tired to stand, so I turn to face the north and sit, the great column now a long way away. Niko sits on one side of me, and Ana sits in my lap.

I know the time is near. I take Ana's hands and place them over her ears. "Cover your ears, Chiquita." I do the same and nod to Niko. He covers his ears, and the instructions are whispered back through the crowd like the lessons of worship. Soon the entire population has their ears covered as we stare at the column. But nothing happens. More minutes pass. Nothing. Something is wrong.

I think about the times I have witnessed the Chosen Ones and crops being delivered. The carrier is pulled up to the door as the driver climbs off. A minute later, the door opens. Maybe it has weight sensors. Maybe they have cameras. I turn to look at Niko and remove my hands from over my ears. I rush back toward the carrier as Niko follows.

"What are you doing?" he asks.

"I have to set it off manually."

"You'll be killed."

I stop, turn, and face him. I look at all the eyes of the others looking to me for answers. Everyone has removed their hands and is walking toward us. I can't let them down. "Sí. If that's what it takes. I don't care what happens to me. We can't turn back now. Don't you see?"

Niko drops his head for a second then looks back up and nods. "Sí." He turns to look at the crowd. "We can't stop now," he yells.

The crowd erupts with cheers as hands, spears, and bows lift into the air. Then it happens. The sound is loud and long. But it isn't the sound of explosions; it's an alarm, and it's coming from the city. They're signaling the Scavs.

CHAPTER THIRTY-FIVE

Niko and I run to the carrier. Many others pile on as we head back to the column. I know what has to be done. We will have to set the explosions off some way on our own. The two lines of guards are already running toward the column. I try to yell for them to stop, but they can't hear me. I see others pouring out of the crowd, every man, woman, and young adult with a spear or bow darting out like string unraveling from a cloth. I see Vet in front of them as the mob keeps pace with the carrier.

I am standing beside Niko at the front of the carrier, at the controls. The others on board are clinging to the side with one hand while clutching their weapons with the other. Suddenly a hole appears in the wooden floor of the carrier. It's only about the circumference of a man's thumb, but everyone stares at the glowing red embers of the wood around the hole, the wind actually making a flame dance out of thin air for a second.

I look upward and I see them, thousands of faint pink dots in the sky, falling downward—no, not falling—speeding downward as if launched from a machine. I hear screams as I see several men and boys go down.

"It's the Fathers," one of the men in the carrier shouts.

I can't believe it. They're raining down fire. More of the Children go down and lie motionless. I fear it will scare them into submission, but it doesn't. It only seems to galvanize their resolve.

We arrive at the column and run toward the east along the southern wall. As we near the eastern door, I see them approaching— Scavs, soldier Scavs near us and as far back as I can see to where they just appear as black dots sliding across the landscape. They will reach the door before us.

As they pass the door, I draw my bow and pull the lever. The first Scav goes down hard. Niko takes out another with his bow. Then he grabs me and pulls me away.

"No!" I scream. "We have to make it to the door."

But it's too late. They are all over the place. The first wave of Children and Scavs come together. At first the Children do well as the arrows and spears take out the unarmed creatures. But the enemy's numbers are great, and the Children with bows cannot load arrows fast enough to protect themselves as the Scavs begin to overpower them with brute force, knocking them to the ground and beating them with their club-like arms.

What have I done? I only wanted peace for the Children, but this is far from it. The Children still charge from the south as the crowd has come to the east side of the column, the side where the Scavs have come, the side where the battle is to be fought. Fire still rains down from the city taking out more of the Children. I am frozen. I can't move.

Niko yells at me as two Scavs run at us. He takes out one with his bow, but I don't move. Perhaps I deserve to die. As the Scav lunges at me, a spear penetrates his gut. I look and see Vet on the other end. The Scav falls to the ground and lies still. I look into Vet's eyes, and I'm surprised at what I see. It is pure determination. With all that's happening he still has hope. He nods to me and my fire returns. I pull up my bow.

"We still have to set off the bubbles," I yell.

But there are more and more Scavs coming at us. I take aim at the chest of the one in front and fire. He goes down, as does the one directly behind him, my arrow penetrating all the way through the first one. I quickly reload. As I look up again, I see the battle line is drifting south as the Scavs are taking the upper hand. I fire again.

Niko takes out another with his last arrow. He tosses the bow and picks up his spear. But there are too many.

Vet sticks another one, but before he can even retract his spear, a Scav jumps on top of him and knocks him to the ground. The creature pounds him quickly on the chest several times, and Vet doesn't move; his eyes roll back.

"No!" Niko screams and drops his spear and lunges for the Scav. He knocks him off of his papa and takes him on hand-to-hand, fueled by pure adrenaline and hatred. Niko punches the Scav in the face hard, but the Scav gives back as good as he gets, swinging around his massive arm and connecting with Niko's chin, lifting his feet off the ground. Niko's back hits the ground with a thud, but he jumps to his feet, leaps behind the creature, and wraps his arms around his neck. The creature swings wildly and spins around but Niko holds fast, the veins bulging in his arms, his teeth clenched tight, his eyes as red now as the Scav's.

I grab for another arrow, but I am out as well. I pick up Niko's spear, but the creature falls to his knees as Niko continues to cut off his air supply. Then the Scav falls over dead.

Another one rushes Niko, and I thrust the spear into his gut, but it doesn't stop him. The point barely penetrates as I try to hold him back, but he is too strong. I can't contain him. He brings down his arm, breaks the spear in half, and keeps coming. An arrow penetrates his chest and his momentum spins around, and he falls on his back at my feet.

I turn and see San, Ari, and Tag running toward us, but it is Ari who is reloading her bow, so she is the one who just saved me. Tag has only a club about five feet long and quickly proves how deadly he is with it as his stout arms pummel the next aggressor to death. San is accurate with his bow as well. But I do not see Cari and wonder if something has happened to her. The three form a semicircle around us for protection.

I look and see Niko kneeling by his papa, tears running down his face. I kneel down beside him. He looks to me for help, but I have none to offer. I don't know what to do.

I hear San yell out and look up to see that a Scav has his hands around San's neck, choking him. He has dropped his bow to try to free himself from the death grasp. Niko grabs his own bow and rips the arrow from the chest of the Scav on the ground beside us, the one Ari killed.

Suddenly the Scav goes down and doesn't move. San falls to his knees gasping for air. The side of the Scav's face is crushed like a crop from the fields. I look up and see Dax, the man from the Market. I breathe a sigh of relief.

Dax rushes toward the mob of creatures. "Come on!" he yells as several Scavs hear and accept the challenge. They rush him, but he crushes them one by one; a single blow is all it takes from him to put them on the ground for good. They retreat, but he follows.

"What do we do?" Niko asks.

I look up at the battle, a horrific scene unfolding. Scavs are all over the base of the column. I can see the large bubbles still stuck to the northern wall covered in Curz's black mix. I judge the distance as I remember the last meeting of the Elect, as Niko showed me how far an arrow would fly. I look at the arrow in Niko's bow, the tip and several inches still dripping blood from where he retrieved it from the body of the Scav. I grab the long red sash from Vet's belt, the one that marks his identity as an Elect, and pull it out. I reach into my two pouches and pull out the flat round stones.

"Give me the tip," I say.

Niko understands and holds the arrow tight, the flat arrowhead pointed toward me. I take the two stones and press them together. The air glows bright and the heat is instantaneous—and extremely painful. My fingers begin to burn as I wrap the red strip of cloth around it. Flames appear, but I keep wrapping, my hands burning so hot I can feel and smell the skin melting. I tie it tight.

"Go," I say as I finish.

Niko stands, lifts his bow into the air, and releases. The arrow flies through the sky toward the column, the tip now a ball of flames.

I see Dax still taking them on, at least ten of them around him, some on his back as they try to bring the big man down. I yell for him to run, but my voice is drowned out by the sounds of battle.

The arrow flies true. As it descends toward the wall of bubbles, the end separates as the stones burn through the stick. But the burning arrow and ball of flame continue on their trajectory and fall into the black-covered bubbles.

Niko pushes me to the ground, my tender hands scooting along the dirt. Then I hear it. The sound is deafening, like a thousand explosions in a matter of seconds. Then there is silence.

I stand to see the results. The air is filled with dust and debris. The explosion took out every Scav in front of the column—and Dax. I turn and see the battle has stopped as everyone, Children and Scavs alike, are in awe. The Scavs run back past the column toward the north. I see the black dots scurrying to the horizon and one lone white dot in the distance—Lucent. The others gather around her as they all disappear over the last line of rocks.

I see chunks of debris falling from the wall. I hear a rumbling noise, which grows louder and louder. Then I see it. I can see it moving. It's working. The column is falling directly to the north. The rumbling sound intensifies.

I think of Lucent, the queen of the Scavs. I think of her pompous arrogance. Thanks for that tip about the column being the same height as the tunnel is long. It was very useful information indeed. I think of that entire race of creatures gathered to celebrate, gathered to feed on the Children. Here comes your delivery. The column begins to fall faster.

"Enjoy your feast, Highness," I shout. "This is for Payo."

The entire city appears as it comes through the clouds, like slow motion at first, then falling faster and faster until it crashes to earth directly on top of the sacred Scav camp, the place where they collect the Chosen Ones, the column taking out all the ones still rushing to get back. The impact shakes the ground, causing everyone to hold out their arms for balance. It makes the sound of a hundred thunderclaps as dust fills the air in a huge cloud, a swirling mist that seems to have a life of its own, reaching all the way up to the overcast sky.

It's over. The crowd erupts with cheers. I see the Children with their weapons raised, shaking them in defiance. In victory. I stare out across the battlefield and see the ones lying motionless on the ground, some killed by the Scavs and some by the Fathers. I see all the dead Scavs. I'm not sure how to feel. There is death everywhere, including everyone I ever knew before coming here. But the battle is ours. Now the Children have no enemies and unlimited crops that automatically replenish every year. No more worship, no more empty threats, no more lies, and no more Chosen Ones.

Niko wraps his arm around me and pulls me to his chest. "You did it." He pulls back and stares at my scorched hands and a single tear rolls down his cheek. I smile to let him know I'm okay.

Others nearby congratulate me. We sit by Vet's body as the rest of the Children come to join us. I see little Ana running our way and don't have the strength to stop her before she gets to us. She sees her papa and falls to the ground and tries desperately to wake him.

"Get up, Papa," she cries. "Por favor, get up."

I wrap my arms around her as she collapses into my embrace.

The wind blows the dust cloud as the giant brown mist begins to drift away. Everyone stops moving as a strange light engulfs them from above.

"What is it?" I hear someone ask.

I look upward and see that the city, as it fell through the clouds, left a large opening in the overcast sky, allowing the sun to shine through. The entire northern land is covered with its strong rays.

"What is it?" Ana asks.

I stare out at the crowd as everyone seems to be in awe of the vision. Some point their faces upward to absorb the warmth. Others hold their hands out wide and others sit or lie in the dirt and soak it in.

"What is it?" Ana asks again.

I look down and smile. "It's our future, Chiquita. It's our future."

About the Author

Although in 2005 Neal was dragged kicking and screaming to the snow-infested plains of the American Midwest, his home is still Blake, Alabama, atop beautiful Sand Mountain. He now resides in Milwaukee, WI, with his wife and three dogs.

Soliloquy Titles From Bold Strokes Books

The Balance by Neal Wooten. Love and survival come together in the distant future as Piri and Niko faceoff against the worst factions of mankind's evolution. (978-1-62639-055-3)

The Unwanted by Jeffrey Ricker. Jamie Thomas is plunged into danger when he discovers his mother is an Amazon who needs his help to save the tribe from a vengeful god. (978-1-62639-048-5)

Because of Her by KE Payne. When Tabby Morton is forced to move to London, she's convinced her life will never be the same again. But the beautiful and intriguing Eden Palmer is about to show her that this time, change is most definitely for the better. (978-1-62639-049-2)

Asher's Fault by Elizabeth Wheeler. Fourteen-year-old Asher Price sees the world in black and white, much like the photos he takes, but when his little brother drowns at the same moment Asher experiences his first same-sex kiss, he can no longer hide behind the lens of his camera and eventually discovers he isn't the only one with a secret. (978-1-60282-982-4)

The Seventh Pleiade by Andrew J. Peters. When Atlantis is besieged by violent storms, tremors, and a barbarian army, it will be up to a young gay prince to find a way for the kingdom's survival. (978-1-60282-960-2)

The Missing Juliet: A Fisher Key Adventure by Sam Cameron. A teenage detective and her friends search for a kidnapped Hollywood star in the Florida Keys. (978-1-60282-959-6)

Meeting Chance by Jennifer Lavoie. When man's best friend turns on Aaron Cassidy, the teen keeps his distance until fate puts Chance in his hands. (978-1-60282-952-7)

Lake Thirteen by Greg Herren. A visit to an old cemetery seems like fun to a group of five teenagers, who soon learn that sometimes it's best to leave old ghosts alone. (978-1-60282-894-0)

The Road to Her by KE Payne. Sparks fly when actress Holly Croft, star of UK soap *Portobello Road*, meets her new on-screen love interest, the enigmatic and sexy Elise Manford. (978-1-60282-887-2)

Swans and Clons by Nora Olsen. In a future world where there are no males, sixteen-year-old Rubric and her girlfriend Salmon Jo must fight to survive when everything they believed in turns out to be a lie. (978-1-60282-874-2)

Kings of Ruin by Sam Cameron. High school student Danny Kelly and loner Kevin Clark must team up to defeat a top-secret alien intelligence that likes to wreak havoc with fiery car, truck, and train accidents. (978-1-60282-864-3)

Wonderland by David-Matthew Barnes. After her mother's sudden death, Destiny Moore is sent to live with her two gay uncles on Avalon Cove, a mysterious island on which she uncovers a secret place called Wonderland, where love and magic prove to be real. (978-1-60282-788-2)

Another 365 Days by KE Payne. Clemmie Atkins is back, and her life is more complicated than ever! Still madly in love with her girlfriend, Clemmie suddenly finds her life turned upside down with distractions, confessions, and the return of a familiar face... (978-1-60282-775-2)

The Secret of Othello by Sam Cameron. Florida teen detectives Steven and Denny risk their lives to search for a sunken NASA satellite—but under the waves, no one can hear you scream... (978-1-60282-742-4)

Andy Squared by Jennifer Lavoie. Andrew never thought anyone could come between him and his twin sister, Andrea…until Ryder rode into town. (978-1-60282-743-1)

Sara by Greg Herren. A mysterious and beautiful new student at Southern Heights High School stirs things up when students start dying. (978-1-60282-674-8)

Boys of Summer, edited by Steve Berman. Stories of young love and adventure, when the sky's ceiling is a bright blue marvel, when another boy's laughter at the beach can distract from dull summer jobs. (978-1-60282-663-2)

Street Dreams by Tama Wise. Tyson Rua has more than his fair share of problems growing up in New Zealand—he's gay, he's falling in love, and he's run afoul of the local hip-hop crew leader just as he's trying to make it as a graffiti artist. (978-1-60282-650-2)

me@you.com by KE Payne. Is it possible to fall in love with someone you've never met? Imogen Summers thinks so because it's happened to her. (978-1-60282-592-5)

Swimming to Chicago by David-Matthew Barnes. As the lives of the adults around them unravel, high school students Alex and Robby form an unbreakable bond, vowing to do anything to stay together—even if it means leaving everything behind. (978-1-60282-572-7)

365 Days by KE Payne. Life sucks when you're seventeen years old and confused about your sexuality, and the girl of your dreams doesn't even know you exist. Then in walks sexy new emo girl, Hannah Harrison. Clemmie Atkins has exactly 365 days to discover herself, and she's going to have a blast doing it! (978-1-60282-540-6)

Timothy by Greg Herren. *Timothy* is a romantic suspense thriller from award-winning mystery writer Greg Herren set in the fabulous Hamptons. (978-1-60282-760-8)